D0250981

# PAINTED SKINS

# PAINTED SKINS

*A Tess Grey Thriller*

## Matt Hilton

This first world edition published 2016
in Great Britain and the USA by
SEVERN HOUSE PUBLISHERS LTD of
19 Cedar Road, Sutton, Surrey, England, SM2 5DA.
Trade paperback edition first published
in Great Britain and the USA 2017 by
SEVERN HOUSE PUBLISHERS LTD

British Library Cataloguing in Publication Data
*A CIP catalogue record for this title is available from the British Library.*

ISBN-13: 978-0-7278-8650-7 (cased)
ISBN-13: 978-1-84751-752-4 (trade paper)
ISBN-13: 978-1-78010-816-2 (e-book)

*All Severn House titles are printed on acid-free paper.*

Severn House Publishers support the Forest Stewardship Council™ [FSC™],
the leading international forest certification organisation.
All our titles that are printed on FSC certified paper carry the FSC logo.

Typeset by Palimpsest Book Production Ltd.,
Falkirk, Stirlingshire, Scotland.
Printed and bound in Great Britain by
TJ International, Padstow, Cornwall.

# ONE

She wasn't running away. She was hurtling towards a new chapter of her life. She wasn't physically running, she was driving, but it was an acceptable metaphor for her purpose. She often thought in metaphors and similes. It was how she had endured her teens and early twenties, by replacing drudgery with bright and shiny fantasy. Who would be Cinderella in the cold ashes, if you didn't believe you'd ever go to the ball?

If she recounted her life in the pages of a book then surely the first chapter would be a tale of misery, but in the best tradition of storytelling the worm was about to turn. Actually, she had turned, bucked the miserable trend she'd been held prisoner to. She'd twisted the plot and was now setting off on a brand-new wild adventure. Who knew, maybe there was a handsome prince waiting on the next page. Not that she was dependent on finding a new man: she could do fine without one cluttering her plans for the immediate future.

Having headed south and circumvented Boston, with a brief stop to eat in Auburn, she was now somewhere west of Worcester, Massachusetts, following the turnpike towards the state of New York, planning on reaching Springfield before she made her next stop. She was many miles from home, and for the past ten or fifteen had avoided looking in her mirrors. That part of her life was behind her now. No looking back. No regrets and good riddance. Her gaze was fixed on the road ahead, though there was little to be seen beyond her headlights but for the distant demon-eyed squint of another vehicle's taillights. Even as she concentrated on the distant lights, the blinkers came on and the vehicle took an off route. Now her way west was clear, and she pressed her foot a little harder on the gas pedal.

There'd been a hot spell back home. Unusual for Maine this late in the season, but the weather was on the change. A front was pushing down from Canada and with it heavy showers and squalls: soon the fragmented leading edge would be followed by heavier and sustained cumulus, bringing with it prolonged rain and likely snow. She'd be glad to see the back of inclement winters; things would be so much balmier where she was heading.

She had no work lined up, but she was confident in her ability to snag a job soon after arriving in California. She was experienced, could lend her hand to most things. If she had to she'd take a job waiting, or tending bars, whatever, until something better came along. She'd enough money to get by on for now, so she wasn't worried.

Road signs were briefly illuminated as she whizzed past. Monson; Palmer; and not too far ahead Ludlow, and she thought that perhaps a short stop in her journey wouldn't be too inconvenient. She'd been sipping juice from a sports bottle but now her bladder felt the size of a cantaloupe. A bathroom break and a few snacks were in order. She began watching for a gas station or rest stop. If all else failed she'd pull into the suburbs of Ludlow.

Distracted, she didn't notice the vehicle that joined the road behind her, and because she astutely refused to look in her mirrors didn't note its fast approach. Only when its lights blazed on high beam, filling the interior of her car, did she realize just how close to her fender it had come.

Her first concern was that she was speeding and this was a highway patrol vehicle. She checked. She was doing fifty-seven, not excessive. Perhaps the cop had been lurking by the highway, bored and begging for something to do to fill his shift, and she was the first motorist to come along, and he'd pounced. But would a cop drive so dangerously close without flicking on his gumball lights?

She nudged her brake pedal.

The following vehicle didn't back off. Nor did it overtake when there was plenty of room to manoeuvre and nothing coming the opposite way.

She gave her car some throttle, pulled away ten yards. The vehicle matched her speed, and again the glare invaded her car. Whoever was behind the wheel flicked the lights up and down, and she blinked at the strobe effect that left ghosts dancing in her vision.

'Idiot!' she snapped. But to be honest, she couldn't say if it were at the reckless driver or at her foolishness at making this journey alone, without protection. Sometimes, she knew, lone women drivers could be vulnerable; she'd simply never considered that *she* could be the vulnerable one.

She switched on her blinker, slowed, hoping this would force the driver to pull around her and continue. Her fender was shunted. She was jerked in her lap belt, head nodding, and emitted an involuntary croak of alarm. Before she could further voice her dismay, her car was shunted again and the steering wheel was snatched from her grip. She grappled for control but the car veered right, the tyres hitting the grit separating asphalt from the soft grass shoulder. A rut in the dirt caught and held the tyres, but only for a moment. When she tried to force the car towards the road again the back end fishtailed. The following vehicle bore in, its front fender striking the back end and forcing her car into a wider arc. It hit the grass, the entire frame juddering, and the noise was colossal as divots of mud kicked for the heavens.

Trees loomed in her vision. Then one filled the windshield, and this time the impact was resounding. She was thrown forward in her seat, chest against the wheel, her forehead cracking solidly against the glass. When she slumped back she was dazed but it was too soon to feel pain. The flash of agony came moments later, and when it arrived it was accompanied by a rushing gale through her hearing. Her eyes were closed, mouth hanging open. An invisible elephant was sitting on her shoulders. Her head lolled, and she forced open her eyelids. Lights still blazed, and after images danced in her vision.

The engine still whirred, and steam belched over the hood, obscuring the tree from sight. As if being guided by another, she reached for the ignition. She was mindful of fire, and switched off the engine. She looked around, too stunned to make sense of anything, only that she was in a bad position. She groped for the door handle, but was held in place by the lap belt. The airbag on her steering column had failed. The car was old, ill maintained: how did you ever know to trust something that had never been tested? She struggled to unclip the belt, felt it pop open, and she leaned against the door. Blood trickled from her hairline. She reached tentatively and found a gaping gash in her scalp. She pulled at the handle with blood-slick fingers.

The door was yanked wide and she almost tumbled out.

Hands grasped her.

Not the hands of a saviour. These hands dug in painfully, ensuring she'd no way to pull free. She was yanked out as savagely as the door had been forced open, and dragged a few yards from the wreck of her car.

Still confused, her thoughts in a whirl, pain now wracking her from head to foot, she blinked at the figure looming over her. He'd transferred one hand to the front of her shirt, drawing the material into a tight fist. His other arm was raised, and in it a heavy flashlight. Its beam dug at the dome of the night sky. Then swooped down in a tight arc, and she knew the truth of it.

She had run from drudgery, directly into the arms of terror.

This was not a fresh chapter in her life. This was the end of her story. And there was no hope of a sequel.

# TWO

Without warning, rain battered down with scatter-shot fury, sending pedestrians running for cover under the awnings on Wharf Street. But the downpour was short-lived and did little to ease the heat, making the atmosphere more humid as the rain evaporated, with tendrils of steam rising from the overheated asphalt. People checked from doorways, their palms held out, then took tentative steps, before spilling again on to the sidewalks. It was early fall in Portland, Maine, and the heatwave was unexpected. Autumnal colours already patchworked the foliage, so the searing heat should have been welcomed, but most only grumbled.

Sitting with the window rolled down, Tess Grey felt a breeze teasing her, but it did a poor job of cooling the interior of the muscle car. The sunlight sent flaming razorblades through the windshield. Her exposed skin prickled. She'd donned shades against the glare. She adjusted in the bucket seat, averting her face from the harshest of the glare but without taking her attention off the bar's front door.

The crowd parted like the Red Sea before Moses when Po strode for the car. Nicolas 'Po' Villere was tall, dark haired, with a weathered face and turquoise eyes. He was a man whose every move appeared languid, until he was angered, then something changed. People knew to get out of his way, even if they didn't understand why, beyond a primal instinct that warned them he shouldn't be provoked. He was an ex-con, and admittedly a killer, but he was a good man. Tess was fourteen years his junior, and her background was on the opposite side of the law-enforcement fence. They were an unusual pairing, but the old adage that opposites attract was true: Tess was his employer, but they were full partners in another sense.

He'd left his Mustang double-parked, Tess ready to fend off any ticket-happy cops from the passenger seat, and headed inside the bar. Tess hadn't been confident he'd find the person they were looking for, and from the stern set of his features she was right.

'Where next?' she asked as he slid into the driver's seat.

'We should go speak to Max again; there was something he was holding back.'

'You want to twist his arm?'

'I tried being nice, maybe I should use a different approach.'

'Good cop, bad cop, all in one.' She smiled at him. 'Maybe I should be the bad cop this time?'

'You know how Max treats women,' said Po. 'If he comes his crap with you I might just end up hurting him.'

'My hero,' Tess said. 'Thanks, but I think I'm capable of handling an a-hole the likes of Maxwell Carter.'

'F'sure,' said Po, 'but then he'll get hurt even more. We need him still able to speak.'

'My right hook isn't what it used to be,' she reassured him, and couldn't help a discreet rub of the scar tissue banding her wrist.

Po didn't comment. She was no less fierce because she was carrying an old wound.

He started the muscle car and pulled out, some in the crowd now watching the growling Mustang with as much wariness as they had its driver.

'Could all be a wild-goose chase,' Tess said, relishing the breeze that buffeted her through the open window.

'Do you think she's dead?' Po asked, as if the answer were a foregone conclusion.

'Too early to tell, Po.' If she were pushed on it, Tess would admit it was a probability that Jasmine Reed was dead – whether or not her body would ever be found was the real question. 'People go missing for all kind of reasons, not all of them bad.'

'Most of them are. You don't hear 'bout too many happy folks disappearing without a trace.'

Tess again rubbed distractedly at the scar on her wrist. She'd no argument.

'How long is it she's been gone now?' Po made a mental calculation. 'Sixteen days?'

Tess didn't answer. Jasmine Reed had made the news, but as a twenty-four-year-old woman, and with no sign or hint of foul play involved in her disappearance, the media and the police soon lost practically all interest. She had a long record of absconding, and Portland PD hadn't done much beyond filing a missing persons report. As a minor, or an adult with a mental or physical disability, she'd have been deemed vulnerable, and her case would have been prioritized. But Jasmine was none of those, and reserved the right to come and go at will: if she'd chosen to leave town without telling a soul, then that was her prerogative. Having been a sergeant with the Cumberland County Sheriff's Office, Tess knew how these things worked, but it didn't mean she had to like it.

Stereotypical responses had greeted Jasmine's disappearance; the general consensus being she'd met a guy and run off to parts unknown with him. It wasn't the first time, after all. She had been raised in the system, a foster child, and a troublesome one at that. Whenever she'd been found in the past, she'd been fit and healthy, and usually with a boy. Returned to her latest foster parents, it was inevitable that a fresh report would be lodged the following weekend when she bugged out with her latest beau. However, and Tess couldn't be the only one to think about it, that was when she was a teenager. She hadn't gone missing in the best part of the last five years. Out of the control of the state, she'd no reason to run. Dropping off the face of the earth like this was characteristic of the teenage Jasmine, not of the well-adjusted young woman she'd supposedly grown into. That she worked the bar in a strip club shouldn't cloud anyone's judgement of her, but it did.

'We shouldn't put this off any longer,' Po said. 'Max knows something, and he's going to tell us what it is.'

'He's our best lead, it'd be stupid not to follow it as far as it goes.'

'F'sure,' said Po. He angled the car away from the Old Port where most of Portland's nightlife was centred around Wharf and Fore Streets, heading instead for the less salubrious bar that Maxwell Carter managed on the outskirts of town. 'So let's go and rattle Max's cage.'

# THREE

Two men in pale suits sat opposite each other in what appeared at first glance to be a gilded prison. The bars were gold-coloured, but the lustre was only from paint. On closer inspection, some of the paint was chipped, and patches of tarnished metal showed where the coating was rubbed thin.

The suits looked expensive, but on closer inspection they too showed wear. There was a sheen of perspiration on the older man's face, and he mopped at it with a folded napkin, frustrated by the task. His prematurely greying hair looked darker than it did in daylight, also slick with sweat.

The younger man appeared untroubled by the stifling heat, though there were dark patches under his armpits and his trousers were streaked with moisture from his palms where they nipped tightly over his thighs.

'Ever thought about talking to Daryl about investing in air-conditioning, Max? It might coax in a few more customers,' the older man said. He was called John Trojak, and he was a stranger to this type of establishment.

'The dancers take off their clothes,' said Maxwell Carter, 'you want them to catch a chill? Anyway, when it's hot like this the johns buy more beer. You've a lot to learn about this business, Johnny. It's unlike any other.'

'It's not my first time in a strip club,' he admitted. 'Not that I've ever enjoyed the experience. Ha, if my wife Veronica suspected I was within a mile of one of these places she'd have my gonads in a sling.'

Max smoothed down the wrinkles in his trousers. 'She sounds like a sensible woman.'

'Yeah? Then neither of you know me well enough.' Trojak sniffed.

The gold bars were as faux as the augmented breasts on some of the dancers featured on the posters decorating the walls. The bars were arranged in a half-moon formation, hemming in the booth seats on a dais. Similar arrangements were set around the room, but all were deserted. It was midday, and the club wouldn't open for hours yet. Secretly, Trojak was glad none of the dancers were there in the flesh, because he found stripping a distasteful career choice. The only other people were an old guy pushing a broom and a tattooed homosexual with an Elvis Presley pompadour replenishing the bar.

'You want me to hook you up with a girl?' Max asked, but his mouth puckered up at one corner. His face was thin, his cheekbones jutting either side of a long aquiline nose. His dark eyes were too small, beady, his lashes barely discernible they were so sparse. He reminded Trojak of a starving mole.

'Talk like that causes undue trouble, Max. Besides, there's only one girl I'm interested in.'

'Uh-huh. I haven't heard from Jazz since last you asked.'

'I was hoping you might've asked around for me. None of the other dancers know where I can find her, huh?'

'I asked. Nobody knows where she's at. She has disappeared . . . just like that.' Max clicked his fingers.

'Bruno isn't going to be pleased,' said Trojak, though he wore a faint smile. He dabbed a trickle of moisture from under his right eye.

'Can't help you, buddy. But I have my ears open. If I hear a thing about her, I'll let you know.'

Trojak stood. He crumpled the napkin and tossed it on the table. 'Appreciated.'

'Leaving so soon?' Max asked. 'You haven't drunk your beer.'

'I don't drink.'

'Your wife again?'

'Nope. Personal choice.' He slipped a hand in his jacket pocket, stepped around the table. 'One of the few I get to make these days.'

Max pushed out a hand, about to offer a shake of camaraderie.

Trojak snapped down on the extended wrist and hauled Max across the table. His other hand had come out of his pocket, and there was a soft click as a blade sprang open from its handle. 'If it were up to me, I wouldn't do this,' said Trojak, as he dug the blade into the back of Max's hand, 'but what Bruno wants, Bruno gets. You understand, old friend?'

Max cried out as the steel pushed through his hand, the tip grating on the table's veneer.

As quickly as he'd delivered punishment, Trojak retracted the blade. Let go of Max's injured hand. He swept up the crumpled napkin, used it to swipe the blood from the blade.

From behind the bar, the tattooed guy stared at them in disbelief. He wasn't about to offer any assistance, but Max shook his head at him anyway. He didn't want Trojak bloodying his knife a second time. Sensibly, the barman returned to his duties. The old guy with the broom hadn't even looked up.

'Jesus, Johnny! The hell you do that for?' Max's skeletal face was bonier than ever. He clutched his injured hand to his chest, his opposite palm pressed against the seeping wound.

'I just explained: Bruno said that if you didn't come clean about the woman, I'd to show you where your lies could lead.'

'I told you the truth! I haven't seen or heard a thing about Jazz.'

'I know, Max.' Trojak leaned closer. 'But you didn't tell me about the *other* woman.'

'The other woman? Who the hell you talking about?'

Holding his free hand about shoulder height, Trojak said, 'The one about yay high. Blonde. Good looking . . . if you like them curvy. Late twenties, I'd put her.'

Max gawped.

'Teresa Grey,' Trojak enunciated clearly.

'Tess? You're talking about the private detective that's poking around?'

'Who else?'

'Well, I told her exactly what I told you, Johnny! I know nothing about Jazz or her whereabouts.'

'Good.'

'So what the fuck's this about?' Max held up his bleeding hand, squeezing the wrist to stanch the blood flow.

'Mind your tongue, Max. There's no need for coarse language. You were punished for withholding vital information. Would've been good to know a detective was looking for Jasmine.'

'Well you obviously did. Son of a bitch, why'd you have to goddamn hurt me like that when you already knew about her?'

'Stop cursing and I'll explain.' Trojak waited until he was satisfied Max had a hold on his tongue. 'Like I already pointed out twice, that was on Bruno's orders. If it were down to me, I'd have simply shook your hand. No hard feelings, old friend.' The knife had been spirited away, and now Trojak extended his hand. 'Happy to do so now.'

'You want me to shake your hand? After cutting me?' Max clutched his injured hand to his chest.

'You're right. Maybe it's not a good idea.' Trojak looked down at his damp suit, and grimaced. 'Hard enough getting sweat out of this crummy material without having bloodstains to contend with.'

# FOUR

'What happened to your hand?' Tess spotted the bulky gauze bandage on Max Carter's hand the second she'd entered the club, but waited until they were seated before raising the subject. The bandage was dotted with blood, both sides of the hand, and she guessed he'd been injured shortly before her return.

'Friction burns.' Max mimed an act of personal sexual gratification.

Tess eyed him, unamused by his lewd behaviour. A few yards away, Po leaned against the bar, and his displeasure showed in the marginal stirring of his body. She glanced at him, winked, indicating she was OK.

'You should get that seen to,' she said, 'before it becomes infected.'

'Hand's fine. Don't know what you're worried about.'

Tess shrugged. 'Personally I don't care what you do. At least you won't need to worry about friction burns when your hand rots off.'

Max's pinched eyes screwed tighter. 'If you weren't here bothering me again I'd already be at the ER.'

Tess doubted him.

Max waved his good hand at the bar. 'Chris has cleaned and packed the wound for me. He trained as a triage nurse.'

Chris was the bartender. He'd served Po the fizzing Sprite, which sat untouched on the bar next to her partner's elbow, then made himself scarce; supposedly heading off on an errand. Tess suspected he wanted no further part of Max's business that day.

'You have your own personal nurse, Max? Nice.' She glanced around the tatty club. 'Wonder what other benefits come from working a sleazy strip joint like this.'

'It's an exotic dance venue, like I already explained. It's called Bar-Lesque for a reason. *Burlesque*. It's not a strip club.'

'Keep telling the city council that, you might get away with it, but you can't kid me, Max. It's common knowledge some of the dancers put on private shows . . . and we both know how they end up.'

'You looking for a job?' His gaze slid over her as greasy as oil. 'Might have to lose a few pounds, maybe get yourself some bigger titties, then I might be able to find a place for you.'

'I hear there's still a bartending job open. Can't expect Chris to pick up all the slack.'

'So we're back to Jazz, then?'

'Why else would I even enter this roach pit?'

'Maybe you just can't get enough of me.'

Tess thumbed at Po, and Max followed the gesture. 'You should be careful,' Tess warned. 'My friend over there's the jealous type.'

'He doesn't sweat me.'

Po leaned on the bar, his butt perched on a stool. One ear was cocked to the conversation, and his gaze was steady on the image in the mirror behind the bar. He was coiled, ready to charge over and slap some civility into Maxwell Carter. It would take the barest hint from Tess. She changed the subject.

'You said Jasmine wasn't one of your strippers.'

'I offered her a spot dancing, but she wasn't up for it.'

'She retained some morals, then?'

'Wasn't it. She was body conscious, I guess.'

'I've seen photos of her. Jasmine was beautiful.' She was a young woman who'd adopted the retro-look, part 1940s glamour, part tattooed vixen. She could have graced a promo video for a neo-rockabilly band.

'The johns enjoy foxy tattooed gals; I told her so, but it wasn't her tats she was ashamed of.' Max's damaged hand was held tentatively, yet he still used it to indicate the region of his lower abdomen and pelvis. 'She once got cut up . . . down here.'

'Surgically?'

'Nope. Nut-job with a knife.' He squeezed a smile.

Tess blinked. She'd heard nothing about Jasmine Reed being subjected to a violent attack.

'When did this happen?'

'Beats me. I never saw her scars, just heard about them.' He made a face, but Tess thought it was through regret not revulsion. 'Told her some of the johns would find them sexy too.'

Tess glanced at her own scar. She'd once been ashamed of it, so could understand why Jasmine might also be reluctant to undress in front of a leering crowd. These days Tess wore her scar as a badge of courage. Perhaps Jasmine did too, and the last she wanted was a scumball the likes of Max Carter ogling it.

'Her attack happened before she started working here, right?'

Max huffed. 'You suggesting it was one of my customers that got heavy with her? No way!'

'Just trying to establish a timeline, Max. So how long did she tend bar for you, before going missing?'

He shrugged. 'Told you already. Eighteen months, give or take.'

'Give or take what, a week, a month?'

'Fucked if I know. I'd have to check the books.'

'So check for me.'

Max held up his injured hand. 'I've more important things to be getting on with. Now if you don't mind, fuck off, will ya?'

Po stood without warning.

He crossed the floor before Max could flinch, and had hold of the bandaged paw. He squeezed. 'Apologize now, pecker head.'

Max screeched.

'I said apologize to the lady.' Po squeezed his hand, exerting crushing force. Blood dripped from the sapping bandages.

'For *what*?' Max howled.

'For your goddamn foul mouth.'

Tess's own mouth was a tight line, but she was peering up at Po. 'I can handle this,' she reassured him.

'Ain't going to stand by and listen to this butthead trying to make a fool out of you,' Po growled.

'Only one he's making a fool of is himself.' Tess turned her attention to the grimacing man. She raised her eyebrows.

'I . . . I'm sorry,' Max croaked. 'I . . . I spoke out of turn.'

'Personally I don't give a crap for your potty mouth. But

you were going to go and check exactly when Jasmine began working here.'

Po hauled Max up by his injured hand, sent him towards the bar with a short jab of his palm between the skinny man's shoulders. 'Git. And be quick about it. If I spend any longer in this crud hole I'm gonna catch a social disease.'

Max went behind the bar and through a door. Tess could hear him muttering from where they waited. 'I had everything under control,' she said to Po.

'Sick of waiting on the punk,' Po replied. 'That a-hole understands one form of instruction, and it doesn't start with "pretty please". Just needed a little motivation to get his butt in gear.'

'We'd better watch out in case he comes back with a gun,' said Tess.

Po picked up the Sprite. A glass was a handy distraction when thrown at a gunman's head.

Max leaned around the doorframe. He blinked furiously; his sparse lashes were invisible. He held up some papers. They were wage records – Tess doubted they reflected the actual amount of cash that changed hands with the club's workers, and were there only for when the revenue man came knocking. He moved from the small office, but kept the bar between them. Po set down the soda. Max fed out the sheets of paper on the bar as if dealing a hand of cards. 'These are the earliest slips I could find,' he said. 'This here is just over eighteen months old, so Jazz had to have been here a full month before that to get her first wages.'

Tess turned the sheet of paper towards her, read it. If it was a copy of the first wages Jasmine earned then she calculated that it was nineteen months and one week since 'Jazz' began working the bar. She made a mental note of the date.

'See,' Po said to Max, 'that wasn't so difficult now, was it?'

'Wish I'd never laid eyes on the bitch,' Max huffed.

Po held up a warning finger.

'I'm not talking about *her*,' Max said with a nod at Tess, 'I'm talking about Jazz. That damn bitch has caused me more trouble than I can put up with.'

'Civility,' Po said, his final warning.

Tess forestalled any further animosity. 'Who hurt you, Max?'

Max glanced at Po, but knew she wasn't referring to him. 'Nobody. I cut myself on some broken glass.'

Tess ignored the blatant lie. 'Someone else has been asking after Jasmine's whereabouts?'

'I haven't seen her, haven't heard from her, and have no fucking – uh – no clue where she is. I wish you'd all just leave me alone.'

'Who hurt you?' Tess asked again.

'You wouldn't know him.' Max's head came up. With the bar firmly between them he'd regained a little backbone. 'And whoever hurt me is my own goddamn business. Now . . . like I said before: get outta here. This is a private club and you're no longer welcome.'

Po looked poised to vault the bar, but Tess touched his elbow. 'Let's go,' she said.

Po sniffed, but turned with her for the door.

She paused. Looked back. Max was gently manipulating the sopping bandage. 'Word to the wise,' she said. 'Seriously, Max. Go get that looked at.'

'Still works fine,' Max replied, and held up his middle finger, flipping her the bird before ducking out of sight in his office.

# FIVE

Chris the bartender was standing on the sidewalk a few yards from the exit, smoking a cigarette. It had rained while Tess and Po were inside, and the overheated road again steamed, sending up streamers as dense as the smoke puffing from Chris's lungs. He nodded them over with a sweep of his pompadour.

'Just getting some fresh air,' he said, and grinned at the irony of his words.

'Can I bum one of those off you?' asked Po.

'Sure.' Chris tapped a Camel from a soft pack and held it to Po. He raised his eyebrows at Tess.

'No thanks,' she said, 'but you guys go ahead.'

In an act of solidarity with Chris, Po lit his cigarette with a Zippo he carried. 'Obliged,' he said as he took his first inhalation. Tess always marvelled at Po's ability to smoke socially, when he could put away the cigarettes for days at a time afterwards. She used to smoke, and had given up after a struggle. She could kill for one, but her addictive personality meant she'd be back to a pack a day if she took a single drag. She stood upwind of the two as they flicked ash into a kerbside storm drain.

'Max his usual effluent self?' Chris asked. At first Tess thought she'd misheard him, but Chris went on, 'That guy opens his mouth and raw sewage pours out.'

'He didn't have much to say for himself,' Tess said.

'Nothing you could repeat to your mama at any rate,' added Po.

'You guys are looking for Jazz, right?'

'You know where she is?' Po countered.

Chris shook his head, his mouth pinched tight on the Camel. He thought hard, and then flicked ash. 'Sure wish I knew she was OK, though.'

'When did you last see her?' Tess asked.

'Day before she went missing.' He nodded at the club, his sculpted pompadour flopping on his brow. 'Right there at Bar-Lesque. We crossed bar duties for a few hours early evening, but then I stayed late and she headed on out.'

'Say where she was going?' Po asked.

'No. Home. I assumed.'

Tess looked over at the club. There were a few guys hanging around on the nearest street corner. When it grew dark she suspected there would be more. 'Any of the dancers ever attract any unwanted attention when they leave?'

'Jazz wasn't a dancer,' Chris stated.

'She was pretty enough to pass as one,' Tess countered.

'She was striking.' Chris rolled his shoulders in admission, then shoved his hair back in place. 'I'm gay, but I'm not blind.'

He checked out the men loitering nearby.

'Those guys are regulars. Often hanging around, bumming smokes or loose change. None of them would go near Jazz.' He made a furtive nod at the club. 'You do know that Max only manages that place? It's owned by Daryl Bruin.'

'You talking about Bruno?' Po asked.

Tess watched Chris nod once in affirmation. She didn't need anyone to clarify who Daryl Bruin – or his alter ego 'Bruno' – was: she'd come across him plenty of times when she was still with the Sheriff's Department. Bruno wasn't so much a mobster as he was an entrepreneur who modelled his business dealings on a fantasy bred from watching too many James Cagney movies. Lately she'd spotted him cruising around town in a vintage roadster, wearing a double-breasted suit and fedora. He affected all the habits of a made man. The guy was a joke, but there were some who bought his act. She imagined that the local street hustlers would stay away from his business, and leave any workers under his protection alone.

'Does his protection extend to the bar staff?' Tess asked.

'Only when it suits him.' Chris leaned in and Tess caught a whiff of his breath. She found the aroma of burning tobacco comforting, it evoked warm memories of her grandfather, but expelled from the lungs it wasn't as pleasant. She averted her face but made out she was checking out the club again. Chris didn't notice. He went on. 'You noticed the wound to Max's hand?'

'Said he cut it on glass and you patched him up,' said Po.

'That's only part of the truth. Have you heard of a guy called John Trojak?'

Tess checked Po for any sign of familiarity. Po pulled on his cigarette.

'He came by a little while ago. He was also looking for Jazz.'

Tess felt the skin round her eyes tighten.

'He's a strange one,' Chris said. 'Comes over all pleasant and amenable, then he sticks a knife through Max's hand.'

'He works for Bruno?' Po ventured.

Chris snuck a furtive look at the doorway, perhaps expecting to spot Max eavesdropping on their conversation. 'I don't know why Bruno is interested in Jazz; it's not as if she was one of his girls. But he wants to find her badly enough that he had Trojak hurt Max.' He appraised Tess. 'You're the detective who stopped Hector Suarez's rampage, right?'

Tess shrugged, being slightly abashed by the notoriety her run-in with the crazy killer had brought her. She had only been one of a small group of people – including Po – influential in bringing him down, and for sending his brother Albert to prison for a long time, but in the media the focus of the story had been centred on her. As a once disgraced cop making heroic amends, she had been newsworthy.

'Seems Bruno wasn't impressed by Max for not telling him you were on Jazz's case.' Chris grimaced. 'Maybe I'm courting danger just by speaking to you like this.'

Here we go, thought Tess, the moment Chris's hand comes out for money. But that wasn't it.

'To hell with Bruno,' he said, and ground out his cigarette on the sidewalk. 'He doesn't own me, and I don't owe him.'

'You think Jazz left because she knew Bruno was after her?' Tess prompted.

'There was no hint of interest from him until after Jazz went missing.'

'She owe him money or something?' Po asked.

'Couldn't say. Never heard anything like that mentioned. Can't see Jazz taking a loan from him. She worked hard: I don't think she was short of a dollar.'

'Yet she worked bar at a strip joint,' said Po.

Chris didn't reply. He too worked the same bar. Perhaps he was offended by the suggestion that his job was demeaning. Po didn't apologize. He was stating a fact.

Tess decided to get things back on track. 'You mentioned Bruno wasn't happy that I'm looking for Jasmine . . .'

'Probably expects you'll find her before Trojak does.' Chris shook his head. 'I overheard what Trojak said before he hurt Max. It wasn't so much through discovering you were looking for her, but that Max had failed to mention it. Trojak knew you'd been to see Max before, and that Max had held back from telling Bruno.'

'You know anything about Jasmine being attacked?' Tess went on.

Chris frowned.

'I don't mean recently. A while ago.' Tess touched her abdomen.

'Oh, right. Yeah, I heard about that.'

'Do you know who was responsible?'

'Nope. She never shared the details; her scars were shameful to her for some reason. Didn't want to talk about them. She only mentioned the attack after Max brought up the suggestion of getting her on stage.'

'Did you see them? The scars, I mean?'

Chris shook his head. 'I'm not exactly the kind of guy she'd have taken her clothes off for.' He glanced at the door. 'Look . . . I'd best get back.'

'Thanks for your time,' Tess said, and held out her hand. There was no need to stall him any longer.

'Thanks for the smoke, buddy,' Po added.

'Yeah,' said Chris as he briefly shook Tess's hand. He wavered, as if he had a last thing to add, but heard the door squeak open and snatched away his hand. Max stood under the awning.

'Coming, boss,' said Chris and moved for the club.

Max whispered something out of earshot. Chris shrugged expansively, glanced back at them, then swerved around Max and out of sight. Max sneered and flipped Tess the finger a second time. He lurched inside, and the door bolts rattled. As he had said, they were no longer welcome inside his club.

'Where are your thoughts taking you?' Po asked.

'Thinking maybe I should've let you twist Max's hand a little longer,' she said. 'Maybe let you snap that middle finger off.'

'Be happy to oblige.'

'No. Let's leave it. Max doesn't know a thing. Chris I'm not too sure about; but I don't want to press him.' Tess suspected Chris was more inclined to supply information without prompting. 'I gave him my card when we shook hands just now. He knows how to get in touch. I think we'd be better off going to see Daryl Bruin, and find out what his interest in Jasmine is.'

# SIX

Flash showers continued to batter the sidewalks, and the heat frazzled the wet splotches to faded grey within minutes. Before long the hot spell would break and the rain would be more sustained. The rain would become sleet, and then the snow would fall. There was a time when Tess loved the snow, but that was before her life had almost been ruined one snowy night. The blizzard had killed her law-enforcement career, killed her engagement to her fiancé, and had come close to killing her. That same night she'd accidentally shot an innocent man. Now, with the first flurries, she couldn't help recalling the horrifying events that had almost destroyed her, and she greeted the first snow with a sour taste in her mouth. Therefore, she was determined to enjoy the hot spell while it lasted, and the less time she must spend in darkened roach pits like Bar-Lesque the better.

Thankfully Daryl Bruin did business from a modern office complex, renting rooms on the top floor of a Fore Street three-storey building, commanding a view over the narrow-gauge railway that served the eastern promenade, and the glittering water of Portland Harbor. When she entered his office, with Po striding alongside her, she was happy to find an airy, well-lit space. Bruin was taking a call, but flapped a hand at them to sit. Tess took the proffered chair, Po didn't. He stood with his sinewy forearms folded over his chest, peering down at Bruin with the slit-eyed gaze of a cat. Through the south-facing windows the sun bleached the office furniture and carpet, and caressed Tess's back with its warm fingers. Ordinarily she would welcome the sensation, but she knew that within minutes, as the sun intensified its massage, she'd grow uncomfortable. She sat back, and placed a hand over the back of her neck.

Her move reminded Bruin she was there, and he made a curt goodbye and placed down the phone. He folded his hands on the desk that separated them, his fingers glittering with white gold, and an expensive wristwatch hanging loose on his bony wrist. He wore a double-breasted pinstripe suit with wide lapels. His brown hair was slicked back and he had a thin moustache reminiscent of Clark Gable's. He was a good-looking man, but probably only to women of a certain age – over seventy. He appeared ready for a fancy dress party, one of those themed where partygoers turned up dressed as gangsters and molls. It made her wonder about his interest in Jasmine Reed and her own penchant for the retro look: maybe he had designs on her to help complete his image.

'I've been expecting you, Miss Grey,' he announced.

'You have?' she countered, and played surprised. It was apparent he'd been keeping tabs on her following her conversations with Max and Chris, but it did no harm to let him think he was a step ahead in the game.

'Well, of course. We both have the same lady's welfare in mind. It was only a matter of time until we met.' He ignored her a moment to check out Po. Po's features were still, but his turquoise gaze locked on Bruin's face. Bruin snorted. 'I'm only surprised that when you turned up you'd feel the need to bring along your bodyguard. Did you expect conflict between us? I'd rather we pool our resources; after all, a problem shared is a problem halved.'

'Nicolas isn't my bodyguard,' said Tess. But she didn't explain further. Po was her working partner, albeit in a silent, off the books capacity. He was also her lover. But Bruin needn't know that. She made a point of looking towards the office door, beyond which she'd only seen a female receptionist on their way in. Speaking of bodyguards, she wondered where John Trojak was. Actually, the term was probably incorrect regarding the man who'd pushed a knife through Max Carter's hand – she had no idea what Trojak's position was in Bruin's company.

Bruin offered Po a smile. 'So what exactly is he?'

'For one, I'm not deaf,' Po drawled, 'and I'm not dumb. You want to know something about me, then ask me.'

Bruin wagged a be-ringed finger at him, his watchstrap clicking on the desk. 'That's a Cajun accent if ever I heard it.'

'Got something against Cajuns?' Po inhaled slowly through

his nostrils, and Tess recognized the slow intake of air as a sign Po was readying for action.

'Nicolas works with me,' she said quickly, to forestall the situation degenerating rapidly out of control.

'He doesn't look like a private detective,' said Bruin.

'*He* looks exactly like a mug,' Po said, choosing to talk in the third person the way that Bruin did.

'Gentlemen,' said Tess, 'I'm sure we can have a conversation without resorting to insults.'

Bruin sat back. 'If I insulted anyone it was totally unintended. I was merely commenting on certain character traits I'd noticed.' He tugged an earlobe. 'I find accents fascinating. I hear Louisiana, but I also hear something else. How long have you been here in Maine?'

Po exhaled, and his arms unhooked to hang loosely by his sides. He leaned forward a few inches. 'We came here to ask you some questions, not to answer them.' He indicated Tess. 'Listen to the lady, answer what she asks, and try not to insult anyone again, intentionally or otherwise.'

Bruin's nose crinkled up, and he displayed teeth too white and straight to be wholly natural. He looked from Po to Tess, and gave a grunt of disbelief. 'I'm sorry. Whose office is this again? What gives *you* the right to come into my office and demand answers from *me*?'

Tess pinched her lips. She still had a hand cupped to the back of her neck, and suddenly felt foolish. She lowered her hand, and smoothed the collar of her blouse before she laid the hand in a half fist on the desktop. She tapped the nail of her index finger on the wood. 'You said you were expecting me, Mr Bruin. Why else would I visit your office if not to question you?'

Straightening his tie, Bruin said, 'I thought perhaps you'd come about the reward.'

Tess glanced up at Po, and saw a flicker of confusion in her partner's gaze. This was new information neither of them had expected.

'I can see that comes as a surprise,' Bruin said, and his lips quirked as if he'd won a small victory. 'I've offered a reward for information leading to the discovery of Jasmine Reed's whereabouts.'

'What's your interest in her?' Tess asked bluntly.

'It troubles me that nobody else seems to care for her welfare.'

Tess touched her chest. 'I care.' She gave a brief nod at Po. 'He cares.'

'Only because you were hired to find her. Otherwise you wouldn't be looking. Nobody would but me.' He raised his eyebrows, stared at her forthrightly. 'Tell me I'm wrong.'

He was right, but only partly so. Tess's detective skills had been purchased, but since she'd agreed to take on the task of locating Jasmine she had become personally engaged in the hunt. Having learned about the young woman's tough upbringing, and the way her disappearance had been ignored by parties who should know better, then she'd grown determined to help. It wasn't right that Jasmine had been written off as of no concern, simply due to her past. She deserved more. Tess couldn't help feeling a connection: throughout her own life she'd been misjudged, especially after the shooting that had gone so terribly wrong that snow-filled night. Everybody deserved a second chance.

'Who hired you?' Bruin asked.

'My client's identity is not your concern, Mr Bruin.'

'I'm guessing it was Jasmine's grandmother.'

Tess didn't reply, but her silence confirmed Bruin's statement.

'Aah, so now the old harpy is interested in Jasmine? That's rich . . . considering Margaret never gave a damn about the girl while she was growing up. Has the wizened old tart suddenly found a guilty conscience?'

'You speak as if you're familiar with Jasmine's upbringing,' Tess said. 'Yet I never heard your name mentioned in any of the background checks I ran. What is it I'm I missing here, Mr Bruin?'

'Oh, I think it's best you simply refer to me as a concerned member of the public.'

Po had returned to his station next to the window. Tess heard his scorn through the short exhalation he directed at Bruin. Bruin glanced over at him, but immediately his attention flicked back to Tess. 'I know Jasmine in passing. She was an employee at one of my business ventures. When I heard that she'd gone missing it bothered me that nobody cared about her. I'm a wealthy man, and I have resources to hand: I thought that if nobody else was doing anything to find her, then it was down to me to do the right thing.'

'Bullshit,' said Po.

Tess ignored his bluntness, though she had thought the same.

Bruin lifted both cupped palms. 'As unlikely as it sounds, it's the truth. I'm a humanitarian at heart. I have philanthropic tendencies, and if my money can help locate a missing girl then it's there.' He leaned forward a tad. 'Now, I'm guessing that Margaret Norris isn't paying top dollar for your services, so here's what I'm suggesting.' He waited a beat. 'You work for me.'

'No,' said Tess.

'You haven't even given my offer a moment's thought.'

'I don't need to. The answer's no.'

'Margaret needn't know, if that's what you're worried about. You can still take whatever she's paying, and I'll top you up. My only stipulation is that when you find Jasmine, then you tell me first.'

'No deal, Mr Bruin. Maybe you're used to buying people's services, but that's not what's important to me. There's something called professional integrity. Have you never heard of the concept?'

He shrugged off her question. 'We're all looking for the same girl. It makes sense that we pool what we know, and find her quicker. Surely that's a concept you don't find distasteful? I just thought that I might reward you for your cooperation.'

Po walked over. Bruin pretended to ignore him, his gaze fully on Tess, but the colour blanched in his cheeks and his pupils enlarged fractionally.

'If what you say is true,' said Po, 'then start talking. You have some guy called Trojak looking for Jasmine. You claim to be a philanthropist, but from what I've seen Trojak isn't flashing cash for information. He isn't rewarding anyone; he's dispensing punishment with a damn blade.'

Bruin finally looked up at Po. He leaned back in his office chair, smug as he rattled the gold watchstrap loose on his wrist, but he wasn't fooling anyone. He was putting distance between them. His fingers curled around the lapels of his suit jacket as he returned Po's stare. 'That's quite an accusation you've made there. Can I ask who told you such a nasty lie?'

He'd no loyalty towards Maxwell Carter, but neither would Po say anything that would endanger the man further. Sadly, Tess thought it might be too late, because it was apparent to all who was referred to.

'Max didn't say a thing. We saw what happened,' she lied, to divert attention from Max. The guy had remained tight-lipped, and didn't deserve to be punished for something he hadn't done. Tess was also careful in phrasing her words: she hadn't seen the act, only the aftermath, but if pushed on it she hadn't actually clarified one way or the other. Let Bruin squirm, he might be more amenable to telling the truth if he thought they would go to the cops with what they'd witnessed.

'I'll have a word with John when he returns,' Bruin offered. 'Though I find it difficult to believe he'd hurt anyone. He's a sweet guy.'

'So am I,' said Po, and allowed the irony of his words to percolate in Bruin's mind.

Bruin squinted up at him again. 'So you are a Cajun, right?'

Po didn't answer.

'This some kind of ancestral homecoming for you, buddy?' Bruin went on.

Again Po refused to offer any information.

Tess wondered what the hell Bruin was getting at: some subtle threat of his own?

'I read *Evangeline* in college,' he continued. 'Do you know it? If I recall it was about the expulsion of the Acadians from these lands.'

'Written by Henry Wadsworth Longfellow,' Po said, and Tess watched Bruin's eyebrows rise in surprise. Po looked like the mechanic he masqueraded as in his day job, but she knew there was much more to him than his skill with a wrench, especially that he was better read in the classics than most. Sometimes people checked Po out, noted the ingrained oil in his knuckles, his weathered features and laconic mannerisms and discounted him as some kind of slow-witted bumpkin.

Usually it was to their peril. 'I've read it. But it wasn't while I was in college.'

Tess wasn't following the discourse too well, and shifted uncomfortably. The intensified sun was doing its best to fry the back of her neck, and she surreptitiously placed her hand over the exposed skin. Po spotted her discomfort. He leaned and placed his knuckles on the desk, so that he negated the space Bruin had opened between them. 'Like I asked already, d'you have something against Cajuns, *buddy*?'

Bruin forced a chuckle. 'Nothing whatsoever.'

Tess stood.

'Seeing as there's nothing further to discuss, I think it's time we left,' she announced.

Bruin wafted a hand towards the exit. 'If you change your mind about my offer, please let me know. But you're right: talking like this isn't serving any purpose for now. I've work to do, as I'm sure have you. Don't let me keep you if it means stopping you from finding Jasmine.' He smiled with as little sincerity as the smile Tess returned.

No handshakes were offered.

Tess moved for the door and Po followed. In her peripheral vision she saw Po crouch, and she'd no illusion about what for. From his boot he retrieved a knife, which he used to scratch something from under a fingernail as he walked. The display wasn't lost on Bruin: he had a knifeman in John Trojak, but Tess also had hers.

# SEVEN

'So what was all that about?' Tess asked as Po drove away.

'I had gunk under my nail,' said Po.

'I'm not talking about your stunt with the knife.'

'The job offer?'

'Everything he said,' Tess corrected.

'The guy's a royal a-hole. He just can't help himself.'

'I'm not sure he's someone to be underestimated.'

'He isn't. But he's still an a-hole.'

'You'll get no argument from me.' As they followed the road, they paralleled the shoreline of Portland Harbor. The sun was arcing for the western horizon, and the sea had grown choppier as the tidal breeze lifted. The water was marked by deep shadows in the troughs, scintillating twinkles at their peaks. Occasional flashes were dazzling. Tess donned her shades. 'His reason for looking for Jasmine was a lie.'

'F'sure.'

'So what's his real interest? You don't think that he's her . . .' She faltered on the suggestion.

'Father? Could be. It would explain how he knows Margaret, and dislikes her so much. Guys don't like their mothers-in-law, as a rule.'

Tess snorted at his lame comment. 'Even if he is Jasmine's biological father, he never married her mother. Margaret can't be his mother-in-law.'

'I wasn't being literal.'

'Speaking of "literal", what was all that *Evangeline* stuff about?'

'Don't know. Maybe he was digging for dirt on me, and thought his best chance of learning something was through lateral questioning.'

'It worked,' she pointed out.

'He knows I'm not the knuckle-scraper he first suspected. He knows I come from original Acadian stock, but not why I returned to my ancestral lands.'

'Your people originally came from Maine?' Tess asked. She'd never given the subject much thought. But now that Bruin had raised the subject of *Evangeline*, a poem following an Acadian girl's search for her lost love, after the forced expulsion by the British of the Acadians during the French and Indian War, it made her wonder about his heritage. She already knew that some Acadians were relocated to Louisiana, where the pronunciation of their name became 'Cajun', but she'd never considered that his ancestors had originally resided in Maine.

'What do you know about your family tree?' he asked, being ironic. 'Can you go back three hundred years?'

She was a genealogist by training, having majored in history and cultural anthropology at Husson University before becoming a deputy. She was certain she could trace back her lineage to the *Mayflower* if she put her mind to it. But it shamed her to admit that beyond her great-grandparents on her mother's side she knew nothing about her ancestors. On her father's branch of the family she knew little beyond her grandfather, an NYC cop murdered during a convenience-store robbery, but for a few unfamiliar names and hazy dates. She stayed quiet.

'He was only trying to be smart,' Po suggested. 'I think he'd have enjoyed himself if he'd had to explain himself to an ignorant fool. He didn't get that opportunity.'

'What about this Trojak guy?' Tess asked.

'What about him?'

'Don't you think we should go and speak with him?'

'Not sure that would be a good idea yet.' Po turned his Mustang off Fore Street, heading across town for Cumberland Avenue, to check in with Tess's occasional employer, Emma Clancy. Following the investigation into the Albert Sower case, Emma had relocated her private investigative business from Baxter Boulevard after her original office was burned down.

'You're probably right. But I'm not ready to speak to Emma yet.' Tess helped rescue Emma after she was abducted and marked for death by Sower's henchmen, and had been rewarded by her, regularly sub-contracting work to her and – in an off-the-books capacity – to Po. However, the case concerning Jasmine Reed was a private job. 'Can you drop me at my place?'

'We're headed that way.' Tess also happened to live on Cumberland Avenue, on the upper floor of a small building housing an antiques and curios shop. 'I should go and check in with Charley while you do what you have to do.'

'You can read me like a book,' she noted with a smile.

'Uh-huh. You want to go and dig up what connections you can to Daryl Bruin. Why not save yourself some time and speak with Margaret Norris? I'm sure she might be able to enlighten you.'

'You could be right. But you know me: it's all about the details. I want to learn what I can so I can determine the truth about him, not just get a jaded impression from a woman who might dislike him as much as he obviously hates her.'

'You wondered earlier if Bruin was Jasmine's father. I don't see it. Unless he was a boy when he slept with her mother, I think he's too young. You will most likely check, he looks older because of the way he styles himself, but I'm betting he's only in his early thirties.'

Tess nodded. But her mind was turning over possibilities. 'This Trojak,' she said. 'He's not averse to using a knife. Both Max Carter and the bartender, Chris, mentioned Jasmine was once attacked and cut badly. You don't think her attacker was Trojak?'

'I wondered. Not sure we can come to any firm conclusion until we speak with Jasmine.'

He drove her to her house, pulling up alongside the kerb outside the antiques shop.

'Want to come on up?' she asked.

'You'll never get any work done then.' He smiled wryly.

She mimed looking at the wristwatch she didn't wear. 'You're still on the clock. Recreation time is for after work, not before.'

'Guessed you might say that. No, I'd best get to the autoshop and check that Charley has everything in hand.'

'Give that old devil a hug from me,' she said, and the frown she received wasn't totally unexpected.

'I'm only happy you don't want me to pass on a kiss,' Po said.

'Nah, this one's just for you.' She leaned over and pecked him on the lips. 'Down-payment for later,' she added.

He gunned the engine as he drove away, and Tess watched from the sidewalk as he headed for a less salubrious area of town. Once he'd turned on to High Street, she pulled off her shades and headed up the slope for the stairs at the side of the building: they allowed access to her apartment without having to enter the shop. Because of the lingering heat the shop door was wedged open, and inside, sitting behind a counter and reading a paperback novel, was the owner, Mrs Ridgeway. Normally when spotting Tess she'd pass the time with chit-chat, and usually Tess welcomed the gossip: the book must have been an engrossing read because she didn't look up, for which Tess was grateful, because she was eager to get on with her research. She took the wooden steps quietly, and made it up to her apartment, her key ready to unlock the door, before Mrs Ridgeway appeared at the bottom of the stairs. Tess fought hard to conceal the sigh of regret that rushed through her body. 'Oh! Hi there, Mrs Ridgeway. Sorry, I wasn't deliberately being rude; I saw you were reading and didn't want to disturb you.'

'Please, Tess. How long have we been friends? Call me Ann.'

'Of course, Ann. Sorry.'

'There's no need to be sorry, no need. In fact, I can tell you're busy, so I won't keep you.' Ann Ridgeway was a small woman, thin to the point Tess was in fear of her drying up and blowing away on the hot breeze. She wore her grey hair cropped short, and her spectacles on a beaded lanyard around her neck. She toyed with the lanyard with the fervour of a Catholic rubbing a rosary. 'I only thought to mention you had a visitor while you were out. I must say . . . I found it all a little odd.'

'Odd?' Tess echoed. Occasionally her brother Alex called by, and one time even her mother had arrived unannounced. As judgemental about Tess's living arrangements as she was about every other aspect of her life, her mother's visit had been blessedly short and she was yet to return. Po had been to her apartment on numerous occasions, but he was her only regular visitor these days. Mrs Ridgeway knew Tess had a small circle of friends, so took note of any strangers who came by.

'He was a strange one. Wouldn't give me a name, and wouldn't state his business, but I caught him up there, peering through the door glass as if checking you were in or not. I didn't hear him knock or ring the bell. Usually I can hear everything: these old wooden buildings carry noises. There are times when I wonder if the place is haunted the odd things I hear when I know you're not home . . .' She chuckled at the suggestion, or maybe it was because she'd realized she was prattling on. 'Were you expecting a visitor?'

'No,' said Tess. 'He wasn't a delivery guy?'

'No. He was wearing a suit and tie. Neat greying hair. Carrying a few extra pounds, too. Not fat, but bulk. I heard him wheezing when he came down the steps, but I don't think it was from the effort of climbing up there. My guess is he was annoyed to find you gone. When I asked what he wanted, he practically ignored me, brushed past like I wasn't there. He looked well presented, but the thing I recall most about him was his smell. Body odour . . . woo!' She wafted a hand under her nose. 'That fella was due a shower and change of drawers if you ask me.'

'Did you notice what he was driving?'

'He had a car parked, but I'm sorry, I don't know about makes and models. If it helps it was blue. Actually, come to think of it, the colour was more like the aquamarine of your gentleman friend's eyes.'

She meant Po. His eyes were noticeable because they were turquoise, an eye colour not very prominent in their neighbourhood.

'And he didn't say anything?' Tess pressed.

'No. Not a thing. Perhaps he pushed a card under your door, but I didn't see him with a pen or paper.'

Curiosity was burning at Mrs Ridgeway, and if Tess allowed it she'd gladly read any note left by the mystery man, but Tess had no intention of urging her up the stairs. 'Well, it's odd as you said. But if his visit was important I'm sure he'll call again.'

'I'll keep an eye out. If I see him again, I'll let you know.'

'Thanks, Mrs Ridgeway . . . uh, Ann. Now, I'd best get inside. This heat, huh? If I don't shower and change, my visitor won't be the only one turning up people's noses.'

Tess keyed open the door, glancing at the floor on the chance a note had been slipped underneath. There hadn't been. She turned back to Mrs Ridgeway. 'The plot thickens,' she announced, then before the old woman could get started again she waved, smiled, and closed the door behind her. She waited, counting to ten, heard soft clunks through the floorboards and guessed it was safe to open her door again. She checked, and Mrs Ridgeway had indeed returned to her novel. Tess expertly inspected her door. There were a couple of scratches on the lock, but they were dull, and had probably been made by her. She looked up and down the jamb but there was no sign that the mystery man had tried to force the door. It appeared he'd only done what Mrs Ridgeway witnessed. There were greasy palm prints on the glass. He'd peered inside, but the glass was opaque and he'd have formed no image of her apartment, just a blur of colours and warped shapes.

She closed the door, and for extra measure shot the bolt.

There was no blinking light on her answer machine. So the visitor hadn't called ahead, nor left a voice message after finding her home vacant. She knew she'd received no call on her cell, nor text message or email. If he had been a random caller – a salesman or canvasser – then he wouldn't have been spying inside. He wouldn't have been so furtive when confronted by Mrs Ridgeway and would surely have stated his business.

So what was his intention?

Who was he?

If it were whom she suspected, then it gave a feasible answer to her first question.

She went to her work station, fired up her iMac, brought up Safari, keyed in a name and location.

John Trojak. Portland, Maine.

There was little online: a few brief mentions of the name, but nothing to clarify if they were the man she was looking for. She checked for images, but there were none. She logged into another program, bringing up her account with Emma Clancy's firm. Because Emma worked almost exclusively on behalf of the local district attorney's office, she had access to databases that most private investigators couldn't resource. Tess had already left some covert programs running, watching for use of the credit cards in Jasmine Reed's name and for hits on her cellphone signal, interrogating database systems for anywhere her name appeared, and finding her vehicle's location via various law-enforcement and government agencies. She was also interrogating social networks. She should really check them for any indication of Jasmine's whereabouts, but the identity of her mysterious visitor was nibbling at her mind. She skipped over the results of her searches, and found nothing of importance, while mulling over the appearance of Daryl Bruin and John Trojak in her case. She entered a local law-enforcement database and immediately got a ping back on Trojak.

On screen was a series of photographs, the most recent relating to a case of domestic violence at his family home. She scowled at the report until something jumped out: Trojak was the victim.

She printed the picture, thought things over, folded the picture once, then headed downstairs to her prime witness. Ann Ridgeway put down her book as Tess entered the shop, took off her spectacles, and allowed them to hang on their lanyard. She'd heard Tess descend the stairs, so knew she wasn't expecting a customer.

'Hi, Ann,' Tess said.

'So you did get a note?' Mrs Ridgeway asked, as she eyed the folded sheet of paper in Tess's hand.

'No, this is something I printed myself just now. I was wondering if you'd take a look at it.'

'Of course.'

Tess handed over the sheet and waited while Mrs Ridgeway put on her spectacles again, then unfolded the photograph.

Tess watched Mrs Ridgeway's face as she pored over the image.

'Well?' Tess prompted.

'It looks as if this poor thing has been beaten,' Mrs Ridgeway said. Her nose twitched a couple of times, and she shook her head. 'Who is he?'

'I was hoping you'd recognize him.'

'You thought this was the man who was here earlier?'

Tess nodded. 'Obviously I was wrong.'

'It's a different person,' said Mrs Ridgeway. 'Even if I ignored the bruising round his eyes and the swelling to his forehead, this here isn't the man I saw earlier.'

At a loss, Tess only frowned. Mrs Ridgeway handed back

the photo and Tess took it, looked down at it, hoping that at this angle Mrs Ridgeway might study it again and change her mind. The man at her door wasn't a big deal, but Tess had been certain she could solve the mystery by identifying John Trojak and tying them together.

All was not lost. Since Trojak had entered their investigation, it was best that she and Po had an idea of what he looked like, because she believed it was inevitable that they'd be meeting soon, and she didn't want either of them to be off guard when he finally showed up.

# EIGHT

'It sounds as if we should be more concerned about his wife causing trouble than worrying about Trojak,' said Po.

'That's not funny.' Tess scowled at him. 'Male victims of domestic violence aren't as rare as people think.'

'I know,' he said. 'Chill out, Tess. I was only joking.'

'It's not a laughing matter. It's a huge problem, only it doesn't get reported as often as it should.'

'Tell me about it,' Po said. But he'd no intention of talking about the subject, or of listening, because he turned away. Tess was positive there was an unfamiliar emotion washing through him. She wanted to reach out to him, to comfort him, but there were periods of his life he was yet to share with her, and he wasn't ready to open up about this one yet. She respected his privacy: sooner or later he'd feel ready to trust her enough to tell her everything. She'd learned some minor details about Po's murdered father, but his mother remained a complete mystery: had he let slip something he'd attempted to keep secret for years?

They were at Charley's Autoshop, in the dingy office at the rear of the workshop area. The room was small, cramped and grimy. The desk was overflowing with oil-smudged paperwork. A couple of chairs, and an ancient PC, practically filled the rest of the limited space, so there was nowhere that Po could escape. He stood with his back to her, as if checking that all was in order in the garage, but she knew he regretted bringing up the issue of domestic violence, and hoped it would pass.

'There was nothing new on Jasmine,' she offered, to change the subject. 'But I was able to learn a few things about Daryl Bruin and his pal Trojak.'

He squinted over his shoulder. He nodded, thankful she'd understood his discomfort and moved on.

'Any reason why they should be hunting for Jasmine?'

'No. But I learned a thing or two why Bruin might feel some

kinship with her, enough that he might genuinely want to help Jasmine, as he said.'

'I don't buy it.'

'Me neither, but we have to consider it.'

Po returned and sat on the edge of the desk; he'd no option seeing as Tess had claimed his chair, and the second one was piled with old paperwork. He stared at her, his features unmoving.

'Well, you going to keep me in suspense all night?' he finally asked.

Tess wiggled her eyebrows. 'Daryl Bruin came up through the same system as Jasmine. After his father booked out, his mom began turning tricks to make ends meet. She fell into hard drugs, died of a heroin overdose when Daryl was seven, and he entered the system, was made a ward of the state. He was a foster kid, in and out of various homes, until he was adopted at fifteen by the lovely Bruin family. Oh, and you were right about him not being as old as he looks.'

'It's that stupid moustache and old-guy clothes,' Po said. 'So Bruin isn't his original name, huh?'

'No. His adoption files were closed, but you know me—' she tapped a finger to the side of her nose '—I have my ways and means. I only know about his former life because I discovered he'd been adopted. I was able to follow his trail back from there, and found the names of the families who fostered him. Back then he still used his mom's name.'

'Don't tell me: Reed?'

'If only it were that easy, huh? And no, it wasn't Norris either; he's no relation to Margaret or to Jasmine's mom, Ellie.'

'Jasmine's dad?' Po offered.

'I did wonder, but it came back negative on them being siblings. Jasmine's mother didn't name the father on the birth certificate, so I met a dead end there.'

'Margaret Norris could tell you who Jasmine's father is.'

'She might be able to, but I'm not sure it would help. See, I found out who Daryl Bruin's father was, and he died before Jasmine was even born. Before she could even have been conceived. No, their fathers are two different guys.'

'So how does knowing any of this help?'

She shrugged. 'Like I said, it gives Bruin a genuine reason

for wanting to help find Jasmine. Maybe he is the kind-hearted philanthropist he made out, and he genuinely does want to help because of their similar backgrounds.' She screwed up her nose, showing she didn't believe a word of it. 'Or there's something I'm still missing.'

'I vote for the latter,' said Po.

'I second the motion.' She grinned. 'But I did find something interesting: you didn't ask me the name of Daryl Bruin's biological father.'

'Trojak,' Po stated.

Tess's grin faded. 'Talk about stealing my thunder . . .'

'It was the only other name I could think of,' Po admitted. 'So what's the deal? They're brothers?' He asked the latter with a hint of trepidation in his tone. They'd just got off the back of a case involving brothers, and Po was still carrying the scars from that conflict.

'No, they're not brothers. Cousins. John Trojak's father is Bruin's uncle.'

'Trojak's the elder of the two? Why's he following Bruin's instructions like a lap dog?'

'Bruin's the brains of the outfit; Trojak's the brawn. Not unlike our relationship when you think about it.'

Po grunted in laughter.

'Maybe his wife's not the only one pushing him around,' Tess said, and realized their conversation was back on thin ice. But Po had apparently moved on from whatever had disturbed him earlier.

'Or maybe he gets to do neat stuff for Bruin that his wife doesn't allow.'

'Could be it.' It was all conjecture, and did nothing to help find Jasmine. But Tess hated a mystery. No, that was untrue. She hated loose ends. She actually *loved* solving a mystery, and the inclusion of Bruin and Trojak had added extra layers to the conundrum surrounding Jasmine Reed's disappearance.

'So . . .' Po went on. 'You learn anything about your visitor?'

She'd told him about the man peering in her front door earlier, and how she'd initially suspected that it was Trojak sniffing around for clues.

'Not a thing. All I have is a brief description of him and his car. I can't do much with either, and maybe I'd be wasting my time doing so. For all I know it was just some random caller who has moved on.'

'Or a prospective client,' Po suggested.

'No.' Tess shook her head. 'My home address isn't listed alongside my business. Clients wouldn't come to my house, they'd contact me through Emma's office, or via my website.'

'Unless it's someone who knows you personally. An old friend or colleague?'

'I don't know. Why be so tight-lipped when Ann Ridgeway spoke to him?'

'Perhaps he had personal reasons and didn't want a busybody knowing his business.'

'Well, there is that. Mrs Ridgeway does like to gossip.'

Po shrugged. The mystery guy was unimportant. But not to Tess. She didn't like loose ends one bit.

'What's the plan?' Po asked.

'I've set an alert on my computer; if it gets a hit on Jasmine I'll get a message on my cell. You about done here?'

He nodded. Charley, the manager and chief mechanic – and unbeknown to most, Po's employee – had already left for the evening. All that was left to do was to shut up the shop. 'What's on your mind?'

'We do a bit more digging,' she said. 'Maybe knock on a few more doors. I really can't sit around waiting for a text message.'

'And there was I thinking of grabbing a pizza and going to see a movie,' Po sighed.

'Ha! The last movie you watched in a cinema was *Ferris Bueller's Day Off.*'

'Actually,' Po said, 'it was *Biloxi Blues*, but I can see how you made the mistake.'

'Y'know, it's a weird thought: the last time you graced a theatre was before I was even born.'

'If it's any consolation I was still a kid myself. My taste in movies has matured since then.'

'I've seen your DVD collection,' she said, and got up to follow him from the office. '*The Goonies* is a positive sign of your continuing maturity.'

Po smiled in good humour, but shooed her towards the exit.

He'd already dropped the roller shutters over the repair bays, so the only way out was through a scarred old door in one corner of the building. He doused the few remaining lights as she pushed out the door. Her Prius was parked alongside the near kerb, while Po's Mustang dominated one of the parking bays in front of the shop. The only other car in sight was parked on the opposite corner, and its colour immediately caught Tess's attention. It was aquamarine. Its headlights were on, and the engine running. A guy peered at her from behind the steering wheel.

She glanced back, checking on Po's progress, but couldn't see him. Electronic bleeps indicated he was setting the alarm panel. She looked back at the car, her attention alerted by a change in the engine's grumble. The car began crawling towards her. 'Po,' she called, 'get out here.'

'What's up?'

Tess wasn't sure if anything was up, but she knew enough not to trust coincidence. The appearance of an aquamarine-coloured car so soon after having a similar vehicle described to her couldn't be ignored. She stepped out past the front of her Prius and stared through the windshield at the driver but couldn't make out any detail. One hand came up, as if she intended hailing him. The driver hit the gas, and the car powered towards her. Tess lurched back, fearful of being smashed against her own car, but the move was overkill. The car didn't come near hitting her, or the Prius, but it was obvious the driver wished to get away before she could get a good look at him.

Breathless she watched the car streak away, and wasn't aware of Po until his hand fell on her shoulder.

'What was that all about?' he asked.

'Don't know. But I think it's the man who was at my house earlier.'

'So if he's looking for you, why not stop and state his business?'

She was at a loss.

Her mind was busy with other matters. One of them was committing to memory the car's licence-plate number.

'I don't know,' she said. 'And I don't mind admitting, I don't like it.'

# NINE

'Any luck, sis?' asked Alex Grey, leaning from the window of his patrol car. He'd drawn the cruiser parallel to Po's Mustang, so he was alongside Tess in the passenger seat. They were on a public jetty on the bayside trail, facing out to where the lights of moored boats bobbed on the inky water of Back Cove.

'You mean in finding Jasmine Reed?' Tess replied.

'Unless you've another job on I don't know about?'

'Nothing,' she said. 'On both counts.'

'I tried getting somebody in missing persons interested in Jasmine again, but . . .' He shrugged. 'I'm sorry, it's a case of the girl who cried wolf too many times.'

'Yeah. I've already been down that track.'

Alex clucked his tongue in thought, and Tess heard Po's chuckle. He found her habit of clucking both endearing and frustrating in equal measures. When she glared at him he said, 'Must be in your genes.'

Observers often commented on the resemblance between Tess and her brother. Sometimes people thought they were twins, despite the difference in height, age, and Alex's obvious masculinity. They were both fair of hair and complexion, but their eyes were different colours. Alex came off the better in his sister's opinion; he had the startling pale blue eyes of their father while hers were a dowdy shade of brown, an inheritance from her mom, but at least without the sour squint. There was no denying their familial connection, and it had been exaggerated when they were in uniform. However, Tess's Sheriff's Deputy uniform had been relegated to mothballs while Alex still wore his Portland PD duds with pride. They had an older sibling, Michael Jnr, but he'd moved out to Dayton, Ohio, with his new family, though he too was a law-enforcement officer, a state trooper. Michael Jnr was as dark as his siblings were fair.

Tess loved her brothers equally, but the connection she had with Alex was special, not simply through how alike they were but because they'd recently worked together in a fashion that meant they were indelibly linked through their mutual friends. Alex and Emma Clancy were an item, and it was Alex who'd convinced his girlfriend to hire Tess when she'd required the services of a trustworthy investigator, and also Alex who'd introduced her to Po when she'd sought a guide to travel with her to the bayous of Louisiana. She owed him, but then she wasn't beyond asking him for another occasional favour.

'There's one thing you might be able to help with . . .' she said and offered him a puppy-dog flash of her big brown eyes.

'Uh-oh. Why'd I know there was going to be a catch?'

Tess had hailed him to a meeting with a promise of coffee and donuts, which she had held on to: he'd get them once he agreed to her request.

'No such thing as a free dinner,' Po said. 'You should know that, buddy.'

'What do you want?' he asked, in a weary tone.

'How's about running a licence plate for me?' she asked.

'You can't do that yourself?'

'I could if I was back at Emma's office, but I'm not. I'm out looking for a missing girl.'

'You know I'm putting my ass on the line every time I do something like this.'

'Of course I know. That's why I appreciate your help so much.' She rattled the bag of donuts. 'Chocolate covered, with candy sprinkles.'

'Yeah. Why worry about my ass when you're going to make it grow as big as a house?' Alex reached for the bag, but Tess retracted it.

'Run the plates first,' she said.

'At least give me the coffee,' Alex said. 'I'm so parched the dispatcher won't understand me.'

She handed across the steaming coffee. Then recited the number she'd committed to memory as Alex greedily peeled back the lid. He sniffed the contents, sighed deeply. He slurped noisily even as he reached for the mike pinned to his chest. He called in and requested details on the aquamarine car as if he was currently observing it on the street.

Words were fed back to him, but directly into his earpiece, so Tess had to wait while he thanked the dispatcher and turned back to her. 'Donuts for details,' he said, and reached across, making a gimme-gimme wiggle of his fingers.

'You do know how clichéd you look?' said Tess.

'Clichéd or not, I love donuts. Give 'em over.'

Alex relayed the details while digging in the bag and pulling out the first of four chocolate-covered treats. The licence tag came back to a late-model Ford, owned by a Jeremy McGuire of Portsmouth, in neighbouring New Hampshire.

'Wasn't a Ford our guy was driving,' Po pointed out. 'It was a Chrysler.'

'You sure you gave me the correct details?' Alex asked Tess and was rewarded with a scowl.

'No reports on McGuire's car?' she prompted.

'None. But that could change. McGuire maybe doesn't know his ride's missing its licence plate yet.' Alex chomped on a donut. 'I'll put out a BOLO on this Chrysler, see if we can give the driver a pull. He has some questions to answer.'

Tess exhaled noisily through her nostrils. If the mystery man was driving around with stolen plates on his car he was definitely up to no good. He was now an issue for the police, but it irked her: she wanted to know what the deal was with him before he was thrown in a cell.

'Do me a favour, Alex,' she said.

'Another favour, you mean. It'll cost you.' He shook the bag of treats.

'Jeez, how many donuts can one cop eat?' Po asked.

'You can bank them for another evening,' Alex promised, 'I don't want to get so fat I can't get into my uniform.'

'Deal,' said Tess. 'Hold off on that BOLO, will you? Give me a chance to get to this guy first, before anyone else pulls him in.'

'You're asking me to ignore my duty when there's a criminal commissioning illegal activity on my patch?' He grinned round a mouthful of dough. 'Six donuts next time,' he said, 'and you don't tell Emma. She has me eating seaweed and quinoa salads, for God's sake. She hears about me bingeing out on junk food and I'm history.'

'Your silence for my silence,' Tess said.

'You got it, sis. But with one caveat: if I do come across this dude, I will pull him over myself.'

'Fair enough,' Tess agreed, 'but I also have a stipulation. You call us to come speak with him before you take him in.'

'Can't see any harm coming from that,' he agreed.

Po started the Mustang, the engine growling like a big cat.

'Right, so we've work to do,' Tess announced. She reached over and bumped knuckles with her big brother. 'Don't eat all those in one go.'

# TEN

There was only one word to describe her predicament that summed it up precisely: Hell.

In the dim space where she squatted, she couldn't tell the passage of time. She'd tried to keep track, timing her days with the number of meagre meals she'd been given, the times she'd urinated and defecated in the tin bucket that had yet to be emptied and spoiled the small room with its rank stench. She'd attempted to number the days by the infrequent visits of her captor, but she had no idea of the potency of his sex drive. Three times he'd come to her, brutal in his need to sate himself, but she couldn't say if the horrific attacks had occurred daily or if there were longer breaks between them. There were other women here, and she'd heard their screams, their plaintive cries, their gasps of agony, and knew she wasn't the only one to be visited by their monstrous dominator.

The cut on her head had scabbed, the bump beneath had disappeared, as had the ache in her chest where it had impacted with the steering wheel the night she was taken, but those aches had been replaced by others, and they continued to pain her, though the abrasions and bruises were nothing to the agony of mental torment.

Three female voices she'd heard to date. But she couldn't be certain that the four of them were the extent of the brute's enforced harem, because she'd attempted to speak to her neighbours and none had replied. They understood the rules. They must not speak to anyone other than their master, and only when commanded to. She had soon learned that lesson, having been kicked mercilessly into submission, and warned what would become of her tongue if she did not obey the rule of silence. She didn't doubt her abductor's capacity to cut out her tongue, but also knew he was reluctant to remove the tissue he'd made her pleasure him with after the beating. She'd been tempted to bite, but a similar reluctance to forcefully remove her teeth was no issue to him. Nobody spoke, nobody whispered; the only time they gave volume to their voices was when he drove them to cry out in pain or terror. There could be other girls secreted in this awful place, but having been held longer, they better understood the folly of disobeying the rules and now remained silent . . . or he had removed their tongues.

How far could a person fall into the foggy miasma of terror before they were lost forever? Her early life hadn't been pleasant, but compared to now she'd been living a dream of relative comfort. If she thought her teenage years had been awful, where she had constantly struggled against anger, frustration and depression, then she'd no concept of what real hardship felt like. How she'd love to step back in time to those days she'd once raged against, because she'd grasp every precious moment as if it was her last.

It was strange – a tiny part of her wanted to lie down and die, whereas another more significant piece raged against her despoilment and enforced captivity, wanted to flee this place, to breathe fresh air, to run, and run, and never stop running.

But she was running nowhere.

How could she when she was shackled to what she'd discovered through the blind groping of her fingers was an old engine block, or other piece of machinery. She could drag it a few inches, but that was the extent of her freedom. She was only loosed from her shackles at visiting time, and then she was placed in leg irons of a different type, while forced to shuffle to another room her captor usually kept unoccupied, her sight taken from her with a rubber hood pulled down to her nostrils, and her voice stifled by a rubber ball wedged between her teeth and held in place by a leather strap. He would remove the shackles, the gag, but never the hood. She had no idea of what he looked like, though she knew he was large, muscular and strong. His slurring voice, alternately delivered at a whisper and in a roar of anger, could be that of an older man, but his virility contradicted it.

Though he was cautious in concealing his identity from his slaves, there was never an attempt at covering his tracks in a manner that suggested he was forensically aware: he ignored the use of a condom, and was neglectful of forcing his victims to bathe. In fact, she was sure that – even discounting his seed – she was a festering Petri dish of his genetic soup because he'd licked her, spat on her, bitten her, and without doubt his blood was beneath her fingernails. She suspected strands of his hair had adhered to her sweat-pasted skin, and his pubic hair had become woven into her own, and the thought that she was plastered with so many of his identifying genetic markers both repulsed and terrified her. Being so blasé about covering his tracks meant a number of conflicting things: his reason for obscuring his identity was more personal, while everything else suggested he wasn't fearful of ever being identified through trace evidence, because their bodies would never be discovered. What was his demented intention: to keep replenishing his stock of sex slaves as they became worn out, and doing away with his castoffs in a final and devastating manner?

On one occasion before she'd been led to the private room where he conducted his filthy attacks she'd heard a distant noise from deeper in the labyrinth. At first she couldn't make any sense of the rushing-roaring sound. It was similar to a storm-force gust pushing beneath the eaves of an ancient house, or floodwaters surging through straining pipes, but her mind conjured another image: blistering white-hot flames roaring up a chimney. Did he have a furnace stoked for the moment he had finished playing with his latest victim, where she would be forced to climb inside, all genetic evidence seared from her, even as her flesh was charred to the bone?

Thoughts of the furnace added validity to the notion that she was in hell, or at least in an anteroom of Satan's fiery domain. It was a thought she couldn't shake. She'd formed an impression of her whispering captor based on the fanciful idea of being stuck in a supernatural realm, one where he was a flaming-eyed demon, whose forked tongue whickered over her skin, tasting her essence, checking if she was ready to be pitched into the bottomless pit, to be eternally consumed by immolating flame. Sometimes she wondered if she was already dead and this was her punishment for every wrong she'd ever done or for every sinful thought.

No, she cautioned, he's just a man – a brutal, deranged, cruel, sexual deviant, but a man all the same – and she was still alive.

While she lived, there was a chance she could still be saved. Persevere, she told herself. Get through this.

Do what you must do to survive.

This isn't hell; it's a precursor to something else.

Stay strong.

She wept in the darkness, silently.

She knew that things could grow infinitely worse before they got better.

But what could be worse than hell?

# ELEVEN

Maintaining good manners was important to John Trojak. He'd been raised to say *please* and *thank you*, and to offer his seat to pregnant ladies, to give way for the feeble or infirm. He called older women *ma'am*, and men *sir*, and if he wore a hat he would doff it in company. Without manners, modern society – a word wholly inappropriate in this case – would be uglier than it already was. He despised foulmouthed people, but recognized that to most the use of course or abrasive language was from a lack of education, when they found erudite conversation difficult and resorted to four-letter words, simply for emphasis. Those who were ignorant he could forgive, with only a regretful shake of his head, but when he was subjected to a tirade of curses for no other reason than the speaker was being intentionally hurtful, then he took umbrage. At that point he'd politely ask the curser to refrain from using bad language in his presence. Sometimes his request was enough, sometimes it encouraged a renewed torrent of abuse; on those occasions he'd resort to a more pointed demand.

Some stupid people misjudged his easy-going nature and politeness, thinking they were signs of weakness. Others thought him a target for their uncouth jokes. He showed them he was neither weak nor a laughing matter. Without, he was pleased to say, resorting to the sort of language they understood.

His ease at dispensing violence when he was averse to swearing might seem odd, even humorous, to Daryl Bruin, but his cousin wasn't averse to using Trojak's double standards to his benefit. Trojak met first impressions during business deals, and when those deals went well he was remembered as a quiet, well-spoken gentleman, but when the deals went bad . . . he was recalled as something else entirely. Thankfully, his reputation preceded him and the times he'd had to resort to strong-arming a competitor or supplier were few, but that was because the initial messages he'd delivered had been so indelibly pressed home. He'd never killed any of Daryl's competitors, but he'd come close, and the fear of the unknown was the most powerful of all.

Because he disliked bad language and uncouth manners so much, his cousin Daryl asked why he stayed with Veronica, instead of finding another woman who matched his sense of decorum. Vero was his wife of twenty-two years. For twenty of their years in matrimony she'd been a loud-mouthed bitch – Daryl's words not his – and in the latter ten years had gone from using her sharp tongue to throwing her fists to teach him exactly what she expected of him. But as well as good manners, and behaviour, Trojak also believed in the value of a promise, and when he'd made his vows, they'd been binding. For better or for worse. In sickness and in health. Veronica's behaviour was through a chemically induced sickness of the mind and heart; what kind of a man would he be if he were to walk away in her time of need?

He loved Veronica. He was sure she loved him equally, in her own way. If she didn't then why would she care so much about what he did – or rather how she perceived what he did – to be wrong and try to set him on the right track? She wasn't an educated woman. If he could forgive the ignorant, then he could forgive his wife. Right?

But he couldn't forgive the idiot who'd almost smashed the life out of him on the corner two blocks from Charley's Autoshop. The fool had driven away so rapidly when Tess Grey and her man had come outside that he'd failed to see Trojak on the sidewalk. Taking the corner so recklessly, his Chrysler mounted the kerb, and Trojak had to flatten himself against a shop front to avoid being struck. The driver glanced at him, but instead of an apology had barked a curse, '*Get the fuck outta the way!*'

Trojak's car was parked just out of sight of the autoshop. Incensed by the crazy driver's antics and foul shout, he jumped in his car and gave chase. His blood was up, his vision tunnelled, and his hearing resounded with all the vicious barbs and threats Veronica had slung at him for two decades. Lord help the man when Trojak caught up with him.

Sense overtook him at some point. He eased off on the

throttle, and fell back. He didn't give up the chase, only length-
ened it, because after his first flash of ignominy he realized
that something more important was afoot than teaching an
ignoramus a lesson. The driver wasn't trying to escape him,
but Tess Grey. Obviously he'd been spying on her and sped
off when his cover was blown. Trojak could guess the reason.
He was after information, and seeing as Tess was engaged in
the hunt for Jasmine Reed, then the driver must also be seeking
her. Daryl's instructions had been clear. Nobody speaks with
Jasmine until after *me*.

The driver hadn't noted Trojak's pursuit, or if he had he
hadn't reacted. If anything, he'd slowed once he was out of
sight of Tess Grey. He obviously did not want to be identified
by her and especially not by law-enforcement officers. He had
something to hide, and not only his interest in Jasmine Reed.

Trojak had a wondering mind. Instead of pursuing, he
followed. He ran his tongue along the back of his teeth,
thoughtful as he kept the Chrysler's taillights in sight. His mouth
was gummy, and he was parched, in need of a drink. No, that
wasn't it. He was experiencing the after-effects of an adrenalin
rush following his close call. When he thought about it, he
could still sense the elevation of his pulse, even feel it through
his fingertips on the steering wheel. He inhaled, exhaled slowly.
Best approach things calmly.

The Chrysler led him a merry chase, and it ended north
of the city in a neighbourhood dominated by industrial units.
The Chrysler pulled down a dirt track and into the lot of a
deserted metal-fabrication workshop. Property realtors' signs
dotted the entrance. Trojak assumed the driver had chosen this
place at random, because it appeared unused. He parked near
the track, and went in on foot, moving through darkness, the
light from the moon enough to negotiate the uneven ground.
Wire fences on either side would make it difficult to hide should
the car return, but Trojak wasn't fearful of that happening.

At the end of the track he reached a gate that stood open.
Puddles left from the cloudbursts dotted a torn-up parking lot,
and glistening streaks on the tarmac showed the Chrysler had
gone round the side of a small complex of wooden buildings.
He could hear running water from a creek, but it wasn't loud

enough to cover the sound of a car door opening and closing. He jogged across the lot, nimbly avoiding the puddles, and set his right shoulder against the corner of the first building. Bushes alongside it offered cover as he moved ahead, treading slower this time. At the back corner he again set his shoulder against the wall, and used the point of balance to lean out a fraction and peer into the darkness. He could make out a small copse of trees that crowded the nearest bank of the creek, and the sound of running water was louder now. Closer by it was a blot of darkness, the moonlight obscured by the building he hid alongside. Trojak allowed himself to settle, and for his vision to grow accustomed to the night. He began to pick out form and movement, and he was aided when the door of the car was opened again and the internal light came on. He watched the driver lean inside, rummage around and then pull something out that he wadded between his hands.

The driver then opened the trunk and pulled out some sort of canister. Trojak knew exactly what he was up to, so it came as no surprise when the canister was upended and liquid was splashed over the car, and then inside. The empty gas can was thrown on to the back seat. The driver stepped back, and busied himself with wadding and twisting the material he'd dug out of the car. It was thrust into the neck of the gas tank.

The driver stepped away, still in silhouette, but there was enough light for Trojak to note that he had cocked his ear. Trojak slipped back out of sight, and was positive he'd evaded discovery. His hand dipped in his pocket and he clasped the lock-knife he kept for moments such as these.

A scratch, a grunt, and then a second scratch caught his attention, and he couldn't resist peeking round the corner again. As he did yellow flame billowed for the heavens, and in reflex he screwed his eyelids tight, and ducked from the wash of heat gusting towards him. As he opened his eyes again, colours danced in his vision from the afterglow of the fire's ignition, and he had to blink to see clearly. The fire reached for the heavens, oily smoke piling above it. Trojak glanced from the car to where he'd last seen the driver.

There was no sign of him.

The fire growled, and the car caught in its searing grip creaked and moaned, but distantly Trojak believed he could hear the crackling of breaking twigs. The driver had torched the car, then chosen an escape route down by the creek. If anyone noticed the fire and alerted the emergency services they'd arrive via the track, and the driver had no intention of being spotted leaving the scene.

'Son of a gun,' Trojak wheezed. If he didn't get out quick, he'd be the one spotted leaving the site, and he'd have some tough questions to answer. He retraced his steps alongside the building. Behind him there was a whoosh as the fire flared, followed a moment later by a heavy thump as the gas tank blew. Trojak rounded his shoulders in reflex.

As he reached the next corner and swung around it, readying for a dash across the puddle-strewn lot, his attention was on the entrance to the track. He caught a flicker of movement in his periphery a split-second too late, and he made a big mistake.

Drawn by the movement, his head jerked towards the tyre iron swooping at his head – it was an instinctive reaction and one that meant he'd no hope of avoiding it. The metal slammed him, and a white flash of agony exploded inside his cranium.

Sickened, Trojak went to one knee, as he pushed out against his assailant with an extended palm. He dug again for his knife with the other.

The tyre iron came down again, this time against the side of Trojak's skull.

And despite all his misgivings about cursing, he had only one word for his predicament: 'Fuck!'

The harsh curse never left his lips. He fell face down on the gritty tarmac, even as a third slam of the bar snatched away his last spark of lucidity.

# TWELVE

They had Emma Clancy's office to themselves. It was late evening now, and Emma and her staff had left, but as a trusted employee, Tess carried keys to the building, as well as the alarm codes. She'd asked Po to accompany her to the office on Cumberland Avenue, so she could access programs unavailable on her computer.

'With this weirdo on the loose, I'm not letting you out of my sight,' he promised, though she knew he'd no love of sitting idle while she scrolled through data. It was only a short stroll from the office to her home, so he could easily take off if he wished, but Po wasn't making idle promises: he was more concerned about the mystery man's agenda than she was. He sat, ankles crossed, hands folded on his stomach, still and silent while she tapped and scrolled.

'Damn it! This is a waste of time,' she finally announced, and pushed back from the desk.

Feeling like a loose wheel, Po squinted over at her, watching as she scrunched her fair hair between her fingers. She leaned back, head flung over the headrest of her office chair, and she let out a prolonged sigh as she rubbed her fingers over her features. Aware of his scrutiny, Tess turned to him, raising her eyebrows, her mouth hanging open. 'The less I find out, the more it worries me,' she said.

'F'sure,' Po replied.

'If Jasmine was still alive, I'm certain we'd have got a ping on one of her credit cards or cell by now. Also, I've been watching the DMV reports for anything about her car turning up abandoned, or whatever, and there's not a damn thing. There's nothing on any law-enforcement databases about a body being found . . . none that matches Jasmine, at any rate. It's as if she's fallen off the face of the earth.'

'Or she's better at hiding her movements than we thought,' Po offered.

'But why hide?'

'Why run away in the first place?' he countered.

'If we knew that, at least we'd have somewhere to start looking from.' Tess stood, knuckling the small of her back.

'I'm not trying to teach you to suck eggs, Tess, but have you checked the latest hospital admissions?'

'I have. Nothing. But good thinking, anyway.' She cupped her face in her hands again, and moaned wearily. 'I'm kind of at a loss, Po.'

'You look worn out,' Po said. 'Maybe you should call it a night. I'll take you home . . .'

'Uh-uh. I'm not ready to switch off yet. There's something I'm missing, I just don't know what it is.' She looked at him for the answer, but it wasn't forthcoming. He merely pinched his lips. 'Is it too late to go and speak with Margaret Norris again? I want to hear about the assault on Jasmine, because that's another thing troubling me: there's no record of it on any police database.'

Po stood, and that was all the answer she needed.

'Just let me switch everything off and we'll get going.' Tess leaned back to the computer. Po sauntered over to the window, peeling open a slither in the blinds. It was dark out, but the streetlights made for decent visibility. He could see his Mustang parked on the opposite side of the road, but no other vehicles. Specifically he was looking for an aquamarine-coloured Chrysler. Regrettably there was no sign of it. He turned back to Tess.

'Been thinking,' he said.

'Yeah?'

'The guy in the Chrysler,' he said. 'What if he isn't here for you?'

Tess eyed him, and he touched fingers to his chest.

'The Chatards?' she asked.

'The bounty on my head still stands,' he told her. 'Who's to say someone hasn't come looking to cash it in?'

'Sounds like a lot of trouble for someone to come all this way from Louisiana for a lousy two thousand bucks,' she said.

He shrugged. 'Remind me to call Pinky, will ya? Who knows, maybe the price has gone up.'

'I don't see it,' she said.

'You do realize that sounds kind of insulting from over here?' He smiled. 'You saying I'm not worth more than a couple of grand?'

'Don't worry, Po,' she said. 'You're priceless.'

'At least you didn't say worthless.'

Tess pushed him out of the door in front of her, and when he wasn't moving fast enough for her liking she nipped his butt.

'Man, first I have to endure insults, now it's sexual harassment,' he quipped.

'Get moving, or I won't goose your butt next time, I'll kick it.' Tess bit down on her joke. After Po's discomfort at speaking about domestic violence it sounded inappropriate. She held back, allowing him to leave under his own steam.

Once she'd reset the alarm and locked up, she crossed the street to where Po had the Mustang rumbling. He didn't watch her approach, too busy scanning the street for anyone lurking in hiding.

The suggestion he was the target of the mystery man wasn't too wild a notion. After his father was murdered, Po killed his slayer – a man called Jacques Chatard. While Po served time in Angola for it, a brother of Jacques tried to avenge him, and paid for his mistake with his life. The Chatard family was unforgiving, and on his release Po left Louisiana and settled in Maine. Blood feuds ran deep in the South, and he knew that sooner or later he'd have to end it, one way or another. They'd learned that the Chatards had placed a bounty on his life while seeking a witness in the case against Albert Sower, and that men were willing to cash in on the prize when two punks tried to capture him at gunpoint in the parking lot of a hotel in Baton Rouge. Tess's intervention turned the bounty hunters' attempted abduction into a resounding defeat. Perhaps after news reached their ears of the gunmen's failure, the Chatards had raised the price in hope of enticing more capable hunters? It was a possibility. Tess was more high profile than her companion; it was a genuine worry that she'd been targeted in the hope that she'd lead the latest hunter to Po. But if that were the case, then why had the man taken off like a scalded cat when Po joined her on the sidewalk outside Charley's Autoshop? She was confident that his scrutiny had nothing to do with Po, but that left her scratching her head for the actual reason he'd been spying on her. Before she climbed in the car, she too made a surreptitious check around.

Margaret Norris lived in North Deering, a large residential neighbourhood bordering the town of Falmouth, only minutes away. The neighbourhood boasted some of the oldest houses in Portland, having been spared the fire that razed much of the city to the ground in the nineteenth century. Oldest property didn't necessarily equate to most expensive, and Margaret's family home was a modest clapboard house, though it had a tiny but colourful garden to the front and rear. Po had previously accompanied Tess to meetings with Margaret, so knew exactly where he was going. He hit the gas as soon as she was settled in the seat of the muscle car, the sudden acceleration forcing her deeper in the plush leather.

Tess's cellphone played a ditty – her brother. She put it on speaker so Po could hear.

'Hi, Alex. What's up?'

'Found the car you're looking for.'

'Where?'

'You know Fall Brook, off Auburn Street?'

Fall Brook was a small waterway that ran through North Deering, and emptied in the tidal Back Cove. For a majority of its course it largely paralleled Washington Avenue, she had no idea where the brook ran from beyond that. 'You'll have to be more specific, Alex.'

He gave her a pointed description of the location, and Tess knew exactly where he was directing her. She had shopped at a nearby commercial strip, and as a Sheriff's Deputy had once or twice attended jobs at the adjacent industrial buildings Alex described. 'A couple of your old compadres have a suspect held at the scene. I'm on my way there now, you want to join me?'

'They have the driver in custody?'

'That remains to be seen. They have the car, except it's burning like a torch. PFD and first responders are at the scene already. You'd best be quick, sis, before the suspect's hauled off to lock-up.'

'Be there in minutes,' Po announced, and the Mustang rocketed.

# THIRTEEN

B urning rubber, overheated metal, seared electrical components, and vaporized chemicals formed a stinging
potpourri of stench that assaulted Tess's sinuses and
forced tears from her eyes. She held a palm over her mouth
and nostrils, tried to breathe shallowly but it didn't help. Her
throat caught, spasmed, and she hacked up a cough as if
she still smoked twenty cigarettes a day. Yet she didn't turn
away, still rapt on the smouldering remains of the car, deciding
if it was the one she'd watched fly past her outside Charley's
Autoshop. Portland Fire Department had doused the fire, and
the broken asphalt of the lot was awash with stinking, floating
debris. The tyres had exploded, as had the gas tank, and the
metalwork was stripped back to its base, discoloured by
the intense heat to a myriad of reds and blues and yellows. Yet
there were some small areas the flames had failed to reach,
beneath the headlights, and around the fenders, and there the
colour was blue-green. Alex and Po – who had an expert eye
for vehicles – assured her it was a late-model Chrysler, even
without having to check out the decal on the front.

'How long until we can properly identify the make and
model?' Tess asked, though she knew that it wasn't a huge
task.

'Not long,' Alex replied.

Even with switched plates, there'd still be a vehicle identification number beneath the hood and etched on the chassis. The
only stumbling block at the moment was that it would take a
CSI tech to look over the smouldering remains before the details
could be fed through the system. Before that could be done,
the car would have to be declared safe to approach by the PFD
commander, and then possibly lifted with a crane to see underneath, having sunk to its axles when the rubber burned off
the hubs. It was a job worth doing. Identifying the exact vehicle
wasn't that helpful on its own, but once they established where

it came from it might help identify the driver – sadly he was long gone.

'Who's the guy in the ambulance?' Po asked.

'Witness,' Alex said. 'Victim. Take your pick.'

'What happened to him?' asked Tess.

'Says he noticed flames as he was driving by, came in to investigate and was struck by an assailant. He was still unconscious when the fire crew arrived.' Alex touched his head. 'Must have a skull like concrete; looks like he took the wrong end of a steel bar to his head a few times. I'm surprised he's awake and talking. Refusing to go to the ER.'

'Stubborn,' Tess said, and couldn't help a glance at Po. 'Any chance I can speak with him, Alex?'

'Hold up a minute. I'll have to clear things with the deputies.' Alex walked away, approaching a Cumberland County Sheriff's Department patrol car. Tess had already checked out the pair of deputies, but they were newcomers since she'd left the department, and she wasn't sure they'd be amenable if she approached them directly. Best that Alex did the negotiating.

Tess waited while Alex spoke with them, all the while catching glances from the two young men. One appeared nonplussed, while the other's eyebrows rose close to his receding hairline. He knew her name, and of the short bout of hero-worshipping she'd received from some of her colleagues after helping to bring Albert Sower to justice. He grinned at her, showing all his perfect white teeth, and a wet tongue curled at the back of the bottom row. She feared that a simpleton had replaced her: but that was only judging the young guy by his goofy looks. When Alex beckoned her over, he was amiable, and seemed genuinely honoured to meet her. He stuck out a hand, which Tess accepted, and made his hellos, courteous and erudite. His nametag read Bronson. 'My buddy Arlin speaks highly of you, Miss Grey, says he wouldn't be the officer he is now without your leadership and support.'

'How is Arlin?' Tess asked, genuinely surprised to hear about her ex-colleague. Arlin was there the night she almost lost a hand. For some odd reason he'd distanced himself after she left the department, and she'd assumed it was through shame at being associated with her: but that was when she'd been enveloped in a self-imposed funk, when she thought her life was going down the toilet.

'He's our shift commander now,' said Deputy Bronson, with a nod at his partner, perhaps seeking agreement. 'He's one of the good guys.'

The second cop sniffed loudly. Her name meant nothing to him then, and his opinion of Arlin wasn't as rose-tinted as Bronson's. But he was more aloof to Tess than he was objectionable. He nodded, without meeting her gaze, then turned back to surveying the smouldering wreckage. 'If you're going to speak with the wit, you'd best do it now. Medics are keen to get on.'

'I'll be minutes with him at most,' Tess promised. 'You get a name off him?'

Bronson was the one to answer. 'Mister Trojak, John Arran.'

Po was standing to one side, with his tattooed arms crossed over his chest, his chin down. In her periphery Tess watched his head snap up, and he took a step forward. Her surprise was no less evident, and Bronson wasn't blind.

'You know the guy?' he asked.

'I know of him,' Tess answered, but she was already striding for the ambulance. Po matched her step for step. Alex was only a beat behind them, and he spurred forward to catch Tess's elbow.

'Go easy, sis. He isn't the one who's been following you.'

'I know he isn't the driver of the car,' Tess responded without stopping, 'but he hasn't been following me? He just happened to be here through coincidence, huh?'

Alex and Po shared a glance.

'Trojak's name came up earlier today,' Po told him.

'In the Jasmine Reed case?'

'Works for a dude called Daryl Bruin,' Po explained. 'Who also happens to be looking for Jasmine.'

'I should speak with him,' said Alex, but was forestalled by Po's outstretched arm, and the palm on his chest. 'Give Tess her minute with him, then he's all yours.'

Alex halted, but it was only to stare down at Po's hand. 'Do you mind removing that?'

Po's mouth turned up at one corner, but he withdrew his

hand. Alex owed Po, but their personal alliance was still shaky. Alex was a cop, Po an ex-con, and Alex wasn't fully comfortable with their association, or the more intimate one that Po shared with his sister. He certainly didn't appreciate being treated as if he should defer to the time-served killer.

'Don't forget I'm only doing a favour for my sister,' Alex said, and there was more to the statement than he voiced. 'And don't forget who's actually in charge here, Po.'

'Duly noted.' Po strode after Tess, who was already leaning into the rear doors of the ambulance. Alex mouthed a silent curse at Po's back.

Catching a glance from Deputy Bronson, Alex offered a nod, telling him everything was cool. He moved for the ambulance, but angled so he was out of sight of the injured man inside. Perhaps he'd learn more from Trojak without showing himself: people said things to other civilians that they'd never admit in the presence of a cop.

Tess stepped up inside the ambulance, a male medic making way for her. The medic went round the side of the ambulance to speak with the driver.

Po stood in the doorway, watchful, silent for now. Alex caught a glimpse from him, but that was all. He gave off a hint of wariness, as if he expected trouble, and if Alex knew anything of the Cajun it was to trust his finely tuned senses. Alex rested his palm on the butt of his sidearm. Po winked at him. You're in charge, his smug smile attested.

'John Trojak,' Tess said without preamble. 'Want to tell me how you just happen to be here?'

'My head almost got stove in,' replied Trojak, and he touched fingers to the swelling on the side of his head. Another wound to the top of his skull held a gauze pad, through which seeped blood.

'You know I'm not talking about being in the back of an ambulance,' Tess said.

'I know what you meant, just letting you know what I'm suffering on your behalf, Miss Grey.'

'You know who I am, huh?'

'Of course. I spoke to Daryl earlier; he said you'd been by his office, and that he'd suggested we work together to find

Jazz. I'd be remiss as an investigator if I didn't check out who I'd be working with.'

'Let's make something abundantly clear at the get go: we aren't working together. And since when were you ever an investigator?'

'Since Daryl asked me to look into Jazz's disappearance.' Trojak transferred his fingers to the top of his head, peeling away the gauze. He studied the bloodied patch, then allowed the gauze to slip from his fingers on to the bed alongside him. 'Head's not as bad as it looks, in case you were wondering.'

'I wasn't.' But despite her snippy response, Tess checked his wound. There was no open cut, only a grazed patch where he had lost some hair and the blood oozed from the abraded scalp. He touched other sore spots, but there was no alarm in his expression. He was going to survive his injuries.

'I heard you went to see Maxwell Carter earlier today, and you hurt him. I think you've misinterpreted what it takes to make an investigator. Don't confuse interrogation with torture, Mr Trojak.'

'Did Max say I hurt him?'

'He didn't have to.'

'Then if Max didn't say I hurt him, where's your proof?'

'I saw the result of your handiwork.'

'Max cut his hand on some glass, I heard. He's a clumsy guy.' Trojak struggled to sit up. In the doorway, Po stirred, his arms unfolding to hang loosely by his sides. The motion wasn't lost on Trojak who eyed him for a long second. 'I take it you're Nicolas Villere?'

Po didn't answer, because if Trojak had spoken with Daryl Bruin then his identity was already apparent. Bruin had probably also warned him about Po's less than subtle display with his knife. Trojak settled himself on the gurney, one arm propped behind him for stability. His suit jacket had been removed, and his shirt was dotted with blood, plus dirt from where he'd collapsed from his beating. 'Would you just look at me,' he moaned. 'Veronica will go spare when she sees the state I'm in.'

'Veronica is your wife?' Tess asked, and couldn't resist a sour smile. 'I just bet she'll make you do your own laundry, huh?'

Now it was Trojak who didn't answer. He was no fool, and would suspect that Tess had already checked him out, and learned of his shameful past as a victim of domestic violence. Tess thought he'd nothing to be embarrassed about, but suspected that wasn't the case. But she wasn't against mentioning her dislike of the woman she'd never met, if it meant it would get a truthful response from Trojak.

'So,' she went on. 'What's the story? How'd you end up here like this?'

'Isn't it obvious?' Trojak replied.

'It's obvious you enjoy the sound of your own bullshit,' Po offered from the doorway.

Trojak's eyelids pinched at Po's final word. He chose not to answer Po; instead he looked directly at Tess. 'I followed the guy here who set fire to his car.'

'You were following me first,' Tess corrected him.

'I came over to try to speak to you,' he said. 'Daryl said you were against working with me. I only wanted to reassure you of my good intentions. When I got to the auto-repair shop, I saw that bozo driving away so fast that I guessed he was up to no good. The son of a gun almost run me over, so I went after him to ask what his game was. I followed him here, saw him torch the car and thought that was it. But then he cold-cocked me, got me good too.' Trojak again touched his wounds, flinching for good effect.

'I don't appreciate you lying to me,' said Tess.

'Who's lying?'

'You are. For one, you weren't coming to the autoshop to speak to me; you had to have followed us there. OK, you might have learned that Nicolas works from the shop, but I doubt it. And if you had, and had come by to speak, then why were you out on the street in a place where you almost got run over? Why not just drive up to the shop itself?'

'I wasn't sure of its exact location. Only knew what street it was on. I got out my car to have a scout around, that's all.'

'Beep-beep,' said Po from the doorway. 'That's the sound of my bullshit detector alarming.'

Rubbing his face with both hands, Trojak sighed. 'OK. You're right. I did follow you guys to the shop, but I didn't know how you'd react if I just walked on inside.' He glimpsed at Po. 'I was waiting for my moment, to approach in the open, where you would see I was no threat. That was when that guy took off as if he was in a drag race and almost ran me down.'

He was still lying, but only partly. Tess chose to ignore the disparity in his story, because it wasn't necessary to push for more. 'Do you know who the man in the car was?'

'Nope. Do you?'

Tess shook her head.

'Shame. I owe him.' Trojak made an effort at tucking his shirt in his trousers.

'You did get a look at him, though?' Tess prompted.

'No. He snuck up on me from behind. Smacked me upside the head with a tyre iron or something and that was all she wrote. Next thing I knew was when a firefighter was standing over me.'

Po exhaled loudly. 'You saw him torching his car, but you never got a look at him?'

'Guy had his back to me. Could barely make him out in the dark, then once the flames went up he was out of there. What can I say, buddy? I can't say what I didn't see.'

'Or you did see him but don't want to admit you know him,' Po pushed.

Trojak again returned his attention to Tess. 'I didn't see him. Actually, that's not entirely true. I got a glimpse of him through the windshield, and the son of a gun swore at me. If I saw him again I might recognize him, but as for knowing him beforehand . . .' He frowned, but his expression looked forced. Trojak did have an inkling who his attacker was, he simply wasn't prepared to admit his suspicion yet.

'Describe him as best you can,' Tess said.

Trojak shrugged. 'White guy. Maybe in his mid- to late-thirties, short dark hair, regular features. No facial hair or distinguishing features I can recall. Just one of those faces can easily lose themselves in a crowd. You see him, think he looks kind of familiar, but you just can't place him, so you forget about him and move on. You know the type, right?' He thought harder. 'Y'know, when I think about it, he was a big guy. When he was standing out there by the burning wreck, I could see his silhouette. He looked broad, but not like one of those muscle guys; more like he naturally grew big, a bit like I did.'

Tess recalled Mrs Ridgeway saying something similar, that the mystery man looked as if he was carrying some bulk.

'Did he say anything to you?' she asked.

'If he did, I didn't hear him or I don't remember. Being clubbed around the head kind of has that effect sometimes.' He offered a smile, maybe seeking sympathy.

Tess stood. There was clearance overhead, but she still stooped. Her nose was inches from Trojak's. 'I said earlier we won't be working together. I haven't changed my mind. Now you've learned what comes of sticking your nose in where it isn't wanted, take note of the warning. Back off from this now, Mr Trojak.'

'You can't make me do that,' he said, eyeing her directly.

'I'm not making you do a thing,' she stressed, 'I'm offering you some good advice. Leave finding Jasmine to me, go back and tell Daryl the same thing.'

Trojak shook his head.

'Buddy,' said Po, 'you had a close call here. Could get closer.'

Trojak turned slowly to stare at Po now.

'That sounds awfully like a threat to me,' he said.

Po's eyebrows rose marginally, but he left things at that.

# FOURTEEN

He was in desperate need of a shower, a fresh set of clothes too. He'd been on the road, staying in fleapit motels and pay-by-the-hour hotels, for the best part of a week since leaving California, and stunk with every long mile and restless night of his journey. He'd hitched rides for the most part, only recently stealing the Chrysler while its owner was left bleeding in a ditch, and had made it to Portsmouth, New Hampshire where he swapped out the plates. He'd suspected that he'd have to dump the car but not as soon as this. He'd made a big mistake in getting too close to Teresa Grey like that, and who was the big guy who'd followed him here and watched him destroy his ride? There was something very familiar about the shape of the head he clubbed. Maybe he should have hit him again. He had slammed the guy's head three times in total with a tyre iron, should have given him a fourth whack for good measure. He was confident that the guy couldn't describe him, he'd got him from behind and he was definitely unconscious when he had hidden in the undergrowth alongside the creek. Covered in pluming smoke, trying not to cough and give away his hiding place, he'd watched the arrival of the first responders, and a pair of Sheriff's deputies. He was in no fear of discovery from the lawmen: they made the assumption that he was long gone, and just stood around the fire probably wishing they had some marshmallows to toast. The fire crew was perfunctory in dealing with the flaming wreckage, as were the medics who worked on the guy he'd downed. He should have checked the man for keys, because he must have driven here – although taking the guy's car might not be a good move, not while he still lived. He'd only be forced to dump it at first opportunity, before it became the subject of a search as part of a murder investigation.

He waited and watched. Was intent on doing so until the emergency crews left and he was safe to emerge from concealment, all the while getting smellier and dirtier. He was wearing a suit and slip-on shoes, and neither were designed for crouching in bushes on a muddy riverbank. He still clutched the tyre iron, working his fingers along its haft, reminding himself to ditch it in the creek before leaving. For now he'd hang on to it, in case one of those deputies made a check of the area. A tyre iron was not much of a weapon against a pistol, but it was all he had. If one of the deputies did come snooping, he'd have to act fast and decisively, and maybe even liberate a sidearm in the process. He'd a feeling he was going to need a more dependable weapon before he was done, and his opinion was enforced after he watched three more people arrive at the scene. One was a cop, the others a mismatched couple. The tall guy concerned him, while the woman made the breath catch in his chest. The man was over six feet tall, built rangy, and his knuckles were pronounced: looked like a natural fighter if ever he'd seen one, and he'd seen a few in his time. The woman was Teresa Grey. There was no doubt about it; he'd recently seen her come out of the garage and look directly at him, and because he'd studied the photographs of her he'd found online after discovering she had been hired to find Jasmine Reed. They had a shared agenda, though Grey had no idea. The photos he'd studied were months old now, featured in news stories where she had helped save the life of a kidnapped woman, but she hadn't changed any. Perhaps her fair hair was a little longer, styled differently, but she was as lovely as she had been when smiling shyly for the camera. Actually, here in the flesh, only a dozen yards from him, she was more beautiful again: he could almost imagine the silky touch of her skin under his fingertips, the delicate scent of her breath as his lips touched hers, the firm resilience of her body squirming under his as he bore into her.

'Easy,' he said under his breath and was unsure whether his warning was to curb his instincts, or if he was talking about how he could take her and do to her what went unfinished with Jasmine. He chose to believe it was the former. It was best that he pushed down any desire for her and concentrated on his task. Grey was a distraction he couldn't allow his base desires to fixate on, not before he was done with Jasmine at any rate. Afterwards, well, that was another story.

Grey got into the ambulance. He wished he could hear what was said between her and the man he'd injured, but from his position he couldn't even see inside. The tall guy had posted himself in the doorway, blocking the view even if he crept to another vantage point, and the cop stood by too, his thumb resting on his service pistol. It was too risky getting closer, so he'd just have to wait.

His vigil didn't last long.

Grey climbed down from the ambulance, stood close to the tough-looking guy she'd been with at the garage, and he noticed that their closeness went beyond comradeship. At one point the tall guy snuck an arm around her waist and gave her a quick hug. She didn't appear averse to the show of affection, even glanced up at him and pouted her bottom lip as she patted his taut backside. Next the injured guy stepped unsteadily from the rear of the ambulance, mopping his face with a wad of gauze as he struggled into his dirty suit jacket. Grey's companion placed himself between the injured man and his woman, and it was immediately apparent that there was no love lost between the two posturing men. The plot thickens, he thought, as he watched the injured man walk away, hailed a few seconds later by the cop who'd been lurking nearby. Some words were exchanged, and details scribbled in the cop's notebook, but then the injured man was allowed to leave on foot. It was the first clear look he'd gotten at the man's face, and he was momentarily taken aback: John fucking Trojak? He knew him from back in the day. What was Trojak's intention in following him? Not good. He was tempted to sneak after him, finish the job with the tyre iron, and take his car after all, but again he told himself to take it easy.

He'd made enough mistakes already, and couldn't afford to make any more based on his rash nature. In hindsight, going to Teresa Grey's home had been a stupid move, especially allowing himself to be seen by the nosy old sow from the antiques shop downstairs. He'd been equally negligent observing Grey and her companion at the autoshop, getting far too close and allowing himself to be spotted, and forcing him into a speedy escape. That had encouraged Trojak to pursue him, and had brought them into conflict. In one damn evening he'd left behind a trail of witnesses, and now two reasons for the cops to hunt him. On its own, the burning of the stolen car would probably only generate paperwork, but the savage assault on Trojak might encourage a more proactive response. Stupid, stupid, stupid.

Keep your mind on what you came here to do, he silently chided. Think, consider the consequences before you make another move. Don't do anything to jeopardize finding Jasmine.

It was sensible advice.

But how could he ignore the smooth, swaying motion of Grey's hips as she walked alongside her companion towards their souped-up muscle car? He had unfinished business with Jasmine Reed, and fresh business to start with this latest rare beauty to catch his attention. Briefly he was torn between which woman he wanted to take most.

# FIFTEEN

Worry, relief, shock and confusion were the most obvious emotions that played across Margaret Norris's face in the few seconds after answering her door. It was late, and she'd dressed for bed, appearing in the gap below the security chain in the partially opened door clutching at the neck of a towelling dressing gown. She wore spectacles, but she'd doffed them in anticipation of retiring to bed, so her features screwed around her nipped eyelids as she peeked up at Tess.

'Yes?'

'Mrs Norris, it's me. Tess. Teresa Grey.'

'Oh, Tess!' Margaret nodded but made no move to unlatch the chain. 'Who's that with you?'

'This is my associate, Nicolas Villere. You've met before, but if you'd rather he waited while you—'

'It's fine, I'm decent,' Margaret cut in. 'But why are you here so late? Oh, don't tell me—' Her face crumpled, fearing that Tess had arrived with the worst news possible.

'We haven't found Jasmine yet, but there are some things I need to speak with you about. I hope you can help, it will speed up the search for your granddaughter.'

'Yes. Yes. Anything I can do to help.' She fumbled with the security chain, realized it was impossible to open while the door was ajar, so made apologies and closed the door. She again rattled at the chain.

'I can wait at the car if you prefer,' Po offered. 'She might be uncomfortable speaking to you with a man present.'

'She said she was decent, no worries.'

There was another clunk, and a soft muttering from beyond the door.

'Just thought that the subject might be a tad sensitive for her to discuss while I'm there.' Po shrugged.

He had a point.

'Maybe it would be best.'

'Could do with a smoke, at any rate.'

Without waiting for an answer, Po turned and wandered down the porch steps towards the small front garden. Before he was off the bottom step he plucked a pack of Marlboros from his shirt pocket, then delved again for his Zippo. He was sparking up before Margaret finally got the door open. She looked expectantly at Tess, then for where Po was.

'My friend is going to wait with our car,' Tess said by way of explanation.

'He can smoke inside,' Margaret assured her.

'He won't,' Tess said.

'I will,' Margaret stated. 'You mind?'

'It's your home, Mrs Norris.'

'Not all of you young kids think like that these days; had a fella round fixing my shower threatened to leave if I didn't cease and desist immediately. Jeez, not as if I had the right to complain about the halitosis he was breathing in my face.'

'Smoking doesn't bother me,' Tess reassured her. Not that she enjoyed the odour that clung to the place when she stepped inside the house. Opening a window or two wouldn't go amiss if Margaret was going to continue chain-smoking. The walls were coated in a thin film of tar, the same colour as caramel up near the highest corners. It was a sepia canvas so unlike the colourful flowers outside.

'Come sit,' said Margaret after closing the door. She led Tess to a small sitting room, neat despite the acrid aroma and blue pall hanging in the atmosphere. Tess sat on a small flower-patterned settee while Margaret took an easy chair opposite her.

'So no news on Jasmine yet?'

'Nothing definite,' said Tess so she didn't take away all hope of finding the young woman. 'But there have been a couple of developments I'd like to talk with you about.'

'Like I said, if there's anything I can do to help, you only have to ask.'

'OK. But I must warn you, Margaret: I don't intend on beating about the bush. Some things I'm going to ask you are going to be blunt, and it will help if you give me an equally straight answer.'

'Be as blunt as it takes, but just give me a second or two.' Margaret lit up a cigarette, perched a glass ashtray on her thighs. Her spindly little legs stuck out from below the hem of her dressing gown like struck matchsticks, her black fluffy slippers forming the burnt heads. She settled back, cigarette held aloft alongside her right ear, and a ribbon of smoke curled through her grey locks. As an afterthought she reached for a pair of glasses from a side table and fed them on with her left hand. 'OK. I can see you now. Go for it.'

'Do you know Daryl Bruin?'

'Sure I do. He's an ass.'

Tess wasn't the only one who intended being blunt. She smiled. 'You know him personally, then?'

'Known him since he was yay high.' The cigarette was used as a pointer level with Margaret's chin. 'Of course he was still Daryl Trojak back then. Just a boy. He came up in some of the same foster homes as my Jasmine did.'

'He's older than Jasmine, though,' Tess pointed out.

'He was one of the older kids at one home Jasmine was sent to. She was the youngest out of four foster kids, Daryl the eldest.' Margaret snorted. 'Didn't like him as a boy and I haven't changed my opinion since he grew up.'

'Has he been to see you, to ask about Jasmine since she disappeared?'

'No. But his weird cousin has on his behalf.'

'John Trojak?'

'Yep. The henpecked one. That simpleton has issues, you know? Doesn't like cursing, doesn't like dirt, doesn't like much other than pleasing that bitch of a wife of his. He was another who asked me to douse my cigarette. I told him to go fuck himself.'

In the time since she'd lit up she'd never taken a draw on her cigarette, and Tess was beginning to believe her smoking was more habitual than through addiction: it explained why more of the smoke was on the walls and furnishings than was ever inhaled. It was an expensive habit, when Margaret could achieve the same pleasure from twiddling a pencil between her stained fingers.

'What did Trojak want?'

'Clues where he could find Jasmine. I told him, if I had any clues would there be any need to hire a private investigator.'

So it was from Margaret that Bruin had learned of Tess's involvement, by way of his cousin. 'What's his interest?'

'Daryl told him to look for Jasmine.'

'But why?'

'Didn't say. At least he didn't tell the truth. Just said that Daryl was annoyed that nobody else was taking her disappearance seriously and he wanted to help.' Margaret laughed scornfully to show her disdain for that explanation. It matched Tess's opinion of Bruin's claim. 'You ask me, Jasmine flitted while owing him money, or she knows something that asshole doesn't want made public.'

Tess had considered the former, but not the latter. She made a mental note to check on the first, but now was the time to push Margaret on what she meant. 'You're talking about her knowing something harmful to Daryl?'

'Why else would he bother looking for her, if not to shut her up?'

'Is there anything you can tell me about what Jasmine might know?'

'If there's anything, she didn't tell me. Don't forget. We weren't close. After her mom Ellie died, I guess Jasmine expected me to take her in. When I couldn't she held it against me. We talk now, but, well, it's not as grandma to granddaughter.' Margaret flicked ash, held the cigarette aloft again. 'At least, we did, up until a few weeks ago.'

When Margaret first hired Tess to find Jasmine she'd mentioned she hadn't seen or heard from the young woman for at least a week before she went missing, but hadn't explained why. 'Did you argue?'

'All the time.' The old woman looked at Tess sharply. 'Doesn't stop me from caring about her, though.'

'Of course not.' Tess argued incessantly with her own mother, but she'd still die for the old harridan if it came to it. Hell, if she didn't bicker with her mom they wouldn't have a thing to say to each other. 'I meant about anything in particular.'

'Sadly we don't need a good reason,' Margaret said.

Amen to that, Tess thought.

'I hear that Jasmine was once subject to a violent assault . . .' Tess allowed Margaret to absorb her words, and to fill the following silence.

'What has that to do with her disappearing now?' Margaret asked blunter than any question Tess had posed.

'Perhaps nothing. Perhaps everything. I hear she was stabbed and yet there's no police report about her attack.'

The old woman shook her head dismissively. 'It happened a long time ago. I don't see why it would have any relevance to the here and now.'

'You agreed to tell me anything I asked . . .'

'I just don't see how going over old ground can help find Jasmine now.'

Tess held the old woman's gaze. Through the lenses of her spectacles the sharpness of Margaret's gaze clouded over. There were subjects she didn't care to come clean about. 'I'm guessing you find the entire episode shameful, Margaret. I understand, but you needn't be ashamed. If Jasmine was a victim then . . .'

'If you ask me she led that boy on.'

'Sorry?'

'Jasmine. She brought that trouble on herself. The way she was back then, she was, y'know, loose.'

'Are you suggesting she deserved to be stabbed?' Tess asked, incredulous.

Margaret's eyebrows danced, and the cigarette that had burned down to the stub dropped a teetering column of ash on her shoulder. Tess neglected to tell her, irked by the woman's attitude to her own grandchild.

'Who was the boy?'

Tess anticipated hearing Daryl Bruin's name. But that wasn't it.

'Put it this way, Jasmine's lies would have ruined that boy. Nasty lies tend to hang over anyone's head. Y'know what people say: there's no smoke without fire.'

'Jasmine's assault was covered up to protect her attacker's reputation?'

'You didn't know Jasmine then. She was, well, she was troubled.'

It's hardly surprising if that's the attitude of her nearest and dearest, Tess thought. She could feel herself bristling. Hell, if this wasn't about a wronged girl possibly in desperate need of help, she would tell Margaret Norris to shove her paycheque where the sun didn't shine. As it was, she needn't be secretive about her displeasure. If Margaret chose to sever their agreement, then so be it: Tess would work the case *pro bono* on Jasmine's behalf and to hell with the sour old trout's money.

'You believed her attacker over your own flesh and blood?'

'I never met her supposed attacker,' Margaret pointed out. 'Never spoke to him. But I knew what Jasmine was capable of. Always warned her that lies would take her down a dark route one day.'

'Being stabbed wasn't dark enough for you?'

Margaret rubbed out the smouldering stub in the ashtray. Immediately lit another cigarette. Tess hadn't seen her inhale once. 'When she was in some of those foster homes, she made some nasty accusations.'

'About her foster parents?'

'The men in particular. Sometimes her foster siblings too.'

'Are you talking about claims of sexual abuse?'

Margaret neglected to answer, but Tess watched the skin of her features tighten. Tess waited. Finally the old woman fed her cigarette in her mouth and her cheeks pinched tightly round it.

'Were Jasmine's claims ever investigated?' Tess prompted.

'They were unfounded.'

'No smoke without fire,' Tess reminded her.

'She was forever crying wolf,' Margaret responded quickly. 'But she was too much like her mom to take seriously. Her mother was just like her, used sex to get her own way, then would cry rape when it suited her.'

'Jasmine was raped?' Tess felt a cold prickle go down her spine. 'I hadn't thought about that.' When Jasmine was stabbed Tess had assumed it was during a mugging or other violent encounter.

'I didn't say she was raped. I said she cried wolf. Turn of phrase. She said the son of one of her foster parents tried it on with her, and she had to fight him off. Said he cut her when she wouldn't put out for him. You ask me, she cut herself. Wouldn't be the first time.'

'She self-harmed?'

Margaret's gaze went to the visible scar on Tess's right wrist, and her nostrils flared in and out. She stabbed her cigarette aloft. 'Teenage girls sometimes do stupid things for attention,' she said.

Tess didn't feel the need to explain that her scar had nothing to do with teenage angst, or anything else. She suddenly understood how judgemental Margaret Norris was, and she was the girl's only connection to her family. She didn't agree with Jasmine's actions but understood why the younger Jasmine might have felt so bereft of love that she had harmed herself: to a troubled kid any reaction – even anger and scorn – was better than no reaction at all.

'When you first contacted me in the hope I'd look for Jasmine, you said you were worried something really bad had happened to her. I believed you, but I thought that was the justifiable concern of a grandmother for her grandchild. But now I believe you were being more specific. Here you are saying how Jasmine was troubled, a liar, a self-harmer, someone who was always crying wolf, so tell me, Margaret, what has changed your opinion?'

Margaret shook her head, smoke again curling through her hair. The lenses of her spectacles reflected Tess's earnest expression.

'You said you'd tell me anything I asked about,' Tess reminded her. 'If you really do care about Jasmine, you *need* to tell me.'

'I can't.'

'Why not?'

'Because that—'

A shout from outside caught the words in Margaret's throat, and she almost dropped her cigarette. Her head swivelled towards the front door.

Pottery smashed, and there was a rumble of footsteps on the porch steps. A thud. A grunt. The steps clattered to the scuffle of feet again and a second dull thud shook the house. Two male voices rose in anger. One of the voices had Tess out of her seat and bolting for the door.

# SIXTEEN

With a Marlboro hanging out the corner of his mouth, Po had rested his hips against his Mustang a few minutes earlier, and took out his cellphone to ring Pinky Leclerc.

The recent incident with the mystery man burning the stolen car and his subsequent assault on John Trojak had got Po worried. He wasn't normally a man to fret, but that was when he only had his own ass to worry about. Things were different now that he and Tess were a couple. She wouldn't thank him for his overly protective thoughts, because she wasn't one to require handholding and would remind him with a stiff reprimand if he ever treated her as the weaker sex. She was tough and brave, both qualities that had attracted him in the first place, but he wasn't stupid. Strength and bravery didn't amount to much when you were up against a stronger and more reckless enemy. He wished his earlier notion that he was the target of a hit was true, but the subsequent events had changed his mind, though he should check. The man had been seeking Tess, no doubt about it, and when she'd spotted him he'd reacted in an unexpected fashion. He'd fled, but at no point was he acting like a prey animal running for its life: he had responded more like an apex predator leading its quarry into a trap. Trojak was lucky to be alive. Another more pinpointed hit of the tyre iron and that would have been it.

'Hey, Pinky,' he said as his call was picked up.

'Nicolas!' Pinky Leclerc's voice was high with emotion. 'So you finally got round to calling me back, you!'

'Been meaning to say hi,' Po reassured his friend.

'At least you didn't wait a dozen years this time.'

'It's only been a coupla months!' While recuperating from his encounter with the deranged knifeman Hector Suarez, Po and Tess had returned to Baton Rouge for a brief stopover on their trip to New Orleans, and had enjoyed Pinky's hospitality.

But since then, Po had been remiss in making contact. Thing was, unless he'd anything specific to say, Po wasn't one for making small talk.

'I hope pretty Tess has been an attentive nurse to you? I told you, you want me to come up there and play Florence Nightingale, I'll be on the next flight, me.'

'I'm good, Pinky. Tess too.' Po flicked his cigarette in a drain.

'Then why ring, you? This time of night, you didn't call me to share pillow talk. Though I'm open to offers.' Pinky smacked a kiss down the line. 'What's up in the dreary north?'

'Working a case with Tess. Missing person.'

'And you think I can help? I'm a lot of things, but I'm no bloodhound, me.'

'Was wondering about the latest news coming outta New Iberia,' Po said.

'Those Chatards?' Pinky sniffed. 'They still grumbling and groaning, them, but that's all. Pissed that they missed you last time you were in N'awleans, but I ain't heard nothing new.'

'There's this guy been hanging around Tess . . .'

'Nicolas, you got to accept something. When you get with a woman so beautiful, you got to expect other men to come sniffing. Even me, with my particular persuasion, I go all jellified round pretty Tess.'

'It's not like that,' Po said, and sure hoped he was correct. He wasn't blind, he'd noted the kind of looks Tess caught from other guys, but he'd never been jealous before. He was confident that their relationship was strong, that her head wouldn't be easily turned. 'This guy's up to no good.'

'So sort him.' This was the other side of Pinky Leclerc belied by his genial manner, his camp demeanour. Where necessary Pinky could be stone cold.

'If it comes to it,' Po said. 'First I thought the Chatards had sent someone after me, now I'm not so sure.' He told Pinky about the man's visit to Tess's house, how he was lurking outside the autoshop and made off when spotted.

'Sounds creepy.'

'F'sure. And dangerous.' He mentioned how Trojak had given chase and ended up almost getting his skull caved in.

'So, I say again, me. Sort that creep good and proper. Those aren't the actions of a man with good intentions.'

'I fear you might be right.'

'What? Nicolas Villere is frightened? Oh, my!'

'Turn of phrase, Pinky.'

'Good. You had me worried for a moment, my fearsome friend. Ooh, did I say fearsome? I meant fearless.' Pinky chuckled to himself, while Po rolled his eyes.

'Do me a favour, buddy,' said Po. 'Before I come across this guy can you just check with your sources that I'm not mistaken about the Chatards sending a hitter?'

'I'll ax around, me.' Pinky thought for a moment. 'Things are a bit slack at this end, wouldn't mind checking out your neck of the woods . . .'

'Pinky, you're always welcome to come and visit.'

'I wouldn't cramp your macho style?' Pinky wondered.

'As long as you don't expect me to accompany you on a tour of Portland's pink triangle.' Po grunted in mirth. He wasn't even sure there was such a place in Maine, let alone his adopted hometown.

'Was going to suggest we go scouting for girls, but I guess now you've got Tess you're out of that game.'

'Wasn't exactly in it before I met Tess,' Po replied. 'And I know as sure as hell you never were.'

'I like girls. Just not in the same way as you. So . . . if I'm visiting the bleak north, how should I dress?'

'Leave your high heels at home,' Po advised.

'Nicolas, I'm just shy of three hundred and fifty pounds, me. If I wore high heels I'd end up nailed to the sidewalk for the duration.'

Po tried not to picture Pinky with his heels driven into the ground, his oddly skinny arms windmilling for balance, but failed to block the funny image. He wheezed out a laugh, and Pinky joined him.

Po told Pinky about the unseasonable warm spell, but how it was beginning to break. 'So maybe you'd best bring your furs,' he added.

'Let me ax around about those punk-ass Chatards, then I'll check on flights. I'll let you know when you can pick me up from the airport. I'll be the one looks like a big cuddly teddy bear, me.'

After he hung up, Po found he was still smiling. Pinky had that effect on him. He looked forward to seeing his old cellmate from the Farm again. He was positive that Tess would be equally happy to see Pinky, if not for the distraction he would cause. Tess had her teeth sunk firmly into finding Jasmine Reed, and Po wanted to do all he could to help her, and having Pinky around could be an inconvenience in one way, but an asset in another. The arrival of this mystery man on the scene, and his unhealthy interest in Tess, was troubling, so it wouldn't harm to have an extra layer of protection around, particularly one as trusted as Pinky.

Teasing out a second Marlboro, Po lit up. He didn't need the nicotine, but smoking gave him a reason to be outside in the North Deering neighbourhood without attracting any untoward notice. Gave him good cover to keep watch while Tess conducted business with Margaret Norris inside. It put him in a great position for watching when the door of a car parked further along the street disgorged its driver on to the sidewalk. Po drew on his cigarette as the guy strode purposefully towards him, albeit with one hand massaging the back of his head.

'What you doing here, Trojak?' Po asked.

Trojak came to a halt a few paces shy of the Mustang. He looked over the muscle car with a nonplussed expression, before tilting his gaze to meet Po's. His expression didn't change, even at the challenging tone.

'Public place,' Trojak answered.

'Some free advice for you,' Po went on. 'Go to the hospital and get that head checked out.'

'Head's fine,' Trojak replied.

'Trust me, it isn't. Otherwise you'd have heeded the advice I gave you earlier.'

'I told your girlfriend earlier; I've good intentions. And I've the right to be anywhere I like.' Trojak nodded at Margaret Norris's front door. 'I've as much right as you have to be here.'

'You were told to back off. When that dude hit you in the head, did your brains plug your ears?'

'Look, buddy,' Trojak said wearily. 'It's obvious you don't

like me. Can't say I think fondly of you either. But there's no need for this. We both have a job to do, I'd appreciate it if you just let me get on with mine.'

Po flicked away his Marlboro, exhaled smoke towards Trojak. 'Same here, buddy. You're getting in our way. Now, if you don't mind, fuck off why don't ya?'

'Is there any need?' Trojak wafted away the smoke.

'Plenty need,' Po told him. 'We're searching for a young woman who might be in urgent need of help, and you're slowing things down.' He hooked a thumb at Trojak's parked car. 'Now do us all a favour and git.'

Trojak shook his head.

He moved to walk round Po.

Po stood in his way.

Trojak moved in the opposite direction.

'Don't be an asshole,' Po warned.

'Don't be so crass,' Trojak responded.

He dodged one way, then immediately the other, but Po wasn't falling for the trick. He grabbed the sleeve of Trojak's jacket.

'Get your hands off me!' Trojak tried to snatch his arm free, at the same time pushing for the garden gate and on to the short path between the shrubs. Po had to swerve around the gatepost, and lost his grip. He lunged after Trojak, who picked up his pace and made it to the porch steps.

'Last warning, Trojak,' Po warned.

'I'm not leaving until I've spoken to Mrs Norris,' Trojak replied and lifted his fist to bang on the door.

Po slapped down the arm.

Trojak spun on him. His finger came up, aimed at Po's chest. 'I've tried to do my best to keep the peace,' he said. 'Been polite. Offered to work with you guys. Take a look at what's about to go down here, Villere. Who's acting the jerk, huh?'

'Move that finger or I'll remove it,' Po snapped.

'Do your worst—'

Po's left hand snapped over the extended finger, and he levered down near the knuckle, while wrenching the finger upward. Trojak had no recourse but sink his butt, while a yelp of surprise curtailed his challenge. Po moved towards him, and now Trojak could only shuffle backwards, or else his finger would snap. Once he was moving, Po released the offending digit, but not before his momentum had taken Trojak on to the steps. Trojak shook his hand, checking his finger still worked correctly.

'Sneaky move,' he said.

'I gave you plenty prior warning. Now do us both a favour and hit the road.'

'Nothing doing.'

Po opened both his hands, fingers curled back.

Trojak bunched his hands.

Trojak attacked, head sunk into his shoulders, arms up. But this time he didn't offer a joint to be easily locked, his arms pistoning. Po sank on to his heels, and met the charge as Trojak barrelled into him. He caught the back of Trojak's head, both hands cupped at the nape, then swung out his left leg, using the move as a dancer would to pivot on his opposite heel. Trojak's weight worked against him, throwing him around, then past Po's body. His leading shin butted Po's extended leg, and Trojak stumbled over the fulcrum, and crashed bodily into one of the porch supports, knocking down a hanging basket and terracotta pot that shattered on the floor. The entire house shook as he shouted a wordless roar, slashing backwards at Po with his bunched hand. Po bobbed back, avoiding the hammering blow, and Trojak had the clearance now to spin and launch a flurry of punches. Po backpedalled, his heels drumming the decking. Trojak's own footfalls were decidedly lighter. But his voice was raised in high-pitched war cries.

Po slapped aside each of Trojak's flying punches. His lean face was set in a rictus grin.

'That all you've got, Trojak?' he asked.

His taunt earned the desired result. Trojak threw himself bodily against Po, and together they hustled the length of the porch, and against the far rail. Trojak hammered Po's ribs in a combination Rocky Balboa would have been proud of. But Po rode the blows, body weaving, and the fists barely scuffed him. Trojak's head came up, lips skinned back from his teeth. Po swung an elbow into it. Trojak's eyelids snapped shut, fighting the white flash of agony through his skull, and were slow to open as he fought the oncoming blackness. In desperation, he threw his arms around Po's middle in a body lock. Po wrenched loose, but only insofar as he could push an arm under Trojak's left elbow. He spun out, and the move folded and twisted Trojak's arm up his back, bent him forward at the waist. Po could have powered a knee into Trojak's exposed chin, or slammed him with a blow to the back of the head. He didn't: there was no need for that level of violence. Not yet.

Po used the back hammer hold to swing Trojak around and towards the steps. He marched his captive the few paces forward, then shoved and Trojak went face first off the porch. He thudded on the path, arms and legs spread wide.

Po stared down at him.

Trojak rolled on his back, wheezing out his pain.

'Son of a gun . . .'

'You going to leave now?' Po asked.

Trojak thought about it, and shook his head. He slipped his right hand in his jacket pocket.

Po again lowered his weight over his heels, but this time his right hand reached for the inside of his boot.

'Pull your knife, Trojak,' he said. 'But you'd better be prepared to bleed.'

Trojak's hand remained hidden, but his gaze bore back up at the challenge.

Behind Po the door yanked open, and Tess spilled out on to the porch. In the opening, Margaret Norris stood with both hands covering her mouth.

'What the hell's going on out here?' Tess demanded.

Po straightened, without dropping his guard. 'Ask the dude sitting on his ass,' he said.

Tess craned past him. Trojak finally withdrew his hand, empty, and used it to prop himself up. He shrugged.

Tess looked at Po again.

'For God's sake,' Tess groaned. 'What is it with men?'

'I asked him to leave, he wouldn't,' Po said by way of explanation.

Trojak struggled to standing. He brushed dirt off the knees of his trousers.

'I've business here. I'm not leaving,' he said, still defiant even after having been made to look a fool.

'What do you want, John?' Margaret finally asked, without leaving the open doorway.

'Daryl wanted me to speak to you again,' Trojak said.

'And if I don't want to speak to you?' Margaret demanded.

Trojak shrugged again. 'Your choice, Margaret. But I wasn't going to leave without asking.'

Both Tess and Po looked searchingly at the woman.

'I've nothing to answer to Daryl Bruin,' Margaret stated.

'But . . . Margaret?' Trojak's eyebrows sought his hairline.

'You've had your answer, Trojak,' Po growled.

Trojak's mouth curled up at one corner, and he turned his face aside. He glanced back at Mrs Norris. 'Daryl won't be happy.'

'I don't care if he messes his shorts with frustration,' Margaret told him.

Po grunted in mirth, while Tess's eyelids also pinched in humour at the lurid image Margaret painted. Even Trojak's lips quirked briefly. 'OK,' he acquiesced, 'at least I can tell him I tried.'

Tess moved past Po, shrugging out of his tentative grasp.

She stood a few feet from Trojak.

'Look, Trojak. I understand you're only doing Daryl's bidding. He's your boss, and you have a job to do. We all get that. But you're setting yourself between a rock and a hard place. I'll ask again: back off. Stay out of this, and it'll be best for everyone.'

'I came here to speak to Margaret. She doesn't want to speak. I'll happily leave now.' Trojak stared at Po. 'But there's nobody going to tell me what to do. I'm my own man.'

'Tell that to your wife,' Po said.

Trojak's nostrils pinched, but he didn't reply.

'And tell that to Bruin,' Po added.

Trojak dusted himself off some more.

'I'm going to leave now because it's my choice to do so,' he said, and looked directly in Tess's eyes.

'Fair enough,' she said.

'Right.' He moved to leave.

'Trojak?' Po called.

Pausing, without looking back, Trojak waited.

'Twice already you've narrowly survived a beating,' Po announced at his back. 'Third time you might not be as lucky.'

# SEVENTEEN

A deluge fell overnight, banishing the heat of the past few weeks to a memory. With the rain came gusting wind from the northwest holding a distinct chill from its Arctic source, and a promise of a harsher cold snap to come. It had gone from summer to fall in a few short hours. Trees that had held on to their foliage were almost stripped bare, and drifts of leaves cluttered the drain covers and kerbs. Floodwater threatened some houses and establishments. In her upper-floor home, Tess wasn't in danger of being washed away, but she'd noticed Mrs Ridgeway had firmly closed her shop's door, and had been out with a broom, sweeping the sidewalk clear of debris. Tess had considered going down to help, but the shopkeeper had things under control in no time.

Mid-morning and it was still dim outside, and Tess had her lights burning in her living room. In the corner her iMac was running, but she'd stepped away to replenish her coffee mug and now a screen saver swirled in myriad colours. She'd also set up her tablet, and her cellphone was plugged in to charge. All were integral tools to her job, working away to trace Jasmine. There had been a couple of interesting hits overnight, but nothing that had panned out when she checked the reports to source. A woman found dead by the side of a road in neighbouring New Hampshire had given Tess cause for alarm until she read that she was African-American, so couldn't be Jasmine. She was a victim of a hit-and-run accident, a street worker in the wrong place at the wrong time. Immediately Tess burned with guilt for the relief she'd felt: the woman who'd died deserved as much pity and resolution as anyone else. A second hit was on an abandoned car, the same model as Jasmine's – but that struck out when the licence plate came back to another owner.

She sipped her coffee, thinking back to the previous evening. Po wasn't around.

He'd returned to her house last night, and stayed until dawn. It hadn't been their most memorable night together, with Tess retiring to bed alone, and Po on the settee in her living room. They hadn't argued. There'd been no need. A silent scolding proved more effective on her man. She'd been getting somewhere with Margaret Norris until the overspill of testosterone between Po and Trojak had erupted into a fistfight. Once Trojak left with his tail between his legs, Tess had tried to engage the woman again, but Margaret had had enough for the evening and shut her out. Tess glared at Po, and Po had shrugged. 'Trojak needed putting in his place,' he'd said.

'I'm only glad I made it outside in time,' Tess told him. 'What was next? You were going to gut each other.'

'I wouldn't go that far.'

'Wouldn't you though?'

Their drive back to her place had been in uncomfortable silence.

Once they were inside, and Po had checked out of the blinds a couple of times he'd slipped on to the settee, left arm stretched across the back. Ordinarily Tess would have filled the gap he'd offered, and the sheltering arm would have become an embrace, leading to intimacy that would take them both to bed. But she hadn't sat. She'd checked her programs. Made some supper. Told Po she was too tired to fight.

'I ain't fighting,' he reassured her, earning a scowl. She adored him, but the man could infuriate her without trying too hard.

'That was a cheap shot,' she said.

Po frowned.

'With Trojak,' she went on.

'What was a cheap shot? He asked for it. I gave him fair warning, asked him to leave. He was the one tried pushing his way inside the house.'

'That snippy dig about his wife,' Tess said.

'Oh. I get ya.' Po pushed his fingers through his hair. 'But it was true.'

Tess wondered who the advice was genuinely aimed at. She wanted to ask about his parents, but it wasn't the right time, not when there was a buzz of irritation in the atmosphere.

'A woman who hits her man is equally loathsome to me as when the shoe's on the other foot,' she said.

'Wasn't advocating he hit her,' Po replied, and appeared suitably abashed.

'I know.' Tess leaned in and pecked a kiss on his lips. He looked up expectantly, his turquoise gaze sweeping her features. She rolled her head away from him, followed it to the bedroom. 'I'm worn out. Need to sleep.'

She expected Po to follow, but he didn't, and she lay alone in bed wondering if she was prodding a hornets' nest of emotion on bringing up the subject of domestic violence again. In the early hours, she slipped from the room, the house quaking under the thunderous impact of rain, and checked on Po. He was where she'd left him, ankles crossed, hands folded on his stomach, sound asleep. She didn't disturb him, but returned to the warmth of her bed. She needed to sleep, but couldn't. Her mind was turning over as she attempted to reorder what she'd learned, and more so fit together what she hadn't yet, about Jasmine's disappearance. The deluge on the roof sounded like a drumroll announcing an oncoming epiphany, but her enlightened moment failed to transpire, and instead the incessant rumble finally lulled her to sleep.

When she rose, Po had left, but not without leaving a handwritten note.

*Back soon*, it said, *with a surprise.*

Po wasn't a flowers and candy kind of guy. What was he up to? Hopefully he didn't return with John Trojak's liver on a platter.

After showering and brushing her teeth and hair she prepped coffee and bagels, and she broke her fast while sharing her time between her computers and the window. Mrs Ridgeway, dressed for the weather in a bright yellow slicker and hat, waved, but quickly returned to her broom duties. She used the shaft to scrape out an accumulation of fallen leaves from the nearest drains, before hurrying back inside and closing the door tight. Business would be slow in the shop. Mrs Ridgeway would probably spend most of the day with her nose buried in another paperback novel, and Tess was prepared to read a similar word count.

Since the two false leads, her programs had picked up nothing of interest. She thought again about the victim of the hit-and-run, experiencing a fresh twinge of guilt at writing the woman off, and it made her think of all thousands of women who were killed or murdered or simply vanished off the face of the earth each year. That sent her thoughts down a different track, and she bent to her iMac to launch a new search.

As Po once pointed out, people went missing for all kinds of reasons and not all of them bad. But it surprised her to find how many people actually disappeared, and once the flurry of search activity ceased were relegated to a memory, sometimes even forgotten about altogether. People who were transient by nature drifted at the best of times, and when they upped and disappeared the search was unlikely even to begin. Tess searched for missing females between mid-teens and late thirties but it was far too large a return to recognize any form of pattern. She reduced it to white women from Maine over the last two years: the list was still extensive, but manageable. She worked her way through, cross-referencing where possible, and eliminated a number of women who turned up elsewhere. She even discovered the current locations of two women listed as still missing and thought she should report her findings to the police – except further digging showed that they would prefer their anonymity to remain a secret: one was escaping an abusive spouse, the other, a married woman, was enjoying a lesbian relationship with a new partner, and reporting their whereabouts could cause more harm than it would solve. An unscrupulous investigator might have contacted them and insist they buy her silence, but that wasn't how Tess Grey worked. She deleted them from her records.

Jasmine Reed's name remained prominently displayed, alongside four other girls and young women missing from Maine. Tess checked on their circumstances. Two were drug addicts who'd been found dead in other parts of the country, one to an overdose, the second at the hands of her overzealous pimp, while the third was married with a young family in Iowa. None of the three cases had been closed by the law-enforcement agencies that had logged the original missing person's reports so she made a note to contact them and hand over her evidence. But for now her mind was concentrated on Jasmine and the last girl on her list, Elsa Jayne Moore, who had only recently been reported missing when her family was concerned that she hadn't contacted them since leaving to begin a new life in California. When she brought up side-by-side comparisons, Tess recognized a type. Both women were young, athletically toned, beautiful, tattooed – and both had been marked in another indelible fashion. Jasmine's scars weren't obvious, they were hidden beneath her clothes, but Elsa had been the victim of a fire, and the dappled scar tissue on her left hand and reaching up from her chest to below her chin was obvious.

It was a long shot, but Tess reset her search criteria, extending her reach into neighbouring states, and adding 'scar' to her list of tags. She sat back, sipping her now tepid coffee, slightly nervous at what her latest search might turn up, hoping that it would return a nil result.

Five more names made her heart sink.

She put aside her mug and her fingers flew over the keyboard. She eliminated three who had scars from minor surgical procedures. But it left two: Carrie Mae Borger and Lucy Jo Colman.

Tess brought up pictures.

Athletic. Beautiful. Tattooed. Scarred.

She sucked in her bottom lip, considering what to do.

Before jumping to any conclusions she again cross-referenced, and also delved into the circumstances of the missing girls' disappearances.

Carrie had been gone three months, last seen at a gas station on the I-91 in Massachusetts. Lucy hadn't been seen or heard from for almost four months. Her last known sighting was also at a gas station on the I-91 corridor in Massachusetts, but further south, alongside the Connecticut River. Neither woman had run away from their responsibilities. Both cases were still open with their respective police forces, though their cases had never been connected.

Four women of a similar demographic, with similar looks and body type, going missing over a period of months was probably coincidental, but when they all also carried obvious scars, and two at least had last been seen on the I-91, the pattern set Tess's antennae twitching. She checked on Elsa Moore. There was no positive last sighting but her final credit card transaction had been to pay for a meal at a steakhouse in Auburn, Mass. Tess brought up a Google map of the region, found Auburn and noted that the mall where Elsa last ate sat alongside the I-90. The I-90 and I-91 intersected further to the west, but was there a connection between the areas where the three women had last been? Had Jasmine Reed travelled either road since making off from Portland? Interstate 91 ran north-to-south along the Vermont and Massachusetts border, and she doubted that it would have been Jasmine's route of choice when escaping Maine. She plotted the I-90 back from Auburn to Boston, to where Jasmine could have driven either the I-95 or Route 1 all the way from Portland.

She could be totally misguided, but she couldn't ignore her instincts. She reached for her cell and called Emma Clancy.

'Emma. It's Tess. Just wanted to throw something by you and have you confirm I'm not nuts. You see there's this pattern I've detected and . . .'

'Hi there, Tess,' Emma cut in. 'Nice to hear from you, but do you want to slow down there a little?'

'This case I'm working . . .' Tess went on.

'The missing Reed girl? Yes, I know it. Have you had a breakthrough?'

'Not one that I was expecting,' said Tess, as she pressed the heel of her palm against her forehead. 'Hell, I hope I'm wrong about this, Emma.'

'What is it?'

'Like I said, there's a worrying pattern to all this. There are other missing girls, Emma.'

'From here in Maine?'

'Not all of them are from Maine. They're spread across neighbouring states too. That's why I don't think they've been connected before.' She briefly explained the process she'd followed, how she'd recognized the similarities between Jasmine and the other women's disappearances. 'Because there's been no indication of foul play, the details most likely haven't been shared across the jurisdictional borders. Jasmine's case has been practically dismissed by Portland PD, it's possible that the other girls' cases have been put to bed as well.'

Emma inhaled deeply, and Tess gave her a moment to absorb what she'd suggested. 'You're implying that we have a serial offender on our hands?' Emma was careful not to mention the words *serial killer*; no bodies had been discovered to date and she hoped that none would.

'The four women I've identified could only be the tip of the iceberg,' Tess said. 'I've only searched a few states up until now. There could be others to add to the list.'

Emma muttered under her breath.

'I can't ignore what my gut is telling me,' Tess stated.

'And I don't expect you to. But I think before you release this particular genie from its bottle you need to do some more checking.'

'I was tempted to send what I know already to the FBI. But first I wanted to hear your take on it. You're right, Emma. I need to make sure before I alert the big guns.'

'They wouldn't thank you for an unsubstantiated workload. But if you were to hand them a fully informed investigation, they wouldn't ignore it.'

'I'm going to stick with this then, Emma.'

'In other words, you're requesting a little free time to do what needs doing. No problem. Things are quiet here, so take whatever time you need.'

'Thanks.' Tess thought about mentioning the recent incidents with the mystery man. 'Did you see Alex last night?'

'No. I was at a civic function; not exactly your brother's cup of tea. We spoke briefly this morning, but Alex is back on duty. Why do you ask?'

'No reason,' said Tess.

Emma laughed without humour. She didn't get to where she was by allowing the wool to be pulled over her eyes.

'It's just that he might have mentioned a couple of strange things that happened yesterday.'

'You mean the guy who was following you?'

'Then he did say?'

'He mentioned something about dealing with an assault victim. Some guy was beaten after following a car thief or something like it. Alex mentioned the incident originated from outside Po's garage?'

'Yeah, that was about it. We don't know who was involved yet, but I'm beginning to think it's connected to Jasmine going missing.'

'You think this person and your serial offender are one and the same?'

'It's a possibility,' said Tess, 'but unlikely. No, I have some more digging to do on this guy too.'

'OK. So keep me informed. If there's anything I can do to help, you know you only have to say.'

'I do. Thanks, Emma.'

'No problem.' Emma was about to hang up, but paused. 'Tess. If what you've discovered with those missing girls pans out, do come to me with it first. I'd like to be the one to get the ball rolling with the FBI.'

'Sure,' said Tess, because the kudos earned from bringing down a serial offender would do the world of good for Emma's company, and a lot of attention that Tess could do without. 'It's the least I can do.'

# EIGHTEEN

P o hadn't returned by midday, and Tess was beginning to grow concerned. She hoped her silly thought about bringing back Trojak's liver wasn't about to come true – or worse, that Trojak was the one who'd taken a trophy of their latest encounter. She was fretting for nothing; his note had been effusive, for him, and she suspected he was excited about whatever the surprise was. She sent him a text, informing him where she was going, but didn't expect a reply. Po surprised her:

BACK SOON. STAY INDOORS.

He was feeling nervous about leaving her unprotected when the mystery man was still on the loose, but Tess wasn't concerned. She was more interested in finding out exactly who it was. She returned his text by way of a sad-faced emoticon and the words: CAN'T SIT HERE ON MY THUMBS, LOVERBOY XX

She pulled on clothing more appropriate to the inclement weather, plus a woollen hat that she jammed over her hair and ears, and headed out into the teeming rain. Without her chariot driver, she had to trust in her own driving skill to negotiate the slick streets as she headed back to North Deering. Her Prius was no muscle car, but it was probably easier to handle in the driving rain and wind. She made it to Margaret Norris's house without any major drama, and parked outside the front gate. Perhaps she should have called ahead, but she doubted that Margaret had anywhere she needed to be in such a downpour.

She lurched out the car, and jogged along the path for the porch steps, head bent low, hands protecting her face from the stinging raindrops. A cascade of rain fell from the overflowing gutters, and she had to plunge under the sheeting water. Soaked. She shook and droplets dappled the porch floor. The front door remained resolutely shut, and there were no lights on inside. She rang the bell, but heard no reply over the tumult, so balled her fist and hammered on the door.

'Mrs Norris? Margaret? It's me, Tess Grey.'

She knocked again, and leaned on the bell push for extra effect.

A car prowled by behind her, rain lashing over it. Tess glanced back, but the rain was so heavy she could barely make out the vehicle's shape or colour let alone the driver. It carried on, and she knocked again at the door.

The small clapboard house creaked and moaned under the storm. But from within Tess was sure she heard a door close. She knocked again.

'Take it easy,' muttered Margaret Norris. 'You're going to take my damn door off its hinges.'

Tess exhaled. Waited.

There was a rattle of bolts, but when the door edged open it hung on its security chain.

'I wasn't expecting you back so soon,' Margaret announced. 'After all that fuss last night.'

'Things got a little out of hand,' Tess admitted, 'but I hope it didn't affect our arrangement?'

Margaret was wearing her spectacles and she adjusted them as she thought. 'I still want you to find Jasmine, if that's what you mean?'

'And I'm still on the job. Have been throughout the night and this morning.' A gust pushed rain under the porch roof, spattering it on Tess's back. 'Would you mind if I came in, Mrs Norris. Things are kind of hairy out here.'

'Where's the caveman?'

Tess smiled at the description of Po: but couldn't help agreeing with Margaret's summation. Po had come across as a primitive brute last night. 'He isn't with me. He's doing something else just now.'

'Beating up somebody else?'

'I think that's a little unfair. Nicolas was stopping Trojak from harassing *you*, don't forget.'

'Yeah, I suppose so . . .'

'So . . .' Tess went on, 'I can come in?'

'I guess.'

The door closed momentarily while the chain was rattled loose. 'Come in,' said Margaret, as she held out a hand, clutching an obligatory cigarette. Tess stepped inside, stamping her feet on the mat while Margaret secured the door.

'Somewhere to hang my coat?' Tess asked, as she shrugged out of the dripping garment.

'Put it through here.' Margaret led the way to the kitchen at the rear of the house.

The woman had been working in the kitchen, the reason she hadn't immediately heard Tess at the door. There were far too many pots on the stove and ingredients laid out on chopping boards to feed one woman. Equal amounts of steam and cigarette smoke vied to dominate the atmosphere. Tess took a seat at a proffered chair, and tugged off her hat while Margaret took her coat and hung it on a hook on the back door. Tess worked the damp wool between her fingers.

'You want coffee or anything?' Margaret offered with no enthusiasm.

'No, I don't intend on staying long. Anyway, it looks as if you've enough to be getting on with.'

'It's a lot,' Margaret admitted. 'I cook in batches these days. Prepare enough meals for a few days. Works out more economical that way.'

It made sense. Tess, like many of her generation, cooked as and when, and usually made too much food, which ended up in the trashcan. By the look of things, Margaret was preparing enough food to freeze or store for later in the week. The old woman parked her cigarette butt between her lips and returned to slicing carrots. 'Keeps my mind off other things too,' Margaret said.

Tess had considered mentioning how she suspected Jasmine might be the victim of a prolific offender, but without firm proof it would be a bad road to lead her grandmother down. Instead, she asked what she'd come about. 'Last night we were talking about when Jasmine was attacked.'

'Allegedly attacked.' Margaret glimpsed up from beneath her eyebrows, between the frames of the misted lenses of her glasses. Tess's eyebrows rose marginally in response.

'You said that Jasmine alleged she was assaulted by the son of one of her foster parents?' Tess left the suggestion hanging.

Margaret chopped furiously and chunks of carrot went flying.

She dashed the diced vegetables into a loose pile with her left hand, used the knife-wielding one to pluck out her cigarette. The loose ash fell on the floor by her feet.

'I hinted that something had changed your mind,' Tess went on, 'and you were about to admit something just before we were rudely interrupted.'

'I wasn't about to admit a damn thing,' said Margaret but she avoided looking at Tess, her body language disagreeing with her words.

'Just before Trojak arrived I said, "If you really do care about Jasmine, you need to tell me",' Tess reminded her. 'You said you couldn't and when I asked why not you started to say something.' Tess racked her memory for the correct phrase. 'You said "Because that", but were stopped. *That* what, Margaret? Or *that* who?'

Shaking her head furiously, Margaret used the knife to scrape the carrots off the chopping board into a pan. 'Who's working for who here?' she demanded after placing the pan at the kitchen sink. 'Why are you asking me all these questions?'

'To help Jasmine.' Tess left it at that.

Margaret put aside the knife.

She stubbed out her cigarette in an overflowing ashtray set on the side of the counter. With nothing better to do with her fingers she pushed both hands through her hair, teasing it the way Tess did her damp woollen hat.

'There was a time when I wasn't as well off as I am now. Not that I'm rich or anything, but I'm comfortably off. Time was when things were much harder. Don't judge me, Tess . . .'

Tess didn't reply.

'When Jasmine made the allegation against the boy, I wanted to go with her to the police. I really did.'

'But you came to another arrangement instead.'

'There you go judging me.'

'I'm not interested in soothing your conscience, Margaret, only in helping Jasmine.' Tess held the old woman's gaze. 'What did you do? Exchange money for your silence?'

Margaret's lips nipped tightly and she reached for her pack of cigarettes. She had second thoughts though, and instead walked over and took the seat opposite Tess. She shook her head morosely.

'It was stupid and selfish of me. But I can't turn back the clock now. Jasmine had told lies before, and I was doubtful about what she told me, so who was it really harming if I accepted a cash handout? Like I said, things were tough back then. I'd lost my daughter, my only grandkid was taken away, and I'd no husband around to help keep a house.'

Tess looked at the tabletop.

'Jasmine had made allegations before,' Margaret went on.

'Maybe she was telling the truth those times too,' Tess said, and couldn't keep the tone of reproof from her voice.

Anger flared in Margaret's face, but it wasn't aimed at Tess.

'It's possible that I helped destroy Jasmine's reputation for a measly five thousand bucks! Do you realize how bad that makes me feel now?'

It did explain why Margaret was prepared to pay more for Tess's time and expertise than she'd ever received from the ill-gotten bribe.

'So?' Tess prompted.

Margaret blinked at her.

'Will you tell me the boy's name?'

'I suppose you'd find it easy enough anyway.' Margaret sighed. 'You've a list of all the foster parents, and I assume you've already questioned them.'

The first thing Tess had done was check with Jasmine's former parents, before moving on to chasing down leads with the likes of Maxwell Carter. None of those she'd spoken to had added anything of value, except to express how it didn't surprise them that Jasmine had taken off yet again.

'Cal Hopewell,' Margaret stated.

Tess pictured Allan Hopewell, now a widower. His wife Cheryl and he had fostered Jasmine for a few short months, but had found the rebellious teen too much to handle, what with already having an older son and daughter who took priority.

'Calvin Hopewell?' Tess looked for confirmation, and received a brisk nod. She churned through the snippets of information she'd lodged in the back of her mind concerning the Hopewells. 'If I'm right, then Cal wasn't exactly a boy when Jasmine lived with the family.'

'When you're as old as I am, anyone under forty is still a child.'

'He was a senior in college, right? That made him at least twenty-two at the time.'

Margaret nodded, but wasn't moved on the definition of whether Cal was still a boy or not.

'Wasn't he hoping to join the military?' Tess went on.

'He was home for semester from Valley Forge Military Academy, on one of those "early commissioning programmes", when Jasmine claimed he hurt her. He was on a two-year programme that would qualify him as a second lieutenant on entry . . .'

'I see now why an allegation of sexual and physical abuse might harm his future. Doesn't mean I agree with it, but I can understand how his parents might want to buy your silence.'

'I took their dirty money,' Margaret said, 'but I'm not proud. Didn't even stretch too long before I was back on the bread line.'

Tess fought down the urge to spit in the woman's face.

'Jasmine was how old when she stayed with the Hopewells?'

'Fourteen.'

Tess stared. Margaret wouldn't meet her gaze, and again reached for a cigarette. Her pack had been left on the kitchen counter, across the room.

'That'd make Calvin Hopewell, what, in his early thirties now?' Tess wondered aloud.

'I guess. Round about thirty-two.'

The mystery man had looked to be in his thirties during the brief glance Tess had got of him as he'd driven away from Charley's Autoshop.

'Is he still with the military?'

'How should I know? I haven't had anything to do with the Hopewells since they paid me off.'

'Thought you might have kept up with the news, seeing as Cal's future was determined by you.'

'I think that's enough of the accusations from you, Tess.' Margaret stood shakily, resting both hands on the table. 'There's only so much I will take before I tell you to get the hell out of my house.'

'Yeah,' said Tess, but there was no chance she'd offer an apology. 'I've said all I'm going to say on the subject. I've enough to be getting on with now.'

Margaret stood propped on her palms. She looked weak, ready to collapse and it wasn't for want of nicotine.

Tess waited, positive there was something the woman wanted to add.

A pan on the hob seethed, the lid rattling, and outside the storm hadn't abated. Tess wasn't sure if the house was shaking or if she was trembling with anticipation.

'Cal came by,' Margaret finally said.

'When?'

'This morning.'

'And you didn't think to call me?' Tess asked.

'I didn't speak to him. I only saw him outside, standing under those trees across the street. I knew it was him, even if it's been years since I last saw him.'

'He's a big guy now. Short dark hair, quite a stocky build?'

Margaret nodded in agreement. 'I spotted him from the window. I wasn't sure it was him at first, but then he looked directly at me and I *knew*.' She placed her hands over her face, fingers digging beneath her glasses to rub at her eyelids. 'Knew I'd been wrong to believe his word over Jasmine's.'

'It's because she heard he was coming home that Jasmine left?' Tess suggested.

'That's what I'm thinking.'

Margaret wasn't being truthful. OK, so she believed she'd spotted Cal Hopewell lurking outside earlier. However, Tess didn't believe it was the first time Cal had made his presence known to her. Perhaps that explained how he knew where to go when looking for the person investigating Jasmine's disappearance, or how he knew about where to find her at Po's garage. Cal Hopewell, without a shadow of a doubt, was the mystery man who'd been following her.

'You said you didn't speak with him this morning,' she ventured, hoping Margaret would admit to an earlier visit, but Margaret again shook her head.

'He spotted me at the same time I saw him. He immediately turned and walked away.' Margaret hobbled to the counter and retrieved her cigarettes, tapping one out. 'I didn't look out the window after that,' she went on, 'just came in here and kept myself busy.'

Margaret was frightened of Cal Hopewell, and for good reason. Despite her lie about doubting Jasmine's claim about being attacked, she had known the truth all along. And that meant she was dangerous to Cal Hopewell, as he was a danger to her.

# NINETEEN

The drive back to her house on Cumberland Avenue was accomplished tentatively. The battering rain was carrying flinty ice: snow wouldn't be far behind. Tess's damp clothes steamed up the car, and she flicked her blowers to full to keep the windshield clear. The wipers battled the accumulation of sleet, wiping bows of dirty ice back and forward and making visibility even worse. Her lights were on full, despite it being barely mid-afternoon. Her Prius was a neat little car for summer driving but struggled in these harsh conditions. She couldn't risk taking her eyes off the road for more than a second, but she could see nothing of value in her mirrors. She parked the Prius on the incline at the steps up to her house, thankful to be back in one piece, but also prickling with concern that Po's Mustang wasn't in its customary place alongside. Where had he got to, and when the hell would he be back?

She would have run from her car to the stairs, but that was asking for trouble. The path was filmed with dirty slush, through which ran rivulets of water. A misstep and she'd go down on her butt. She locked the car, pulled her collar up and her hat down to her ears, and walked at a crouch for the steps. The sleet hitting her cheeks stung like crazy. At the roofline the wind attempted to force entry to her home, and she heard a moan of defiance from the eaves as the house withstood the attack and directed the force downward. Heavy droplets flung from the gutters pattered her, some of it invading her mouth. She spat at the gritty taste, and cursing the storm, she went up the stairs, noting distractedly that all was in darkness in the antiques shop: Mrs Ridgeway must have given up and gone home.

As she pulled out her door key, a car swept along Cumberland Avenue, sheeting water. Tess glanced back, hoping it signalled Po's return. She could barely make out the model, but it was a chunky SUV, not a black muscle car. The car continued by and Tess immediately forgot about it as she unlocked her door and let herself inside. She'd only been out in the storm for half a minute and already she was soaked through and almost chilled to the bone. Gratefully she absorbed the ambient warmth wafting from her living space. She pushed the door shut, sealing out the storm, and stood for a moment, dripping on the welcome mat. Only a nutjob would have gone out in that weather, but she thought the trip had been worth the risk. She dialled the thermostat up a few degrees, dumped her purse in the living room, then shed her coat and hat and kicked off her boots, pulling on sneakers. She found a towel in the bathroom and scrubbed the damp from her hair and the chill from her face. A hot shower wouldn't go amiss, but it could wait. She switched on the coffee maker as a consolation prize, and went directly to her work station. In a hurry to get started, she dumped the damp towel on the floor and brought her computer out of sleep mode.

Her internet connection was a tad sketchy, down to the weather. Hopefully it wouldn't fail before she was done. She keyed in 'Calvin Hopewell', added a few more pertinent tags, and hit 'search'. There were a number of false leads, but some that made her sit up and take notice.

'Oh, my God!' she wheezed as she spotted one particular link, and her gut soured when she followed it to a news webpage. The page was in German and she had to translate it first, but already got the gist of what to expect from the initial report. While stationed in Germany, no less than two girls had accused Second Lieutenant Calvin Hopewell, 7th Marine Regiment, of aggravated sexual assault. Reports of the alleged crimes were brief, because through a lack of evidence in one case and the withdrawal of the complaint in the second, Hopewell was released without charge. Possibly the military knew there was more to the reports than Hopewell answered to, because he was whisked out of Germany and sent off to Helmand Province, Afghanistan, before he could cause further scandal. If he misbehaved whilst there, nothing was recorded – or it only appeared in sealed documentation she had no access to. Hopewell next turned up, still at the company-grade officer rank, while based at Twenty-nine Palms, California, the Marine Corps Air Ground Combat Center, assisting in the training of marines on oversea assignments, under live fire scenarios. Hopewell again brought down the Corps' good name when he was arrested for sexual assault and battery on a chalet maid at Lake Havasu, a popular destination for servicemen and women during downtime. Commissioned officers, even at company grade, carried the special trust and confidence of the President of the United States, and the actions of Second Lieutenant Hopewell were scandalous, a severe embarrassment, and could not be tolerated. Court martial and dishonourable discharge followed, as well as a term in the Marine Corps' brig, Camp Pendleton, before he was kicked back on to Civvy Street with little more than he stood up in.

The disgraced marine had been released two days prior to Jasmine Reed's disappearance, and the coincidence was too much to ignore, considering Hopewell had since turned up in his hometown for nefarious purposes. Had he somehow contacted her and placed the fear of God in her concerning his imminent return? Did he feel he had unfinished business with his once foster-sister, a debt he now wanted to cash in now that the truth about his nature was out?

She found two photographs of Hopewell online. One where he stood proudly in his dress uniform, clean cut and happy, the other from a newspaper reporting on his arrest where he was dishevelled and sullen. From the brief glimpse she had of him as he'd driven away from outside the autoshop, she was sure he was one and the same. But for full confirmation, she printed the photos with the idea of showing them to Mrs Ridgeway. Sadly her shopkeeper neighbour had called it a day, as she recalled.

As she stood in her living room, staring down at the images in her hand, the power went out.

There was no flicker of warning, no dimming of the overhead lights she'd turned on against the gloom. Her computer screen went blank. The background hum of machinery in her kitchen ceased, not that she was immediately aware because of the constant drumming of rain and the rattle and moan of the wind through the eaves.

Tess stood with her mouth open. Listening. Caught out by the loss of a basic necessity to modern life. Thankfully it wasn't full dark, so she hadn't been plunged into momentary incomprehension. But she was still grasped by indecision.

The storm was to be blamed for the loss of power.

Had to be.

She went to her window, peering out through the blinds at the buildings on the opposite side of the street. They had power; she saw lights burning behind various windows. So the problem wasn't to do with the grid, but her house. The shop downstairs was on the same electricity supply, but both the shop and her private quarters had separate breaker boxes and meters. Hers was in a closet in the hall. Had the rain found its way inside, shorting a wire and tripping a fuse? She was about to go check when her gaze was drawn back to the street. A rain-washed figure stood on the sidewalk below her window, staring up at her.

The instant she saw him, he turned quickly and walked away.

He'd been wearing a ball cap pulled low on his head, a padded anorak with the collar up, and a scarf wrapped around his lower face. The rain was battering down, obscuring everything. By all rights she shouldn't have recognized him, but she was under no illusion whatsoever. The violent would-be rapist, and disgraced military officer, Calvin Hopewell was right outside.

Her first instinct was to ring the police, but she didn't reach for her phone. She leaned closer to the window, plotting his direction, but already Hopewell was out of sight, and again she was under no illusion. He'd gone round the side of the building, alongside the small yard servicing the shop downstairs. Tess rushed across the living room, through the small vestibule, and into her bedroom. She leaned against the window, peering out. Droplets the size of bird eggs pummelled the glass, washed out the scene below, but she caught a flicker of movement, low down alongside the back of her house.

Steps led up the side of her building to her front door, but fire-safety regulations dictated that a fire escape must be provided from the rear. Tess rarely checked the fire escape, had never used it. Hopewell was down at the base of the ladder, assessing it as an entry route to her home!

The power cut took on a more sinister possibility. Had he cut the mains where they fed from the junction box to the house? What was his intention: to stop her calling for assistance? Didn't he know that a landline telephone worked whether the power was on or off? And hadn't he heard of cellphones?

She should call the police immediately.

But she didn't. She went directly to her bedroom closet and pulled down a sturdy lock box from the top shelf. She dabbed her grandfather's birthdate on the keypad, and pulled open the lid.

Inside the box was her grandfather's old NYPD service revolver from when he was a patrolman, plus spare ammunition. Although she was familiar with the Ruger .38 Service Six, she fumbled it, her fingers shaking with anxiety as she fed the shiny brass shells into the six chambers. The gun was licensed for home defence, and if ever there was a time to put it to use, it was now.

Her damaged wrist ached, more likely psychosomatic than actual pain. But her grip on the butt was firm, and her index finger held steady alongside the trigger guard. The last time she'd fired the gun she hadn't felt at ease pulling the trigger, but hopefully her aversion to shooting was behind her now. Not that she intended killing Hopewell, just using the gun to hold him under arrest until the police arrived: but if she had to . . .

She returned to the window. The storm still thwarted her view, the rain cascading heavier than ever. She listened, and could hear the metallic thrum of rain impacting the escape ladder, but no indication anyone was climbing it. So Hopewell had assessed but given up on the fire escape? The only other ways into her house were via her front steps or the narrow stairwell within the building at the rear of the antiques shop: the doors at top and bottom were kept locked to ensure her and Mrs Ridgeway's privacy, but the locks were cheap and the doors flimsy, psychological barriers at most. She padded through to her living room, checked out the front window but there was no sign of her stalker. She approached the main door, listened, the revolver held ready by her side.

There was too much noise to distinguish the creak and rattle of the stairs from footfalls. She went back to her work station and snatched up her cell.

There was a text from Po:

BACK SOON

Not soon enough, she thought and tapped in a reply:

NEED YOU NOW

Again she thought about summoning the police, but they'd respond on lights and sirens, alerting Hopewell, and he'd flee. That should be the best option, but the man was up to no good, and she wanted to find out what he wanted from her and why. If he were arrested and taken away he'd be charged for car theft and for the assault on John Trojak, but she'd never learn his reason for being back in Portland so soon after Jasmine went missing.

She'd been a Sheriff's deputy, and was used to dealing with dangerous individuals, but she could not forget that Hopewell, for all he'd been disgraced and drummed unceremoniously out of the military, was a trained marine: he might not prove the easiest man she'd ever arrested. Show caution, she reminded herself, not fear. He's only a man, and the gun in your hand makes the difference – unless he'd armed himself appropriately.

Where the hell was Po?

She had to occasionally remind him that she didn't require his constant protection, but there were times when she preferred he was there, even if in his usual silent capacity. Now was one of those times.

'It's down to you, girl,' she whispered under her breath. But the caution she'd so recently counselled pinged a warning.

She hit Alex's number even as she again returned to the door and stood close enough that she'd spot any movement through the frosted glass, but would stay hidden from observation.

'Whassup, sis?'

'Alex,' she whispered. 'Don't want you to go overboard on this, but the guy from last night is back.'

'The one who burnt the car and . . .' His voice had risen an octave.

'Calvin Hopewell,' she said, realizing she hadn't yet

shared her discovery with anyone but Margaret Norris. 'I just spotted him outside my house. Alex, I think he's trying to find a way in.'

'What? Who's there with you now?'

'I'm alone.'

'Where's Po?' His usual passive criticism of Po's relationship with his sister was suddenly replaced by anger because Po wasn't around when he was goddamn needed.

'On his way back,' Tess assured him, 'but I don't know how long he'll be.'

'Forget him. I'm on *my* way,' said Alex, but with no hint of where he was travelling from.

'Stealth mode, please,' said Tess. 'We don't want to frighten Hopewell off.'

'Keep your doors locked, and your phone on,' Alex huffed out, and she realized he was running to reach his patrol car.

Tess laid her phone aside on a nearby table, the line still open to Alex. Obeying one out of two of his instructions wasn't bad. With her revolver held ready, she undid the lock and teased open the door. Immediately icy drops of sleet spattered her, and her face pinched against the assault. She forced her eyes to remain open, as she scanned first the stairs, then the ground to the rear of the landing. There was no sign of Hopewell: had she only imagined the movement near the fire escape? Had he sloped off once he'd realized she'd spotted him out of the window? She had to make sure. She grabbed her coat and pulled into it, juggling the revolver but reluctant to put it aside while she dressed. She thought she heard Alex's voice from her phone, but didn't catch what he was saying. 'I can't see him at the moment,' she said loud enough for her voice to carry to the phone, 'I'm going to take a look around.'

Alex's voice squawked caution, but Tess had already ducked outside again, her gun held up, ready for anything. The wind slammed her, buffeted her side to side. She steadied her feet on the slick boards of the landing, and peered around, again checking the space behind her, but was unable to determine if her stalker had taken shelter beneath the steps. There was only one way to do so, and it meant going down. She dashed moisture from her face, squinting as wet leaves swirled around her like wasps disturbed from their nest.

About halfway down, she reversed on the steps, now checking through the gaps between the risers, watching for movement in the gloom in the recess beneath. Her breath caught, but only for an instant, because she recognized the flutter of cloth as from a tarp she'd placed over some garden furniture stored beneath the stairs. On quieter, sunny days during summer she occasionally grabbed one of the lawn chairs and sat out at the top of her drive, usually with a good book or her earphones on as she listened to the songs downloaded to her iPhone. This year, and despite the heat of the last few weeks, she'd never pulled out any of the furniture, too busy for lounging around. As she reached the ground, she made a quick sweep of the drive, before edging round the bottom of the steps. Hopewell could be crouching behind the stack of furniture. A brief check assured her he wasn't.

Come out, come out wherever you are, she thought, and took a quick peek around the back of the house. The deluge had turned the short strip of lawn to mud, from which stood brittle sun-blanched strands of grass, now fouled with the dirt splashing up. There were fresh footprints in the muck, but of the man who left them there was no trace. Tess tried to make sense of where he'd gone from the tracks, but they were overlaid too many times to make any sense of: Hopewell had paced back and forward as he surveyed the back of the house, seeking ingress, but then headed away. She glanced down near her own feet, but there was no hint of muddy footprints there, so he must have returned the way he'd come, round by the service yard.

'Let him go,' she advised herself.

But she ignored good sense, and went along the rear of the building. At ground level the windows had been blocked from within, Mrs Ridgeway not wishing to offer a sneak thief a view of the goods she stored in the back rooms. The service yard was small, little more than a storage area for the trash cans until they were pushed to the kerbside on collection days. Along one side was a six-foot wooden fence, which didn't offer any security but blocked the view of the junk for those in the next

building along. At each end was a gate, but neither was regularly
locked. The nearest was open, and Tess couldn't swear if she
closed it last time she dumped her trash, or even if the wind
had rattled loose the catch. A single but indistinct footprint
marred the ground inside the yard, almost obliterated by the
teeming rain.

So Hopewell had retreated back through the yard after
checking out the ladder? The far gate looked shut, but her stalker
could easily have closed it behind him as he left. She glanced
down at the muddy print, now barely visible on the poured
concrete that was awash with water sluicing off the ground to
the rear. How long ago had Hopewell gone through the yard?
Fifteen or twenty seconds at most. Which meant he could still
be out front or . . .

Tess spun around, expecting the man to come on her from
behind the wooden fence. He didn't, but she was no less
alarmed. She'd left her door open when she'd come downstairs.
Hopewell could have easily made his way around the front,
waited until she'd gone off on her ill-advised search of the
back of the building then slipped up and inside her home.

She ran along the rear of the house and headed for the stairs,
her teeth mashing her lips at her stupidity as she tried to see
up to where her door stood ajar.

She was distracted for barely a second, but it was all it took.

From the alcove beneath the stairs, a figure lurched at her,
and the impact of a palm against the side of her neck almost
knocked her down.

The son of a bitch had gone round the front of the house,
but he couldn't be sure that he'd make it inside in time to
surprise her, so had hidden in a place she'd already checked
for intruders! The thought flashed through Tess's mind, even as
she fought to catch her balance on the slick ground. The figure
bore into her, two hands about her, grasping her neck, and she
was lifted from her feet. Stunned, she forgot about the gun in
her hand, and instead, clawed and clubbed at her attacker. His
charge took her a few yards on to the hard stand where she'd
parked her Prius, and her spine took the brunt of the collision
with the hood of her car. What little air was left in her lungs
exploded in a wheeze of pain.

The next few seconds were a scrabble of panic and confusion that seemed an eternity. Her attacker forced his weight on top of her, and one of the hands clutching her neck was released to range over her body, between her legs even. The hand snaked up under her coat and pushed under her shirt, fingers digging into the flesh of her abdomen. What in God's name was in the maniac's mind? Was he going to try to rape her right there over the hood of her car?

But then the hand was gone from her flesh and bunched in her hair.

Tess realized her eyes were screwed shut.

She forced them open as a hot wash of sour breath bathed her, and set her off blinking again. The sleet tapped her eyelashes and forehead, and she shouldn't have been aware of the tiny sensations while her entire being was under assault.

Tess pushed out at the face hovering inches from hers.

A voice grunted a surly command, but the words were lost on her. Not that she'd ever succumb to obeying him.

'Get the hell off me or I swear to God I'll—'

Sudden realization that she still held on to her grandfather's Ruger changed her from squirming victim.

She forced the barrel up and jammed it into the soft flesh beneath her attacker's chin.

'Do you know what that is, you sick son of a bitch?' she snapped.

The clutching hands released her and the figure moved backwards a few inches, as Tess forced the gun harder against his neck. His open hands lifted away from her, showing that he would be a good little would-be rapist now she'd taken back the power he'd had over her.

Tess was still unbalanced, her butt on the hood of her car, but her feet elevated off the ground. She squirmed down the hood, her coat riding up her back, baring her against the chilly, wet metal. As her heels found the floor, she pushed up off the car, but was unsteady, and the barrel of her gun slipped from its target.

'Hold it right there!' she ordered as she sensed her captive tense for escape.

He held his open palms out to the sides, bowing his head so she'd no clear view of his face between the peak of his cap and scarf. It didn't matter if she got a good look at him: it was Cal Hopewell. She knew without question.

'OK,' she said, trying to force an officious edge to her tone. 'Keep your hands where I can see them and turn around.'

Hopewell ignored her.

'If you don't think I'll use this, you're mistaken,' Tess warned, with a wag of the gun barrel.

'You're not going to shoot an unarmed man,' Hopewell replied, smug in the certainty he was correct.

'An unarmed man who just tried to throttle me, and God knows what else!' Tess settled her footing, held the gun an inch or so nearer to him. But she was also conscious of getting too close. Caught off guard, she knew a skilled fighter could disarm her before she got off a clean shot, and she trusted that an ex-marine had training in close-quarters combat.

'You won't kill me in cold blood,' Hopewell replied and he took a step backwards, his hands still out to the sides.

'One more move, you sick bastard!'

Distantly a siren competed with the wind to be heard.

Hopewell's head snapped up.

'Yes,' Tess told him, 'you hear right: I called the police. They'll be here in seconds. Now do as I goddamn said and turn around.'

'Shoot me, please,' he said, as if he was requesting a coffee from a barista. 'Go on. Do it.' He curled his fingers, made a go-ahead gesture. 'Otherwise I'm leaving.'

'Stand there, goddamnit,' Tess barked.

Earlier, she'd asked Alex to come quietly, now all she wanted was the siren shrieking like a banshee and her brother running to assist in the capture, because Hopewell was right. She couldn't shoot him in cold blood, and the smug bastard knew it. If she'd handcuffs or something else to secure him with she'd be in a better position, but just as she'd done moments earlier, Hopewell regained the power he'd momentarily lost. The gun no longer demanded fear from him.

Alex, or another responding officer, was still a minute away. But another vehicle suddenly loomed out of the rain – a pickup truck, with the logo of Charley's Autoshop. Two figures were indistinct behind the windshield.

There was a shared instant when Tess and Hopewell glanced at the new arrivals, before their gazes snapped back.

The balance of power had shifted again, and Hopewell knew it.

He turned and fled, even as Po hurtled from the driving seat and charged up the drive towards Tess.

Tess's attention was on him a split-second too long, and by the time she brought the revolver round, Hopewell was already sprinting out of sight behind her building.

'Who the hell was that?' Po demanded as he skidded up to her. His concerned gaze swept her, in an instant taking in her flushed cheeks, her dishevelled state, the gun in her hand, and making up his mind. Before Tess could confirm it was the man who'd been following them, Po was off in pursuit.

There was only one option left to Tess: she followed.

# TWENTY

**P**o's shoulders were rounded, his arms hanging loose by his sides but his fingers curling into fists so tightly that Tess was positive she could hear the creaking of his ligaments. He turned and looked at her, and his sparkling eyes had taken on a deeper hue, the blue of an ocean at midnight. His face, normally lined, was creased deeply, and his mouth held rictus-tight. Tess had never seen him so angry.

Partly she was glad that Cal Hopewell had given them the slip, because she wasn't positive she could have stopped Po from killing him.

He muttered something foul under his breath, but then his gaze held on her, and she watched as the lines smoothed out of his features, replaced by a frown of concern.

'Did he hurt you?' he asked gently.

'Going to have a stiff neck in the morning, but, no, I'm OK.' Tess realized she was still wielding her revolver, and quickly checked for observers before slipping it in her coat pocket. They were a distance from her home on Forest Avenue, near Deering Oaks Park, where the trees swayed wildly in the breeze. After he'd fled, Tess had barely gotten a look at Cal Hopewell, and had concentrated instead on keeping Po's lanky frame in sight. The chase had taken them across lawns, over fences and down service alleys, before they'd spilled out on to Park Avenue, and Po had paused to survey the terrain like a stalking panther. Tess had almost caught up then, wheezing with effort, before Po had strode to the intersection with Forest Avenue, where he'd again scanned for movement, without luck.

His chest rose and fell. His hair was plastered to his forehead, and rain had soaked his shirt and jeans. Tess was equally drenched, and probably looked in a worse state than she felt, except she wasn't exaggerating when she mentioned expecting a stiff neck, she felt as if Hopewell had used her skull as a bowling ball.

'The son of a bitch! What did he want?'

Tess fed an arm through his elbow, and they hugged briefly, neither of them caring less that they were soaked through. 'He didn't say, but I can guess.'

'Did he . . .?' His words faltered.

'Touch me?' Tess squeezed him tighter, and felt his hands cup her hair. His touch was gentle but still uncomfortable. 'He tried,' she said, 'but I didn't let him.'

Po swore savagely, and she could feel the heat flaring in him.

'Where were you?' she whispered.

'As soon as I saw your text I headed back as quickly as possible.'

'I know. I'm not criticizing. I was worried.'

'You needn't worry about me,' he reassured her. 'It isn't anything to do with the Chatards.'

'I know. I found out who that guy is.'

Po extricated himself from their hug, but only so he could peer down at her. He placed his hands protectively on her shoulders.

'I've been busy while you were off gallivanting,' she told him, but added a meek smile to show she was only teasing. She briefly explained what she'd discovered about Jasmine's attacker being the disgraced marine Calvin Hopewell. 'I think he was there watching when I went to Margaret's, and he followed me home again. He knew I was alone, and made up his mind to try to break in. With this storm, there was little chance of any witnesses. It was lucky I spotted him before he made it inside.'

Po swore again. Ordinarily he watched his language around women and children, but he could be forgiven: it was his only way to express his enraged passion. 'And I wasn't there to help in time,' he growled. 'I'm so sorry, Tess.'

'I'm not blaming you: I'm certainly not disappointed with you. I'm only glad you're back.'

Po rolled his shoulders. His pride was stung, she could tell, but he nodded in acceptance.

'I'm still sorry I didn't catch up with that son of a bitch.'

'He's gone now,' Tess said. 'There's nothing we can do about it. But we now know who he is: Alex was coming over too, I'll tell him about Hopewell and the police can have him.'

'Come on, then,' he said. 'Let's get back. We're only getting wet out here.'

'Could we get any wetter than this?' Tess said, feeling exactly like the proverbial drowned rat. Her feet squished inside her sneakers.

'It was this darned storm that held me up,' Po explained as they began retracing their route. 'I've been stuck out at Portland International waiting to pick up your surprise. Flights were all running late due to the high winds.'

Tess glimpsed up at him. 'My surprise, eh? I got a brief look at the truck you arrived in.' She grinned. 'Thought it was odd that you'd chosen to bring over the pickup, but, come to think of it, not when I realize who that could be in the passenger seat.'

'My Mustang ain't built for carrying someone as humongous as Pinky Leclerc,' he joked.

'Pinky's here?' All residual emotion after fighting off her attacker was instantly dispelled by joy. Pinky Leclerc had that effect on her. 'Wow, I can't wait to see him!'

'He's looking forward to seeing *his* "Pretty Tess" too. If I didn't know otherwise, I'd swear he's got a crush on you.'

'No, it isn't like that. Anyway, we both know who he's really got a crush on.'

'You've gotta love the big lug,' Po smiled.

'Funnily enough, that's what he says about you.' Tess bumped hips with him as they walked, and Po laughed, his rage thankfully dispersed – for now.

Flashing lights filled the rain-washed scene. Out of the downpour a Portland PD cruiser materialized, and moments later pulled over the road to draw up alongside them. Alex Grey's face was bleached white with concern, and Tess saw the relief in his eyes as he powered down the window and checked her over.

'Am I pleased to see you,' he announced.

'Must say I'm happy to see you too,' Tess replied. 'Have you got room for two in the back? We're getting soaked out here.'

'Sure, jump in,' said Alex, and hit the lock releases.

Po frowned, not pleased at the mode of transport, but he wasn't a fool. He followed Tess on to the rear bench seat, while

Alex turned round to view them through the wire security screen. Tess slicked the water from her face, then was momentarily unsure where to place her wet hands. She surreptitiously wiped them on her damp thighs.

Alex wanted to know exactly what had gone on, and Tess told him in as few concise words as possible as he drove them back towards her house.

'And you guys chased Hopewell out there to near Deering Oaks Park?' Alex asked.

'Unfortunate that he got away,' Po drawled, and caught a squint from Alex in the rear-view mirror. 'Maybe fortunate, then,' Po concurred.

Alex relayed Hopewell's details and a description gleaned from Tess to colleagues already engaged in an area search. Once he released the mike, he said, 'So who the hell's the behemoth I found sitting on your drive?'

'You didn't treat him as a suspect, I hope?' Po growled. 'He's a friend.'

'Soon as I arrived, he assumed the position. Took me a minute or two to get any sense out of him, and he explained how he was with you, Nicolas Villere, but you'd abandoned him to chase a better-looking fella. I left him with a colleague, can't say what has happened since then.'

Where Pinky came from, he was possibly used to being treated as an immediate suspect by any cop who didn't know him. From what Po recalled of law enforcement in Louisiana they weren't as tolerant of minority races and ethnic diversity as they were up here in the north; but his direct experience of dealing with southern cops was decades out of date, so things could have changed.

'His real name is *Pinky*?' Alex wanted to know.

'His real name is Jerome, but he wouldn't thank you for it,' Po replied. 'Anyway, Officer Grey, what's wrong with being called Pinky?'

'Nothing, I suppose,' Alex shrugged as he glimpsed in the mirror. 'But is he . . .'

'Gay?' Po asked, and lifted an eyebrow of reproof.

'I was going to say "for real",' said Alex, and caught a grunt of mirth from Tess.

'He's unique,' she said, and Po nodded his approval.

'You might say that,' Alex agreed. 'Now I think of it, he's the guy helped you out down in Baton Rouge, right?'

'One and the same,' Tess said. 'Pinky's great. You'll love him.'

Alex didn't reply. He ruminated; probably understanding that the assistance Pinky gave to Tess and Po had also placed him in Pinky's debt.

Pinky was waiting by kerbside when Alex pulled up outside the antiques shop. He was dressed in an enormous parka coat with a fur-lined hood thrown back. His small head sported a woollen bobble hat, which made it appear pointed, and added to the strange appearance of his silhouette. He suffered from a medical condition that had bloated his body from mid-chest down, forming his legs into thick tubes while his arms were oddly skinny by comparison. He made jazz hands when he spotted Tess grinning up at him from the confines of the cruiser. She slipped out and was engulfed in his warmth as he lifted her skyward in a hug.

'Oh, pretty Tess,' Pinky announced, as he set her on her feet again and held her at arm's length so he could study her, 'such a sight for sore eyes, you!'

'I'm a mess,' Tess replied, because she knew she was. 'And what on earth are you doing standing out in the storm like this? You'll catch your death of cold.'

'Ha! You call this a storm? Do you forget where I come from, me? This is a sun shower by comparison!'

Po clapped Pinky on the back. 'Let's get inside, old pal. Tess for one needs to get out of this damned rain.'

A second police cruiser was parked at the rear of the auto-shop truck. Alex conversed briefly with its driver, and then waved him off, the cop going to join the search for Hopewell. Alex followed them up the stairs to Tess's house. Her door was still open, as she'd left it, and her phone was sitting on the hall table. Tess carried it with her while she peeled off her coat and went in search of towels. Although it wasn't his place, Po played host, offering seats and hot drinks.

Alex was keen to go hunting for the man who'd assaulted his sister, but somebody had to take an initial report from her and he'd volunteered. He shook hands with Pinky, and made an apology for his earlier brusqueness.

'Not to worry, I enjoy being roughed up by a handsome hunk in uniform, me,' said Pinky, to a startled look from Alex. Po grinned unashamedly, happy not to be the object of Pinky's affection this time.

Tess was absent for a few minutes, drying off and changing her clothes, and only when she joined them in her living room did she understand why the three guys were all blinking at each other in semi-darkness: the power was still off.

'Nobody thought to check the breaker box?' she asked, and gave Po then Alex a disapproving look. 'If you want something done . . .'

'I'll check,' said Po. 'You tell Alex what went on here.'

Alex stalled him. 'You're going to have to call the power company,' he said. 'My colleague checked around, and found the supply wires to the building were chopped through. Going to have somebody from CSI over to dust for prints.'

'We know who's responsible,' said Po.

But Tess shook her head. 'We still have to gather the evidence.'

'Got candles?' Alex asked.

'I've got storm lamps,' said Tess, and raised her eyebrows at Po. 'They're through in my junk closet.'

'So I'll fetch them instead,' he griped, and sloped off towards her kitchen.

Pinky clapped his hands excitedly. 'It'll be as if we're camping out in the great outdoors!'

Alex seemed about to say something, but Tess beat him to the punch. She thumped him on the shoulder, and his mouth snapped shut.

'Can I point something out?' asked Pinky, with a grandiose wink at Tess. 'I once said for such a woman as you, pretty Tess, that I'd be prepared to change my ways. Well, I needn't now, not when presented by this handsome hunk here.'

'Uh, I'm spoken for,' said Alex a tad too quickly.

'Fear not, I was only pointing out your apparent likeness, me. You are siblings, yes?' He waved a finger between them. 'But who is the elder?'

'Him,' said Tess, 'though you wouldn't think it.'

'Oh! I was fooled by his youthful good looks,' Pinky leered.

'I meant judging by his immature behaviour,' Tess explained and Alex grumbled in good nature.

Po came back lugging some battery-powered lamps, and set one down on Tess's work-station desk. Another he set atop the mantelpiece – an original feature for a now defunct fireplace.

Alex fished out his notebook, and a pen, and looked expectantly at his sister.

Tess held up a finger. Pulled out her cellphone that was ringing.

She didn't recognize the number on the display, but saw it had a Portland area code.

'Hello?' she asked warily.

'Is that Tess Grey? We spoke yesterday,' whispered an urgent voice. 'It's Chris Mitchell, the bartender from Bar-Lesque. Max Carter's club?'

'Chris? Yes, hi! This is Tess.' She looked quizzically at her friends, who were all eyeing her expectantly: over the phone she could hear the rasp of breath. 'Chris . . . is there something wrong?'

'There's somebody here asking Max about Jazz again,' whispered Chris. 'I thought I should let you know . . .'

'John Trojak?' Tess asked.

'No, somebody else. Uh! Things are getting kinda heated over here . . . Oh!'

Behind Chris's other voices were raised, and there was a sudden racket of chairs and tables scraping across the floor, something heavy crashing down.

'Oh my God!' Chris screeched into the phone. 'He's stabbed him. Oh god oh god oh god! Help, Tess, help! Oh dear god, there's blood everywhere!'

# TWENTY-ONE

The whispering devil returned after two days.

In her fanciful manner, Elsa Jayne Moore had imagined a number of reasons for his nonappearance, none of them good for her sick-minded abductor. She hoped that the police had captured him, or that he'd been killed in some random but blessedly appropriate accident, or that he was ill, and lying in some sick-bed thrashing and moaning in agony, bathed in sweat and the heat of a raging infection. She dreamed the bastard was incapacitated or dead, and it would be just punishment for his wickedness. But also she'd grown fearful. If he were imprisoned, dead, ill, or incapacitated in some other fashion, then what would become of her and the other girls he'd secured in their cells? Would anyone find them before they perished from thirst or starvation?

Before he left, he'd double-checked the chain shackling her to the rusty engine block. Double-checked the lock on her door, even thrown over an extra layer of security in some kind of lever she heard bolted and then secured with a padlock. She was certain that similar precautions had been made with the other captives. His final warning came at a rasp through the tiny slot in the metal door through which he checked on his prisoners, ensuring they were effectively restrained before entering their cells. 'Silence,' was all he said, and the promise of retribution that one word held was enough to command obedience.

He'd left water, and a meagre supply of food, but crackers and cookies didn't last long: Elsa had consumed the biscuits in the first few hours he'd been gone, and half the water. Only when she didn't hear his shuffling progress through the labyrinth that first night did she think to conserve her water supply. But now that had gone. She hadn't felt a need to move her bowels, but she'd urinated, and her pee she guessed must be dark and cloudy through dehydration. It probably stank, but she'd grown nose blind, accustomed to the stench by now. When she heard the unlocking of a distant door, and the steady crunch of boots along the corridor that followed, the relief that flashed through her was surprising. She desperately needed to drink. It was a horrible notion, but she understood that her survival was reliant on her abductor when it came to the most basic of necessities.

Strange that she could juxtapose the notion of saviour over the deranged beast responsible for her torment. She wondered if the other girls were as relieved to hear his progress through the labyrinth. She stirred, coming from her crouch, with her chain clutched between her fingers, ensuring it didn't clink or rasp together. In the dimness she couldn't tell if there were any signs that she'd attempted to scrape a weak spot in her shackle. If he noted her attempt at escape, her punishment would be brutal and immediate. She didn't think she need fear too much: the floor was hard-packed dirt, and apart from a few small pebbles she'd found nothing to rub the link against, and had quickly given up. Nevertheless she cupped as much of the chain to her abdomen as she could.

He didn't come directly to her cell. Why would he when she wasn't his favourite? As mad as it sounded, she should be relieved that he found one of the other girls more deserving of his time, but in an absurd way she was also pinched by envy. The uncoupling of the other girl's cell door was noisy, heavy clanks and the screech of rusty iron. His commands were too low to be heard from her cell, but she imagined what he wanted. When he entered, his slaves must turn away and face the back wall. She pictured the girl doing so now, but with no idea of what she looked like it was her own figure she watched assume the position.

Who had he gone to first?

Was it to the girl whose name she'd learned? The one who'd been brave enough to speak with her?

They were forbidden to talk, and for the first few hours after he'd left the girls had obeyed the prime rule. The only sounds were water dripping from a pipe somewhere, the groans and creaks as the ancient structure settled on its foundations at the end of the day, and the scuttling of rodents through cavities in the walls. Elsa was first to find voice, but it was barely above a whisper as she tried to coax from her depths the nerve to call out to her fellow captives. As time went on, and the ambient sounds were all that she heard in response, she grew more courageous. 'Hello?' she called, her voice timid, and as thin as sheer fabric. 'Hello? Can anyone hear me?'

Silence reigned, the hush now deeper as the others held their breath against the expected roar of anger. As Elsa had, they wondered if this was some kind of test, their master was listening for the first hint of disobedience, one for which he'd make an example of the slave who'd dared to defy him. The breath caught in Elsa's throat, and she screwed her face tight in anticipation of an impending attack. The dripping water ticked, the walls creaked, but that was all.

'Hello? Anyone? My name is Elsa Moore. What are your names?'

Nobody answered.

'Please? I know you can hear me. I'm Elsa. Please, to stop me going out of my mind, will somebody answer me?'

'Shhh!'

'Please?' Elsa croaked. 'Your names? That's all I need to hear. Just so I know I'm not alone in this. That *you're* not alone either.'

'Shhh . . . he might hear . . .'

In the darkness, Elsa shook her head. 'He isn't here. He has left. This rule about not speaking: he forces us to stay quiet so nobody hears and finds us. Don't you see?'

'He might still be listening,' came a whispered voice from somewhere to her left. 'Microphones.'

Elsa wouldn't believe their captor was the least bit sophisticated. His dungeon was dilapidated beyond repair, with no electric lights in evidence. What were the chances he'd installed listening devices, or worse, CCTV cameras? Her shackles and chains were ancient, rusted, things he'd found close to hand: he hadn't gone to any effort when designing his cages, except to ensure there was no escape. It's why she thought he demanded silence so rigidly, because he had no way of soundproofing the prison.

'He can't hear us,' Elsa tried again. 'He isn't here. He might not even come back.'

'Shush. Please? Just stop!' said another woman from down the passage to her right. 'He'll hurt us.'

'He has already hurt us,' Elsa snapped, more emboldened now that it appeared she was correct: the devil had left the pit, and he wasn't the all-seeing, all-hearing, all-knowing fiend she'd imagined. 'Physically, mentally, sexually, he has *abused* us. Well, I won't allow him to take my spirit!'

'Then he'll take your tongue instead,' said a fourth voice. 'Is that what you want, Elsa?'

'He won't do that. It's only a threat, one he uses to keep us down. He's a goddamn coward, a snivelling weakling! Don't you see?'

'How long have you been here?' asked the last woman to speak.

'I've lost track,' Elsa admitted. 'I don't know any more.'

'I've been here longer. Do you think you're the first girl to be held in that room?' The woman waited for the shocking truth to hit Elsa. In response there was a subdued sob from one of the other girls who'd since fallen silent again.

'Wh-what happened to her?' Elsa asked, already fearing the truth.

'Trust me. He doesn't make idle threats.'

'He . . . he cut out her tongue?' Elsa moaned.

'Worse.' The woman halted. No doubt picturing the fate of the missing girl. 'Please, Elsa. Be quiet now. For all our sakes.'

'Yes. OK. I'll do that,' Elsa agreed at a whisper. 'But please, before I do, just tell me your name.'

A long pause followed, and Elsa leaned forward in anticipation.

'OK,' the woman finally acquiesced. 'But this is the last thing I'm going to say. My name is Jasmine Reed. My friends call me Jazz.'

Now, as she recalled their brief discussion, Elsa wondered if having been his prisoner for the longest time, Jasmine was his favourite toy. There was no benefit, except perhaps that Jasmine would be fed and watered first. But what would be forced from her in exchange? She hated to imagine what her friend was

about to endure, while yet another part of her, the opposite
to the one that had flashed with envy only moments ago, was
thankful that when he visited her cell soon, he'd have sated one
sick desire and the most she could expect was a beating if
he need sate another.

Jasmine's cell was many yards away, but even across the
distance and through the muffling walls Elsa heard the first slap.
Others followed, and then the whispering devil broke his primary
rule, crying out an animalistic shriek. The rattle of chains
followed, then the sound of Jasmine being dragged bodily from
the tiny cell. Jasmine didn't bleat for pity, she snarled and
screeched like a wild cat, but her defiance dwindled as she was
dragged deeper into the bowels of the labyrinth.

Elsa dropped her chain to cup her hands over her ears. She
wept for Jasmine, and for herself, and for the other girls whose
faint sobs echoed hers. She didn't want to listen, but she did,
and she dreaded hearing that strange roaring of flames rushing
up a flume. Mercifully the arrival of a storm shook the building,
and any hint of Jasmine's terrifying fate was buried beneath
the tumult of noise from rattling beams, flapping tin-sheet
and the shuddering moan of the ancient structure as it strove
to remain upright.

Elsa forgot about her desperate thirst for water.

As the building shook and swayed overhead, she stood,
naked, bruised and beaten half to death, but defiant. She threw
back her head and screamed, a wordless promise.

Now she knew another thirst, this one for revenge on the
beast who'd dared brutalize her new friend Jazz.

# TWENTY-TWO

'There's never a dull moment here in Portland,' Pinky grinned. 'I should visit more often, me!'

Pinky had accompanied Po in the pickup truck, following while Alex and Tess raced to the scene in the PPD cruiser on lights and sirens. The pickup was parked outside the police cordon set up around Maxwell Carter's club, where Tess was forced to wait for news. Onlookers, ready for a night on the town despite the horrendous weather, stood under every piece of available shelter nearby. Tess had joined Po and Pinky in the truck, wedged in the narrow gap between them as she observed the drama.

Chris Mitchell was unhurt, but he was bloody to the elbows, and his normally immaculate hair was hanging loose around his face. His experience as a nurse had saved Max Carter's life, but the wounded man was critically injured and had been rushed to the nearest ER. Tess watched Chris speaking to a plain-clothed detective in the alcove next to the club's front door. He looked shell-shocked, and she suspected he would require medical attention when the adrenalin wore off. Before he grew incapable of stringing a cohesive description of events together she hoped to grab a few minutes with him. It irked her to be on the outside of the police investigation, but that was just the way it was. Alex was in the Bar-Lesque, helping his colleagues, and he might not be free to update her any time soon.

More than an hour had passed since Chris's urgent call and Tess's race across town to help, not knowing whether he would survive an encounter with Max's attacker because she'd hung up to summon an ambulance, while Alex called for immediate back up over his radio. Even after they arrived, she got no news on what was happening inside the club because responding officers had beaten them to the scene and Alex had raced inside to join them. She watched Max Carter brought out on a gurney, medics working on him as they loaded him into an ambulance and took off with the siren wailing. Some time after that an old black man came outside to sit on the kerb with his face in his hands, and then Chris emerged. Chris crouched by the old guy, speaking comforting words. The rain pelted them both, but it was as if the old man didn't notice, maybe he needed the rain to cleanse some of the images he'd witnessed from his mind. Chris patted the old man on the shoulder in consolation, then stared at his own bloodied hands and his shudder of revulsion was obvious even from where Tess sat. He stood out of the rain, partly slumped in the alcove where he and Po had shared a smoke. He was joined by a uniformed officer, and shortly after by the detective who continually prompted him for details about what happened.

'Believe it or not,' Tess assured Pinky, 'Portland's usually a safe place to live. It's not always like this.'

'Only when you are around, eh, pretty Tess?' he joked, and nudged her with an elbow. 'That's what comes with mixing with the criminal element: like attracts like.'

'I'm no criminal,' Po muttered.

'Ha!' said Pinky. 'Criminal is as criminal does. Don't tell me what you do is totally lawful, Nicolas, despite now being on the side of the angels.'

'And I'm no angel,' said Tess, and then shot him a wry smile.

'He he!' Pinky said, and shuffled his butt deeper on the bench, enjoying the ringside seat.

'The cop's leaving,' Po pointed out.

The detective had indeed finished with Chris. He patted his left bicep, indicating they were done, and sauntered back under the awning. Chris remained where he was, staring skyward a moment. Again a shudder swept through him, and he visibly exhaled. He dug in his vest pocket, but his features remained stricken.

'Coming?' Po asked.

'Try to stop me,' Tess answered, and gave him a nudge. It was easier to slide out after him than to wait while Pinky exited the cab.

For the umpteenth time that evening, Tess was battered by the storm. Bent slightly, hands ineffectively covering her hair, she jogged across the street with Po following closely, while Pinky elected to stay in the warmth. A uniformed cop watched them approach, but didn't stop them joining Chris.

Chris spotted them coming, and relief flooded his features.

But it wasn't for Tess's appearance. To Po he said, 'How's about you return the favour and give me a smoke, buddy?'

'F'sure,' said Po, and dug out his pack, shaking out a Marlboro.

Tess shook rain from her hair as Chris gave way for her in the alcove. He bent, cupping his hands to protect the flame as Po sparked up his Zippo. Gratefully he threw back his head and shot a torpedo of smoke at the sky.

'Jeez, I needed that,' he said.

'Looks like it,' Tess said, but wasn't referring to the calming effect of the nicotine. Up close the blood on Chris's arms looked like crimson gloves, and there was more spattered on his vest and jeans, and even a fan of it on his throat. Undoubtedly he had been trying to stem an arterial spray of Max Carter's lifeblood. 'You weren't hurt?'

'No. I'm fine. Well, as fine as I could be after watching someone have their throat slashed.' Chris took another deep pull on his cigarette.

'It's a good job you were there to help Max,' Tess said.

'That all depends on how you define good.'

'I meant that you were able to save him,' Tess said.

Chris nodded, eyelids closed.

'Maybe I should've done something before that maniac broke a bottle and rammed it in his neck.'

Tess and Po shared a glance.

'You said this guy was asking about Jasmine Reed?' Tess prompted.

Chris nodded, hugged himself with one arm while settling the cigarette between his lips again. Once he'd taken a drag, he said, 'He wasn't as nice about it as either you or Trojak.' He smiled at the absurdity of his words, considering Trojak had resorted to violence, and Po had offered it more subtly. Tess thought about how Po had lifted a glass, and how nasty things could have turned out if he'd resorted to using it as a weapon. Horrible, she thought.

'Can you tell us what was said between them?' asked Tess.

'Not really,' Chris said. 'I was prepping the bar and Jeff was mopping the dance floor when the guy came in. I told him that we weren't open yet, but he just ignored me and pushed his way into Max's office. I heard him ask where Jasmine was, and then they were arguing. That's when I rang you, and while I was on the phone Max came bursting out the office with the guy hanging on to him. The guy forced him up against the bar, yelling at him about why Jasmine ran away. He had a gun – I'm sure it was one Max keeps in his desk drawer – but he shoved it in his belt and grabbed the nearest thing to hand instead. He smashed a bottle and stuck it in Max's throat. Well, after that, I was kind of shocked, can't get things straight in my head.'

'Did the guy just leave?' Tess asked.

'Must have.' Chris took another grateful inhalation of smoke. 'Least he wasn't there any more while me and Jeff tried to stop Max's bleeding.'

'Is Jeff the old guy over there?' Tess indicated the elderly black man who had moved from his perch on the kerb and was speaking to a uniformed cop out of earshot.

Chris nodded. 'He does a few odd jobs, pushes around a broom, mainly for beer money.'

Tess dug in her pocket, pulled out the folded sheets of paper, unfolded one, and held it out to Chris. 'Is this the man who attacked Max?'

She'd decided to show the picture of Calvin Hopewell after his arrest, not the one where he was a clean-cut officer in his parade uniform. Chris's pupils dilated in recognition, and his face drained paler again.

'That's him. He wasn't dressed like that, he was wearing a ball cap and coat, but I recognize the face. Shit! I don't think I'll ever forget it!'

Tess folded the photo and put it away. She looked at Po. After losing Hopewell near Deering Park he must have gone directly to front Max Carter in the club. The guy was on a mission, or a downward spiral where his frustration was making his actions more desperate: neither prospect was good news. In the short time he'd been back in Portland, Hopewell had acted violently on at least the three occasions they knew about, and perhaps more they didn't. And unless he was stopped, he would undoubtedly resort to violence again, and the next time there might not be a trained nurse around to save his victim's life.

'We should check on Margaret,' said Tess, and Po's eyelids pinched in agreement.

'Who is that nutjob?' Chris asked.

'You remember when I asked you about when Jasmine was assaulted?' Tess asked.

'That was *him*, the same bastard that hurt her?'

'His name is Calvin Hopewell,' Tess said. 'Does it ring a bell?'

'Jazz never mentioned him, but wait . . . yeah, one time Bruno was here, I recall him mentioning Hopewell's name to Max.'

'Daryl Bruin and Max talked about him? You don't remember what was said?'

'No. I wasn't paying attention; I tend to keep to myself when Bruno visits. But I do remember Bruno being unhappy about Hopewell coming back.'

'Coming back? When exactly was this?'

'Don't know if I can be exact, but it's only a few weeks ago. Maybe just before . . .' His face sank.

'Just before Jasmine went missing,' Tess finished for him.

# TWENTY-THREE

'So finally the cops have taken an interest in Jasmine's case, huh?' asked Po as Tess pottered in his kitchen. Because the power was still off at her place, Po had extended an invitation to settle in at his until repairs could be made to the supply. He lived in a surprisingly roomy ranch-style property on a densely wooded plot with a view over Presumpscot Falls, and even with the inclusion of his surprise visitor – Pinky – he still had plenty of spare rooms. When Tess had previously stayed over they'd shared the master bedroom, but for her convenience – and appearances' sake – he'd offered her a spare room from where she could work, and store the clothes she'd brought from her house after they left Bar-Lesque in order to regroup.

'Only through association with Cal Hopewell,' said Tess. 'But in one way it also strengthens their opinion that Jasmine has deliberately gone missing, to avoid the mad man. They're looking for Hopewell, finding Jasmine is still down to us.'

'You tell them your theory that Jasmine could've been taken like those other girls you mentioned?' Po stood with his scarred and tattooed forearms folded over his chest, butt against the kitchen counter, ankles crossed.

'No, I only told Alex that Chris Mitchell identified Max's attacker from the photo I showed him. It isn't the way a formal identification is normally made, but Alex was arranging for Chris to go to the precinct and look through some mugshots. In the meantime he's put out a BOLO for Hopewell: there's enough to treat him as a suspect for now. I'll also have to do a formal identification at some point, for when he attacked me, but that can wait. Hopefully for when he's in custody and in a line-up.'

'So they're not looking for the other girls either?'

'It's only a personal theory at this time,' Tess explained, 'and possibly a wild one. I did tell Emma about it, and she asked me to find something more conclusive that she could take to the FBI.'

'Unlucky,' said Po.

Tess handed him the coffee she was preparing, waiting for him to continue. He didn't.

'I'm not getting you,' Tess said. 'Who's unlucky? Me?'

'Jasmine.' He sipped his coffee. It was black and hot, the way he enjoyed it. Tess had made hers with milk.

'I'm still lost.'

'If she ran away from one monster only to fall into the hands of another.' Po's eyebrows rose and fell. 'Kind of supreme irony, huh?'

'Stranger things have happened.'

'Oh yeah?'

'You think I'm wrong about there being a predator taking girls?'

'I don't doubt you for a second, Tess.'

Not so long ago they'd both entertained distrust of each other, but that was no longer an issue. She'd no reason to think he was being anything but sincere now.

'So . . .?' he asked.

Tess shook her head, wondering why he didn't just come out with what was on his mind rather than all these open-ended prompts. Then again, it was simply his way, and she guessed he was hoping it would get her thinking on the problem at hand.

'So,' she said, and set down her coffee cup. 'We've a few threads to follow, some things to ascertain first, and a couple of return visits to make.'

'The priority is Margaret Norris,' he stated. 'Hopewell might go after her next.'

'There's a patrol car sitting outside her house for now. I rang her while you were showering, and she's agreed to go and stay with a friend for a few days until things settle down with Hopewell.'

'She still good with us looking for Jasmine?'

If Jasmine had deliberately run away to escape Hopewell's return to Maine, her grandmother might feel it unnecessary to continue paying a private investigator to find her. She might assume that once Hopewell was no longer a danger, Jasmine would come out of hiding. Tess hadn't hinted that Jasmine could be in danger from another man entirely; if she had then it would add an extra layer of concern Margaret could do without. But neither had she discussed dropping the case, because it simply wasn't her way. Jasmine could indeed be safe and sound, living in anonymity someplace, but where there was even an iota of a chance she'd fallen into the hands of a predator, Tess wouldn't turn her back on her. Paid, or unpaid, she'd pledged she'd find Jasmine – and now she thought on it, the other missing girls as well.

'I'm looking for her,' Tess stated, and it was enough for Po.

'OK,' he said, and his affirmation held as much weight as hers.

'So,' she said, with a wry curl of her lip. 'We need to speak to Daryl Bruin again. Trojak too.'

'My favourite people.' Po sniffed. 'Bruin knows something he isn't saying.'

'F'sure,' Tess replied, and Po squinted at her usage of his dialect. Tess smiled; she'd been teasing, but she wondered how many other of his traits she'd absorbed since they'd become a couple. And now that Pinky had arrived she thought it wouldn't be long until she referred to herself as 'Tess, me'. She chuckled at the notion, and immediately looked for the big guy. Pinky was through in the guestroom, and by the mumble of his voice was either talking to himself or was on a cellphone. He was on an impromptu vacation, but likely business back in Baton Rouge still required his attention. How on earth, she thought, did an ex-cop become the lover of a convicted killer, and best friend of an arms dealer? Hell, whatever the fates had in store for such a grouping of friends, she wouldn't have it any other way.

'Not so sure about Trojak,' Po put in. 'The guy's a douche, but he's being used.'

'I tend to agree.'

'Only tend to?'

'Turn of phrase, Po.'

He winked, sipped coffee.

'So when do you want to go ruffle Bruin's feathers?' he asked.

'First thing in the morning. It's getting late now, and in this horrible weather I'm betting he's settled in at home.'

'You have an address for him, or just his office?' He shrugged marginally. 'You want, I can take Pinky out for a tour, maybe knock on Bruin's door as we pass?'

'I could find his home address like *that*!' Tess clicked her fingers. 'But I'd prefer we met him at his office.'

Po checked the time on the clock on his oven. 20:51. Still early, but maybe not for a home visit. 'That girl's going to be out there another night,' he pointed out.

Tess hung her head. It was a fact that wasn't lost on her. 'Nothing we can do about that now. Not that I'm going to stop looking. I'm going to go check my programs, follow those threads I found earlier and hopefully come up with something conclusive Emma can work with.'

'So I'll just hang,' he said, but without recrimination.

'You've a guest to entertain,' she reminded him.

He paused, thinking, then gave her a searching look. 'I couldn't put him off coming.'

'And I don't expect you to. Pinky's your best friend, and mine.'

'It's just I thought it might be inconvenient just now.'

'Not in the least,' Tess assured him. 'It keeps you out from under my feet while I'm working.'

'Huh! Nice to be appreciated,' he said, but with a twinkle in his eyes.

She stroked his cheek, felt the stubble of a full day's growth under her palm. He put aside his coffee, and pulled her into his arms. She leaned back her head to accept his kiss, but he turned her, and sent her on her way with a slap to the butt. She giggled, looked back at him coyly. 'Don't work all night,' he warned, then with a wink he lowered his voice to add, 'I'll leave my bedroom door unlocked.'

Tess collected her latte from the counter, and used it to toast Po's idea.

She met Pinky in the hall.

'Did I just hear Nicolas promise to leave his door unlocked?' he teased.

Tess felt her cheeks colouring.

Pinky winked. 'Wouldn't it be funny if he woke up with a different bunkmate than he was expecting?'

'You wouldn't dare.'

'Ho ho!' said Pinky. Then with a lascivious grin, 'Maybe he's not the only one who should lock his door, pretty Tess.'

'Pinky, you are shameless,' she laughed.

'Shameless and proud.' He leant to nudge her gently. 'Hey, you couldn't give me the number for that hunky bartender, could you? He looks as if he might enjoy some company this wild and stormy night.'

Chris Mitchell wasn't overtly gay, he wasn't camp or effete in any outward manner that she'd noticed, and yet Pinky must have recognized the signs. That, or he simply liked what he'd seen: she thought Chris's good looks and athletic build were probably more alluring than the bloody gauntlets he'd been wearing. 'I'll see if I can introduce you guys,' she promised, then reached up and patted Pinky on his cheek affectionately.

He shambled off to greet Po in the kitchen, and Tess left them to get on with their guy stuff, heading for the spare room where she'd set up her iPad and a spare laptop, through which she'd patched in to the programs she was running at home.

An alert icon was jumping up and down on the laptop's screen, so Tess immediately hit the keyboard to waken it.

The latest item her search had thrown up dismayed her. She sat heavily in the chair in front of her temporary work station as she read the report.

That very evening a hiker had stumbled over the remains of a woman in a shallow grave near the shore of Quabbin Reservoir in Massachusetts. The police had released few details yet, but the location of the grim discovery forced a heavy weight on Tess's heart. When studying the map earlier while plotting the disappearances of the girls she'd already listed, she'd been aware of a huge body of water sitting neatly between the angles formed by Interstates 90 and 91. Was this discovery a coincidence, or was this the first tangible proof that a savage predator was working that self-same catchment area through which Jasmine might have travelled? She had no way of telling, but she was prepared to go with her gut, particularly now that a body had been found. For no good reason she could think of would a woman's body be interred in a shallow grave: this was the foulest of play.

'Is it you, Jasmine?' she asked the screen, and her voice was forlorn.

She didn't want to, but she looked deeper, at the first photographs released from the scene.

An arm, discoloured and gnawed on by wildlife, protruded from the earth. It was slim, toned, a young woman's. It was gloved in intricate tattoos that absurdly blended with the carpet of wildflowers that formed a backdrop. In a ghoulish sense there was artistry in the entire image, totally by accident and unwarranted, and it brought a deeper sense of sadness to Tess. She clicked on the next image, and this one made her briefly close her eyes, before she again forced herself to look. The woman's head had been partly uncovered – possibly by the hiker after making the shocking find, who had dug to reassure himself he must be wrong about what the arm signified, and then realizing the awful truth when the face was disclosed. Tess had no way of telling if the bloated, bruised and cut face was that of Jasmine Reed, and even if the dead girl could speak she would be unable to clarify. The gaping mouth was hollowed out, the poor girl's tongue severed uncleanly at its base.

# TWENTY-FOUR

Sliding a thumb under the right shoulder strap of his suspenders, Daryl Bruin snapped it against his chest as he observed his cousin John Trojak with no attempt at hiding his disappointment. Bruin had oiled his hair, but it wasn't his only feature that was slick. He wore a film of perspiration on his features, and his underarms were practically dripping, staining his expensive button-down shirt. His excessive perspiration had nothing to do with the temperature: more fear of losing everything he'd worked so hard to achieve. He'd had a poor start in life, and into young adulthood, but he'd learned quickly that if you wanted anything in life you had to reach for it, grab it by the throat and never let go. His ethos had stuck with him, and when he thought about the small empire he'd built himself on the back of all that hard work there was no way he'd give it up without a fight. Shit! How could one damn mistake – out of hundreds – come back to haunt him like this, to threaten him with destruction?

He snapped his suspender against his chest again.

'You understand how important this is to me, Johnny?' he asked.

Trojak was standing by the picture window in Bruin's office, as if peering out over the mouth of the Fore River towards South Portland, but absorbing none of the sights: not that there was much to see except a few distant twinkling lights dancing in the darkness. It was after ten o'clock, pitch black out, and still pouring down. He was watching Bruin's reflection in the plate glass, as if ashamed to meet his gaze directly.

'Do you understand, Johnny?' Bruin asked, sharper.

'Yeah,' Trojak replied, but there was no conviction to the word.

'I don't think you do. I really don't think you understand the consequences, or what they'll mean for you.' Bruin laced the fingers of both hands together, leaning forward over his desk. 'If I go down, you go down too.'

'I didn't have any part of it,' Trojak retorted, finally turning his head to stare over his shoulder. There was disgust in his gaze.

'Who employs you, Johnny? Who signs your damn pay cheque? Who keeps Vero in all the fine things she demands? You? Are you responsible for all those things?'

Trojak nipped at his bottom lip, but his eyes were flat.

'I don't need reminding, Daryl.'

'Oh, but I think you do. You'd be nothing without me. Look at what I've given you: a job, a home, *stability*. Where would you be if I hadn't given you all those things? Stacking goddamn shelves at Walmart!'

'There's no shame in that,' said Trojak. 'Many good people have to stack shelves to earn a living.'

Bruin balled a fist, hammered it down on his desk.

'Is that all you goddamn aspire to? No! That's not what you meant at all. Are you saying what you've done for me is shameful?'

Trojak fully turned and stared at his cousin. 'Why don't you ask yourself the same question?'

Bruin's hand slapped against his chest. 'There's *nothing* I've done that I'm ashamed of. Nothing!'

Trojak lifted his eyebrows.

'You've the temerity to judge me?' Bruin demanded. 'Look around you, Johnny. This—' he swept an arm, encompassing not only the office but everything he owned – 'did not come from making easy decisions. But they were the *right* decisions. The right decisions for me, and for you, you ungrateful son of a bitch.'

Trojak's eyelids flickered at the curse.

'Look at you!' Bruin went on. 'You couldn't even hold down a normal job. Stacking shelves? Don't make me fucking laugh! How long are you going to last dealing with all those foul-mouthed ignorant customers? You'll have a knife in somebody's guts first day on the job.'

'I'm not nuts.'

'Aren't you?' Bruin laughed scornfully. 'Go tell that to Max.'

'You told me to punish him.'

'I didn't tell you to nail his fucking hand to a table. That was on you, Johnny, not me.' He sneered. 'What was on your mind? You thought Max needed punishing for his part in what happened?'

'You're twisting things, Daryl. You're afraid that when the police come for you, you'll be charged with all the things you've made me do. You told me to hurt Max for holding out on the detective; how'd you think that was going to end?'

'See!' said Bruin, hammering his desk again. 'I knew it. I knew you'd try to throw all the blame back on me. Take some fucking responsibility for your own actions, Johnny. That's all I'm asking of you. That's all I've ever asked, goddamnit!' He sat back in his plush office chair, the air wheezing out of the cushions as he settled. 'That's all, Johnny.'

'I can't help it if I can't find Jasmine,' Trojak said, and his tone had lost its defiant edge; now he sounded more like a child seeking encouragement. 'I've done my best, Daryl.' He touched a sore spot on his head. 'I don't know what else you expect from me.'

'Your goddamn best, Johnny! That's what I expect. I need you to try harder.' Bruin placed his face in his hands, wiping away the slick film of sweat. He showed his wet palms. 'Look at me, man. I'm worried, Johnny. Worried for the both of us.'

'I don't know what to do,' Trojak admitted. 'I've tried every way I can think of to find Jazz. Don't forget, I'm no detective, Daryl. I tried to speak with Tess Grey; she knows what she's doing, but she won't work with me. She's no fool, but even she's having no luck finding Jasmine.'

'You have to make your own luck,' Bruin said wearily. 'That's what I've been trying to impart to you all these years. Take the fucking initiative, why don't you?'

'Please don't curse.'

'Fuck you. Use some of that prissy attitude to get motivated! If that doesn't work, feel those goddamn bumps on your head again and use them to put a little fire in your belly!' Bruin stood, pushing back his chair with the backs of his legs. 'Come here, Johnny.'

Trojak faltered, wondering what was coming next. But in the end he obeyed, walking slowly to meet Bruin, who came around his desk. Unexpectedly, Bruin hugged him. Trojak stood rigid, his eyeballs almost protruding from their sockets.

Bruin stood away, but left both hands resting on Trojak's shoulders. 'We're family, right? Me and you against the world.'

Trojak nodded, but with a caveat. 'And Vero.'

'You love Vero, right? And you love me? Well, look . . .' Bruin reached up and dug his fingertips into the back of Trojak's skull. Trojak shuddered against the pain flaring through his wounds but held his composure as Bruin made his point. 'Cal Hopewell did that to you. He hurt you, Johnny. He took the initiative like I always say to you, and he hurt you.' He squeezed his fingers tighter and this time Trojak was forced to flinch away. 'Now he's going to hurt the two of us, and that will hurt Vero much worse than him hitting you around the head a few times. You heard what he did to Max, right? Stuck a bottle in his throat? Well, Johnny, that's nothing to what he'll do to us if he ever admits what happened. If you can't find Jasmine, then find Cal. Hurt him before he can hurt *us*. All of us.'

Trojak's agreement was almost imperceptible.

'But how do I find him?' he asked.

'The same way you did last time. That sick-minded son of a bitch never could keep his dick in his pants. From what I hear he's got a boner for Tess Grey. You watch her, he'll turn up sooner or later for her.'

'But what about that Po Villere dude?' Trojak asked.

'You afraid of him?'

'I'm not afraid of anyone, or anything, except maybe losing Vero.' Trojak's nod was firmer this time. 'I'm not going to allow any of them to ruin everything for Vero.'

'She'd never forgive you if you did.'

'My wife has nothing to worry about. Neither have you, Daryl. I'm on this.'

'Good, Johnny! That's what I need to hear. That's the John Trojak I want at my side. Against the world, right?'

'Right,' said Trojak, then with a sly grin: '*Damn* right!'

Daryl clapped a hand on his cousin's bicep. 'Off you go, then.'

Dismissed, Trojak left.

Bruin sat again, peering now at his own reflection in the plate glass. Outside, Portland was awash with rain. The storm though still wild wasn't as intense as it had been, but the conditions might assist Trojak. When people were sheltering their heads from icy rain and wind they tended not to be alert to their surroundings. Maybe this time the idiot would actually come through, and if he played things right could get to Hopewell or Jazz by hanging on to Tess Grey's coattails. One of them needed to be permanently silenced, preferably both. Bruin wasn't kidding when he warned that if either spoke about that fateful day then he would be finished. He didn't give a shit if Trojak fell with him, and it'd be just desserts if that sour bitch Vero ended up panhandling the streets for her next fix, but he felt he'd motivated his stupid cousin enough to get the job done. Trojak was a complex individual, but only when trying to make sense of his skewed thought processes: there was a man who despised bad language but would happily stick a knife through a supposed friend's hand; who wouldn't lift a hand to save himself from the battering fists of his shrew of a wife, but would face anyone else fist for fist, knife for knife, without a waver of concern; who would show defiance when asked to do something, but would always go off wagging his tail if Bruin patted him on the head like a good little puppy dog.

Did he regret using his cousin in this way?

Like fuck, man!

It was as he'd told Johnny earlier, to get where he was Bruin hadn't made the easiest decisions. But they were the *right* decisions. And to save his own ass, and everything he'd earned, he'd gladly put his cousin's life on the line. He'd happily order the deaths of the two people most likely to destroy him. If it came to it, it'd be best if Johnny wasn't around at the finalization of all this, because once Hopewell and Jasmine were out of the picture, and if Max perished from his wounds, he'd be the only person left who knew Bruin's dirty secret.

No. That wasn't entirely true.

There was also the detective and her bodyguard to worry about, because through their pursuit of his adversaries they might learn something they shouldn't.

It was confirmed then, once Trojak had done his bidding, Bruin would give him another pat on the head, and sic him on Tess Grey. Hopefully Po and Trojak would kill each other in the fall out, and all would end swimmingly for Daryl Bruin.

'Yup, Bruno, that's the *right* decision,' he told his reflection.

# TWENTY-FIVE

'**W**e need to get off our butts and do something,' Tess announced as she strode into Po's spacious sitting room.

Po and Pinky were lounging in reclining chairs in front of an immense flat-screen TV that dominated the wall above the original fireplace. On screen Dean Martin and Jerry Lewis were up to some crazy antics. Pinky was giggling with child-like glee, but neither was Po immune to humour, because he also huffed out a laugh reminiscent of steam escaping an overheated boiler. He bit down on the laughter at Tess's sudden declaration and squirmed more upright in the seat, planting his feet.

'What's up?' he asked as Tess bustled past en route for the kitchen.

'While we're taking it easy, girls are dying,' Tess said, and disappeared through the doorway.

'It's like I said, me.' Pinky held aloft one surprisingly long and thin index finger. 'Never a dull moment.'

'Just ambiguous ones,' Po added. 'Wonder what's gotten her bent all outta shape.'

Pinky shrugged, glanced again at the TV and chortled at Jerry Lewis's ungainly dance moves while in the background Martin romanced a pretty girl. He'd only one eye on the old movie though, and one on Po as his friend stood, and took a step after Tess.

Po halted in his tracks as Tess reappeared, shoving her arms into her coat sleeves. Po noted the ashen colour of her cheeks.

'You going to slow down and tell me what the hell's happened?' he demanded.

'We need to do something,' she repeated, still as vague about her sudden change in demeanour. She went to stride past him.

Po grasped her by her shoulders, forcing her to stop and face him. 'What was that about girls dying?'

'Those missing persons cases I was looking into,' Tess explained. She had to swallow bile. 'One of the girls has been found. She's dead, Po. Murdered.'

'Oh, man,' he wheezed, though he'd always been aware that they could face this horrible outcome. 'Is it . . .?'

Tess shook her head, but he'd already curtailed his question. If the victim were Jasmine, she would have already said so.

'It's not her. But I'm positive it's one of the other girls I was looking into.' She told him about the recent news report she'd discovered, and how the location and the victim's profile fitted what she'd already pieced together.

'Did you tell Emma Clancy?'

'Yes. She's going to request as much detail from the investigative team over in Massachusetts as she can: she'll share it with me. But it's still too soon to bring in the FBI.'

'And that doesn't suit you?' His tone suggested otherwise.

'Yes and no,' she replied, unconsciously rubbing her scarred wrist with her thumb. 'Of course I'd love all the resources they can bring to the case, but still . . .'

'It means they'd probably order us to keep our noses out of it,' he finished for her.

'For the FBI to take over they need a pattern, usually three bodies, or proof that the crimes are being committed across state borders,' Tess went on, 'and for now I can't prove my theory.'

'You feel strongly about it, though.'

'When am I ever wrong?' she asked.

'In our relationship? Never.'

They were both being ironic, but it served its intended purpose. Po smiled at her and she exhaled, pushing her fingers through her hair.

'OK. OK. We have to think about this,' she admitted.

A wild goose chase wasn't helping anyone. But neither was she prepared to sit waiting for another murder victim.

'Margaret Norris is safely out of the way for now,' she said, 'and Calvin Hopewell's still a no-show. I want to go back and see Daryl Bruin.'

'It has gone midnight,' Po reminded her.

'Fuck his beauty sleep,' she retorted.

'I'll take you,' Po said.

They looked at Pinky.

'Hey! I'm happy keeping company with Lewis and Martin, me,' he assured them, and made a shooing motion of his hands. 'Got a full box set here to binge-watch. *Sailor Beware* is up next, a personal favourite of mine . . . if you get my drift?' He winked, and jiggled his eyebrows.

'*Mi casa es su casa*, Pinky,' Po told him, 'but I'd appreciate it if you don't empty my beer cooler.'

'Oh, I have my limits, me,' Pinky said, one hand on his heart, 'I solemnly promise I'll save you the dregs from the bottles.'

They'd driven to Po's place alongside the Presumpscot River in the pickup truck. They took it back to the autoshop and transferred to Po's Mustang. Earlier Tess had claimed she'd easily find Bruin's home address, and proved her point with a few swift motions on her iPad while Po drove. The falling raindrops looked as thick as Tess's fingers in the wash of the Mustang's lights. Po had the wipers on full, and the heating blowing to keep the windshield clear. His mirrors were obscured by teeming water, but Tess noticed him continually glancing at them, alert to a possible tail. She too checked occasionally, but apart from a small number of taxicabs nobody was out in the storm.

Bruin's home was on Munjoy Hill, a prominent feature on the skyline of the Portland peninsula, only a few minutes away from his penthouse office on Fore Street. When they arrived, Bruin's tall Victorian was in darkness but for one porch light. Across the way was a cluster of condominiums and apartments sold on the strength of their sea view over Eastern Promenade and to the many islands beyond: this night the view was relegated to a few dozen yards at most.

'Time to wake up Mr Sleepyhead,' Po announced as he switched off the engine. With the cessation of the steady V8 growl the drumming of rain was more evident. Tess didn't appear in a particular hurry to face the storm again.

'You think he's even home yet?' she wondered.

'Only one way to find out,' said Po.

He was out of the car and up the short incline to the front door in seconds. Even over the storm's constant roar she heard him hammering on the door. She watched for lights flicking on inside, but the place remained in darkness. Po hammered again, then leaned and hollered through the mailbox flap. He looked back at her, hands open in question. She waved him to the car. He jogged back, then slid into the driver's seat, dripping wet.

'He owns a number of bars and nightclubs, it stands to reason he'd be late home,' Tess reasoned.

'He's down a manager at Bar-Lesque,' Po suggested, 'you think he's gone over there to oversee things while Max is laid up?'

'Could be. But he doesn't strike me as the type who'll roll up his sleeves. You ask me, Chris Mitchell has had to step up on Max's behalf.'

'You heard how he's doing?'

'Chris?'

'Him too, but I meant Max. He pull through?'

'To my shame, I haven't given Max's condition much thought.'

'He's a royal prick,' said Po.

'Still doesn't deserve what happened to him,' Tess countered.

Po looked nonplussed.

'I think Chris will be fine,' Tess said to change the subject. 'He was shocked, and hardly surprising, but he used to be a nurse. He'll have seen worse. He'll pull through in no time.'

'The guy's too good for that place. Nah, not the club: he's too good to be on Daryl Bruin's payroll, I mean.'

'You got a job open for him at the autoshop?' Tess teased.

'Huh, if I do that, Pinky will become a permanent visitor.'

'As if you'd mind.' Tess gave him a sly look. 'Come to think of it, if he was chasing Chris, I guess he'd leave you be. When we got together I didn't realize I'd be contesting for your affections with your old cellmate.'

'Believe me,' said Po, 'there simply is no contest.'

'So? All that time in Angola together, you never got as far as heavy petting . . .'

Po scowled at her, and she couldn't hold back her laughter.

'Don't worry, Po, your status as a full-blooded heterosexual male is firmly established in my mind . . . despite what Pinky claims.'

'Eh? What the hell did he say?'

'He he!' She mimicked their copious friend, wagging a finger alongside her nose.

Shaking his head, Po hit the ignition and the Mustang growled to life.

'We should swing by Bruin's office,' Tess suggested. 'Maybe he burns the candle at both ends, but I'm betting it's where he feels most in control.'

Po took them down Washington Avenue to Mountfort Street past the cemetery, and on to Fore Street where it paralleled the narrow-gauge railway tracks. As office blocks went, the one housing Bruin's top-floor office was largely unimpressive, and would have been lost in a larger city. It was an old structure that once served as an administrative centre for one of the ferry companies, which had since been gentrified and adapted for upscale clients. It stood out like a sore thumb above the surrounding dwellings, its facade glittering like molten silver in the rain. Lights blazed on the third floor.

Po pulled into the parking lot, and nodded at another vehicle spared the worst of the elements by a private shelter. Tess had no clue about makes and models of cars, but even to her eye the vintage roadster was gorgeous. 'Wow!' she said. 'Looks as if Daryl Bruin's business is more lucrative than I'd have given it credit for.'

'Yup,' said Po. 'Apparently there's good money in tits and ass. That there's a thirty-five Chevy Phaeton. Probably took someone a lifetime of digging around wrecking yards and swap meets to find all the spare parts. Bet you a dollar to the cent Bruin didn't dirty his hands restoring that beauty. Snapped it up at auction, I bet.'

'How much does something like that even cost?'

'Standard, in need of light restoration, you're probably looking at thirty to forty grand. But that one's been modified, lowered, overhauled and I'm betting there's a new engine under the hood. Probably has all mod cons, MP3 player, GPS, air con . . . the works. Don't expect much change from a hundred grand plus your Prius if you fancy doing him a swap.'

Tess held up her hands in surrender.

'I don't much care for hotrods,' Po went on. 'Too much style over substance for my taste.'

This was coming from a man driving a customized 1968 Ford Mustang?

He caught Tess's quizzical frown.

'American muscle,' he said, patting the steering wheel affectionately – but she didn't understand where the difference was. She slipped out before he got too deep into a subject close to his heart, and one that she was bewildered by. She used to think Pinky had a funny way of speaking, but if she tried keeping up with a conversation between Po and Charley at the autoshop it was akin to trying to decipher an alien tongue.

Po joined her at the door, while she pressed a buzzer for Bruin's office. Last time they visited his assistant had let them in, but this time the man himself answered.

'Your fifteen-minute promise better stand, buddy,' Bruin snapped through the intercom. 'I don't care about the goddamn storm either, you're late by three minutes and that means I eat free pizza.'

Tess shared a glance with Po, and he held up a finger. He quickly checked they weren't being observed via CCTV, but then if they were Bruin would have realized they weren't the pizza delivery guy he was expecting.

'A deal's a deal,' Po said, affecting a higher-pitched, local accent. 'S'long as you still tip me, sir, you can eat. Take it up with my boss if he complains.'

Bruin buzzed them in, with a curt order to 'bring it up'.

'That was an unexpected boon, huh?' whispered Po as they stepped inside the office block. 'I doubt he'd have let us in otherwise.'

'Maybe we should've fetched breadsticks,' Tess replied, and headed directly to the elevator for the short ride up to the penthouse.

The elevator opened into a narrow corridor, and directly opposite was the first of two sets of doors allowing access to Bruin's office suite. They stepped up to the first, and Po rapped on them. After the faint click of a lock uncoupling, Po pressed the doors open. They entered the small vestibule where Bruin's assistant usually acted as his gatekeeper. The inner door opened and Bruin bustled out, dressed in pleated trousers, buttoned-down shirt and suspenders, and shiny black Oxford shoes. His greased hair was slicked back, but failed to hide a bald spot on top as he dug in his wallet for a few dollars.

'Like I said, you're late . . .' he began, but as his head came up his face grew still. He was holding out a couple of rumpled dollars.

'Goddamn cheapskate,' Po called him.

'Hey, what are you guys doing here at this time of night?' Bruin countered.

'Seems as if you're used to doing business at this hour,' Tess said. 'Is there a problem?'

'That depends on you. I'm wondering if I need to call the cops.'

'Got something you want to admit to them?' Tess asked.

Bruin fed the two bucks back into his wallet.

'My conscience is clean,' he replied, and jerked his head for them to follow. 'I'm trying to do some damage control, get people moved around to fill staffing levels affected by this storm. Not to mention having a manager down at one of my clubs. Ah, well, you're here now. You may as well say your piece then get out of my hair.'

Po leaned on the doorframe, arms and ankles crossed. Tess accepted the seat she'd previously sat in. This time she didn't have to contend with spearing sunlight blistering her neck; she could feel the chill radiating out from the windows instead. The rain made a constant patter behind her. Bruin took his seat, but with a lingering stare over his shoulder at Po. 'Why don't you come on in?' he asked.

'I'm good right here.'

'You're making me nervous. I've got the feeling you'll sneak over and slit my throat when I'm not looking.'

'Trust me,' said Po, 'if I intend cutting your throat I'll be staring in your eyes when I do it.'

Bruin grinned madly, showing his teeth. 'I really do think I rubbed you up the wrong way with that *Evangeline* crack.'

'You don't fuss me, Bruin.'

Tess sighed, sitting back in her chair and drawing Bruin's attention.

Bruin raised his eyebrows at her.

'Calvin Hopewell,' she stated.

His response was a beat too long in coming. He lowered only one eyebrow. 'Who?'

'You know who. It's the person who cut Maxwell Carter's throat, and who almost bashed in your cousin's head.'

'Hmmm,' said Bruin.

'What's your beef with him?' Tess asked.

'Couldn't say.'

'Won't say,' Tess corrected him.

'I'm only extending my hospitality to you and your friend,' Bruin pointed out. 'I let you in out of the rain when I could've had you kicked out of here for trespassing under false pretences. I'm not obliged to answer your questions. That reminds me! What the hell is keeping that pizza guy? I'll tell you, he needn't ask for no tip.'

'Stop being an ass, Bruin,' said Tess.

'Just saying it as it is. A deal's a deal. If they don't deliver within fifteen minutes I get to eat free, but this is beyond the joke.' He glanced at his gold wristwatch, and shook his head. 'I should get compensation, let alone tipping the delivery guy for poor service.' He forestalled Tess's retort by holding his hand flat towards her. 'I'm only pointing out something important. I'm a man who believes a deal is binding. I offered to pay you to help track down Jasmine Reed, and you refused my offer. I'm wondering if you've given it second thoughts, and that's why you're really here.'

'You can shove your cash up your butt,' Po growled from the doorway. 'All two measly dollars of it.'

'Fair enough,' said Bruin, again concentrating on Tess. 'Then any offer of a deal's off the table. But that also means I've no reason to speak to you, let alone answer your questions.'

'Calvin Hopewell,' she said again, undeterred.

'Don't know him.'

'I beg to differ.'

Bruin made a zipping motion of his lips then threw away the imaginary zip-pull over his shoulder.

'You're making things more difficult than you need to,' Tess warned him. 'See, I know you know Calvin Hopewell. Need I remind you that you were fostered by his parents for a few months?'

Bruin's gaze went flat.

'I didn't say I wasn't. I just didn't connect the name to one of half a dozen families I was passed to and from.'

'When you lived with the Hopewells, did you come in contact with their son Calvin?'

He made a frog-like grimace. 'Not that I recall.'

'He'd have been a few years older than you, Daryl, maybe already away at Valley Forge Military Academy. Ring any bells?'

'I remember an older girl called Beth. Face like a carthorse and the butt to match. But a dude called Calvin? Nuh, means nothing.' He fed his thumbs under his suspenders and rasped up and down them. 'Back then I had such a large extended family it's tougher recalling names than saying goodnight to all the goddamn Waltons.'

Bethany was Calvin's older sibling, now married with children of her own and living in Europe, Tess had learned from the files she'd studied concerning Jasmine's various foster families. She knew Bruin was lying, as Chris Mitchell had already mentioned overhearing him speaking to Max Carter about Hopewell's impending return. But that was a piece of information she preferred to keep to herself.

'You don't recall Calvin being home when you lived with the Hopewells? OK, let's assume I believe you. But what about Jasmine Reed?' Tess waited for his next lie.

'Jasmine wasn't there when I was. Maybe she came along later.'

'So you remember that, but not if Calvin was there?'

'What can I say? Maybe my memory is selective.'

'I bet,' said Po from the doorway.

Bruin turned his head, to peer back him. 'What's that supposed to mean?'

'Let's assume I don't believe you,' said Po.

'No. Let's assume I don't give a shit what you think of me,' Bruin said.

'I'm thinking of coming over there and ripping that stupid moustache off your top lip.'

Bruin blinked slowly. 'Insults I can deal with. What does

concern me is being threatened in my own office. I think it's high time you both leave.'

'Fine by me,' Tess said and stood abruptly. She nodded at Po that it was time to go. 'I've clarified what I wanted to hear from Mr Bruin.'

'Could have told you he was a lying piece of dirt without traipsing out here in a storm,' Po said.

Bruin laughed at the latest of Po's insults. Then dismissively, he reached for his cellphone and dabbed in a number, reminding them he had important calls to make. 'You can show yourselves the way out,' he said without looking at them. 'It's the same way you sneaked in. Don't let the door hit you in the ass.'

Once they were back in the elevator and the doors had swished shut, Tess squeezed Po a smile. 'I didn't expect much from him, but what was more interesting was what he didn't admit. I think that visit was worthwhile, don't you?'

'The only thing that would've made me happier was if you'd let me yank off his moustache and slap the truth out of his lying mouth with it.'

'Another time,' she promised. 'I hope I'm there when you do it, because I think he'll deserve it.'

'He got you thinking about something,' Po stated.

'Yes. Timescales.'

'You're going to have to explain.'

'I need to do some more checking on it,' she replied, 'but there's one thing I'm sure about.'

The doors opened and they stepped out into the entrance foyer.

'How did Jasmine know about Hopewell's release from jail, and his impending return to Maine, if someone wasn't keeping tabs on him? I'm thinking somebody warned her off.'

'Not Bruin.'

'No. He's too eager to speak to her, or worse. Somebody she came into contact with at Bar-Lesque I'm betting.'

'Max? Can't see him giving a damn about her welfare.'

'Not Max. Not Chris Mitchell either.'

Po's frown deepened, but it wasn't for Tess's enigmatic teasing. A figure blocked some of the external exit light.

Trojak? Tess wondered.

But Po's mouth turned up at one side, and he pushed the door open before the new arrival could hit the intercom button.

Drenched through, a skinny youth stood on the threshold, lugging a large vinyl bag over his shoulder. The bag carried the decal of a local pizza delivery service.

'Ah,' said Po, holding open the door. 'Mr Bruin won't be eating free tonight. Here, buddy, how much do I owe you?'

'I'm really sorry for arriving late, sir,' said the young man as he delved in the bag and hauled out a box large enough to conceal a manhole cover. 'I've a twelve-inch classic pepperoni deluxe right here!'

'What kind of guy's going to complain about you being late on a night like this?' said Po and handed over enough cash, plus a weighty tip – more than the miserly two bucks Bruin would have. 'He'd have to be a complete a-hole, right?'

'Definitely not a concerned philanthropist,' Tess added.

# TWENTY-SIX

It was time to put aside dark fantasy, Elsa Moore concluded, and face the grim reality of her situation. Hiding behind the facade of her imagination was akin to burying her head in the sand – well all that assured was that she'd present her rump for another serious assault, and she'd had enough of that already to last ten lifetimes. Thankfully her abuse hadn't been sexual on this occasion, but at the toes of the whispering devil's boots as he'd kicked her mercilessly. And all because she'd had the temerity to ask after her friend Jasmine, and what he'd done to her.

It wasn't that he was enraged that she'd the nerve to question him; it was how she'd learned the other girl's name. The psychopath didn't require covert listening devices or hidden cameras when the slip of Elsa's tongue had proven they'd broken his cardinal rule.

To save the others a beating, Elsa admitted she was the one who'd pushed Jasmine into revealing her name, but that none of the others had spoken. He didn't believe her, and the other girls had been severely punished too.

Now Elsa lay on her side in the filth, unable to sit down or even crouch on her haunches. It was a miracle that he hadn't broken any bones, but her butt and thighs were swollen and sore, abraded and even cut in places. As he'd thrown wild kicks at her she'd curled into a ball against the back wall as far as her chains would allow, but it hadn't been enough to save her. She'd lost count of the blows. As a parting shot her abuser had sent her toilet bucket spinning, then stomped it flat, and the floor beneath her was now muddy with her own waste. She was fearful of her wounds becoming infected, but with no fresh water she could neither clean herself nor slake her raging thirst.

How long was it since he'd left her cell to punish the others? She couldn't tell. An hour, perhaps two? She was in intense pain, and she knew it would get worse before it began to ease.

She'd grow stiffer too, and before long would be unable to walk
– let alone run. Yet now was the time to try to escape, because
he'd believe her too hurt, too cowed, too weak, to attempt to
flee. His berserk attack had left him gasping for breath, and
he'd stalked back and forward as if he were the caged beast,
throwing his fists at the ceiling, kicking out at empty air in his
madness. He'd then come to a sudden decision and practically
sprung from her cell, slamming the door behind him and
securing locks, but in his haste he'd forgotten to check her
restraints, and left the tin bucket in a flattened lump on the
sodden earth.

The other girls had gone silent, biting their lips to stifle
their whimpers. Elsa expected they were aiming dark thoughts
at her because of her disobedience, rather than at the one that
truly deserved them. They were angry with her, and hardly
surprising, but she was equally pissed at them. If they were
going to get out of this predicament alive they had to unite,
not allow the beast to continuously segregate them, and set
them against each other. Jasmine, she hoped, would understand. She'd been brave enough to fight their captor, though
God knew what fate that had led to. But it gave Elsa strength
to similarly fight: she'd rather die than go on being a rough
play toy for the whispering devil.

Stop calling him that!

He's just a man. A sick-minded freak, but still just a man.

Moaning, she uncurled. Pain trickled through her limbs
before exploding in scarlet flashes behind her eyelids. He hadn't
hit her face, and yet that was where most of the agony was
centred. She rubbed her temples with trembling fingers. Her
skin was slick, plastered with coagulated mud and pee, but her
mouth and tongue were arid, a desert. The pain in her skull
was dehydration induced, as was the weakness in her arms.
Tentatively she pushed up to her knees. The skin of her haunches
felt too tight for her, which was incredible considering the
pounds she'd lost in weight since held here. She was tempted
to give in, to lie down, but her head shook in counter-rebellion
to her limbs, her hair thrashing her cheeks. She got the flats
of her palms beneath her and pushed, coming to a stoop with
her feet under her. The pain. The pain. She chewed her lips,

trying not to surrender to it, shook her head again and turned for the engine block.

The rusty old metal weighed almost as much as she did, perhaps more in her current emaciated state. At full strength and vigour she might be able to haul up one end, but she'd no hope of that now. She didn't have to. Prior to the attack, her captor had instructed her through the slot to turn her back and retreat to the far wall. Once she was in position he'd unlocked the door and entered, and he'd unclipped the chain securing her to the block: an act that usually meant a visit to his pleasure room. He'd normally fix shackles to her feet, and use the length of chain attached to her wrists to guide her before him like a dog on a leash. But she'd incited his ire, and taken a hellacious beating for it, but the bastard had been so incensed that he'd neglected to reattach the chain to its lock.

Dull light found its way inside her cell through chinks near the ceiling, and the longer she'd stayed cooped inside her vision had adapted to it. Squatting, grimacing against the fresh pulses of pain in her thighs and buttocks, she traced her chain to its source. One end disappeared under the engine block, and was wedged tightly, and one loop was wrapped around the engine, but she found the free end where it had been unlocked and allowed to fall in the dirt. She sat in the muck, braced her feet flat against the rough metal, and pulled. The chain didn't move an inch from where it was pinned to the earth. She wasn't finished trying though. She wrapped links around the ones between her wrists, and gripped the chain again a few inches down its length. Using the leverage so that the rusty links didn't tear the skin from her hands, she again braced and pulled. The pinned chain gave a couple of inches, but so did her thighs. They shook, and then almost contracted in on themselves and the colossal agony of muscle cramps racked her. She cried out, drawing her ankles to her butt and digging her fingertips into her thighs, as she fought the spasming of the muscles. It seemed an age before she felt ready to try again, and when she did it was tentative. Her backside slid away rather than place any counterweight on the engine block, and she knew it was a subconscious rebellion against experiencing the cramps again.

'What doesn't kill you makes you stronger,' she said, using an oft-used quote whose origin she couldn't credit. 'Or it just hurts like hell,' she added and giggled silently with a hint of madness.

She settled herself, got a grip on the chain again, after ensuring the shackle between her wrists would save her from most of the chafing, then pushed with both feet until she got her knees braced: only then did she haul backwards, allowing the arching of her spine to add strength to her shuddering arms. The chain sprang loose from under one side of the block, but was still pinned tight at the other. It didn't matter, she was making progress, and energized. She repeated the process, groaning, dying to shout and scream at the damn stubborn chain, and suddenly she went flat on her back as the chain tore free.

She sat, gathering her breath, grinning in triumph.

Her captor had thought himself clever. He'd looped the chain counter-clockwise so that where it crossed it would be buried beneath the engine block, making it more secure, but he was wrong. It meant she had only to unhitch that one length of chain before the entire thing came free. Still sitting she spooled in the cumbersome chain and placed it in her lap. She was free of the dead weight, but that was only one of a list of barriers. Now she had to escape the room, the labyrinth, and her demented abuser. Still, she was on the way now, headed in the right direction.

She checked the door first.

It was impregnable as far as she could tell, and that was without the extra locks and bolts on the other side. But was it? She felt for the hinges and they were not recessed. Her fingertips found the heads of ancient screws, but without tools she'd no hope of unscrewing them: they'd been there so long they were corroded and held solidly by the expansion of the damp wooden doorframe. Even with tools she would probably never defeat them. The hinge pins! Her fingers fluttered again, and sure enough she could feel the brass heads of pins. If she could press them out she could force a gap between door and frame.

Good luck, she told herself sarcastically. She required a hammer and screwdriver to knock the pins out. She had neither.

But she had a heavy length of chain and a distorted tin bucket.

She scrambled for the bucket, picked it up, and upended it so that the last dregs of urine spilled out, then moved to drier flooring. The bucket was lozenge-shaped now, with the sides buckled, but it largely held its integrity. It would need work, but for the first time in for ever she saw a glimmer of hope. She stood on the base end, got her fingers around the buckled rim, and began working it slowly and silently back and forward against the crease line, one ear cocked for any hint that the whispering devil – no, the demented sicko – was returning.

# TWENTY-SEVEN

'You mentioned timelines,' said Po, as he and Tess arrived outside her house on Cumberland Avenue. Finally, and thankfully, the storm had begun to subside, although the wind still retained most of its bite.

The power supply had been reconnected by a contractor she'd called earlier in the evening, who'd charged an excessive fee for turning out so late at night and in the middle of a storm. He'd coordinated with the local power company because Cal Hopewell had used a spade to chop repeatedly at the main cable entering the building so that the rainwater got in through the metal shielding and shorted out her supply, so Tess had steeled herself to expect another bill from them too. It was necessary and immediate work, though, and had to be paid – she didn't want to be held responsible for Mrs Ridgeway losing another day's trade. When Hopewell was finally brought in, she was tempted to sue for compensation but was happier to see him returned to prison for his crimes. And if her suspicions were correct, somebody else would join him.

'Let's get inside and I'll explain,' she said.

Po drove his Mustang on to the ramp behind her Prius. She hadn't checked her car for damage: Hopewell had forced her over the hood and it had possibly been scratched and buckled. Fixing her car was another expense to sue Hopewell for, she thought whimsically, though Po would likely carry out the repairs for little more reward than a sweet smile.

Po carried Bruin's liberated supper up the steps behind her, and Tess let them in. Her house felt cold and damp, and her first task was to go around throwing on lights and the central heating. Calling out the contractor on short notice had been worth every cent. Most of her equipment had been decamped to Po's ranch house, but she'd brought her iPad and cellphone back with her: she plugged in the tablet at her work station, but keyed in to the databases she'd been pouring over the last few days on her iMac.

Po was seated on her settee, eating congealed pizza, when she turned to him.

'Want some?' he asked around a mouthful of stringy cheese. She shook her head.

'It's good,' he said, and wagged a slice at her.

She ignored the temptation, though admittedly she was hungry. All of that cheese and dough on her stomach this late at night and she'd be good for nothing. She fetched a yoghurt drink from her fridge, and although it wasn't as chilled as she'd like, she downed it voraciously while ordering events in her mind.

'Bruin's a damn liar,' she announced as she wiped away a yoghurt moustache on the back of a finger then licked it clean.

'Already established,' Po said, and took another bite.

'He claimed that he didn't know Calvin Hopewell's name: a lie. Then he changed his tune, but still said he didn't recall Calvin being resident when the Hopewells fostered him: another lie. He also said that Jasmine came to the home after he'd already moved on; well I need to check, but I'm pretty sure that on that occasion he was telling the truth.' At Po's nonplussed expression, she added, 'OK, only partly telling the truth. Wait here a moment.'

'I ain't going nowhere,' Po assured her. 'Still got pizza to eat.'

Tess dug under her work station, sifting through the drawers where she'd placed some of the old documents she'd previously interrogated. She found the sheets of paper she was looking for, scrutinized them a moment, and then nodded to herself. She carried them to Po as if they were objects of great value: in a way they were, because they were a hinge-pin to solving the connection between Hopewell, Bruin and Jasmine.

She sat alongside Po and he set aside the pizza box. He smelled strongly of garlic, tobacco, and damp denim, but it wasn't unpleasant. Tess angled the papers so he could see them too.

'I knew it,' she said, and indicated what she was referring to first on one sheet of paper, then the next.

'Jasmine was fostered by the Hopewells three times?'

'Uh-huh,' Tess said. 'Granted, the first and latter times were only for a few days. The last time corresponds with when Calvin would have been home from military college, and was when he must have attacked her. She also stayed with the Hopewell family as a younger teen here' – she indicated the middle term – 'after Bruin had already left the home. But look at these earliest dates where Jasmine stayed for a couple of weeks on what has been logged as "respite care". He lied to us: Bruin and Jasmine did cross paths in the home for a short time.'

'Giving him the benefit of the doubt, he might not remember her if she was a young child and he was in his late teens by then. Plus if she was only there on a short-term basis he might not have come into much contact with her. The difference in age isn't a big concern now, but to kids it would have been a wide gulf that separated them.'

Tess nodded in agreement, but she wasn't done.

'Portland's a small city. What's the population, around sixty-five thousand people?'

'I guess,' said Po, 'but that doesn't include the outlying areas. You're probably looking at a couple hundred thousand or more. What's your point?'

'It sounds a lot of people,' Tess agreed, 'but isn't when you ask yourself how many of them are active foster parents. I'm guessing that Maine Child and Family Services has only a small but invaluable resource they can pull on when placing children.'

'F'sure. Kids in need of care probably rotate through the same families time and again.'

'Yeah,' said Tess, because his thoughts were heading the same direction as hers. 'Children in the system will possibly pass each other along the way, with some of them making lasting connections even when they're later separated. They probably bump into each other on any number of occasions over the years.'

'You're suggesting that Bruin – or even Daryl Trojak as he was called then – has known Jasmine since she was a little kid, and did form some kind of attachment with her. One that was later exploited by both him and Cal Hopewell?'

'Jasmine was deemed troubled back then, a wild child: don't

you maybe think she had a damn good reason for rebelling if she was being continually abused?'

'It's quite an accusation to throw at him,' Po cautioned her. 'It's proven that Hopewell's a goddamn beast, but without proof we can't say that about Bruin.'

'He's desperate to find her before anyone else does,' Tess replied. 'That tells me he's equally desperate to shut her up. We have to ask ourselves why?'

'When Hopewell assaulted Jasmine, you're suggesting that Bruin was also there?'

Tess shrugged. They'd no way of knowing.

'When it threatened the boy's future, the Hopewells paid off Margaret Norris to dissuade Jasmine from reporting her abuse,' Po reminded her. 'I don't recall hearing Bruin making a similar pay off.'

'You're on to something there, Po,' she told him and pecked him on the cheek.

Tess put aside the papers. Po adjusted in the seat, laying one hand protectively on her thigh, and she nuzzled into his side. He lifted his arm and slung it around her shoulder and they sat together.

'You should be getting back,' Tess finally said, reluctant to be separated now they'd finally earned a few minutes of comfort. 'You can't leave Pinky alone all night. Not when he's your guest.'

'You ain't coming back with me tonight?'

'I'll be fine here.'

'Not if Hopewell comes back.'

'I don't think that's going to happen. Not with the police searching for him. He's probably gone to ground, or even left the state by now. He'd be mad not to.'

'I think he's already proven that madness is his main commodity. I'm not comfortable leaving you alone.'

'I'll keep the doors locked, your number on quick dial, and my granddaddy's gun under my pillow.' She leaned in for a kiss and he met her. Slowly they extricated, and Tess said, 'If you stay here I'll never get any sleep, and I'm almost dead on my feet. Even if we leave now and head back to yours, it'll be hours before we get to bed. I need an early start, Po, so it's best if I do that here.'

'You aren't convincing me,' he replied, but gave her a knowing grin. 'I know your head's buzzing with possibilities and you have work to do, and I'm being an inconsiderate inconvenience.'

'That's what I love about you, Po. Always so understanding and supportive.'

'I'm a goddamn soft-assed fool, you mean?'

'They're admirable traits in some quarters,' she told him.

He stood reluctantly.

'First hint of trouble you call me,' he warned her. 'Keep your gun under your pillow, I'll have my cell under mine.'

Taking the remains of the pizza, he went to the door and Tess saw him off with a lingering kiss. He went down the steps and into the Mustang and the engine growled to life. Tess stood in the open doorway, hugging herself, and waited as he backed out on to the road where they shared a goodnight wave.

Sleep beckoned her.

Yet it was hours away, despite what she'd told Po.

He was correct when he'd said her mind was buzzing. She was confident she was on to something with the connection she'd made between Bruin and Hopewell, but it didn't help her find the missing third piece of the puzzle.

She went to her work station and brought up the police report she'd found earlier. Back then the details had been sketchy, but more had been added.

A tentative identification of the murdered woman had been made, naming her as Carrie Mae Borger, one of the girls from Tess's list, and who'd gone missing only a few days before Jasmine.

There was no sense of satisfaction discovering her hypothesis was probably correct, quite the opposite. Learning that a predator was snatching and murdering women made her feel sick to the stomach, but she was also hit by a second sensation she couldn't deny. It was a tremor of excitement. After following their cold trails, she was finally on to something important that could lead her to Jasmine, and quite possibly to Lucy Colman and Elsa Moore. She only hoped she wasn't too late to help them, before they ended up like Carrie, in shallow graves with their tongues cut out.

# TWENTY-EIGHT

S leep crept up on Tess in the pre-dawn hours, but it was troubled by dreams that jerked her awake, her pulse thumping, and panic tightening her chest. She could not recall the details, only that she was imprisoned in a dark, desolate place, from where she could not escape: she could hear passers-by walking high above her, unheeding of her plight though she screamed for help. After each abrupt awakening she lay in bed, the covers pulled up to her chin as she waited. She was unsure what she expected, but it wasn't something pleasant. She had a feeling of being watched, as if some evil presence hovered in her peripheral vision, but when she glanced to catch it straight on it would shift away, remaining always out of reach. She'd drift back asleep, still seeking the malevolent entity and slide directly into that horrible place from where she couldn't escape again.

She was finally woken at 7.48 a.m. by the insistent ringing of her cellphone. She expected it to be Po, eager to check on her, but it was Emma Clancy, to whom Tess had pinged a text message in the wee small hours. As she fumbled to slide the answer button she disconnected the call instead. She struggled from under her damp bed covers and placed her bare feet on the floor, sitting a moment, head swimming. Still slightly fuddled by her uncomfortable night, she tried to bring up the missed call log to return the call, but Emma beat her to it. Tess almost dropped the phone when it rang loudly.

'Hi, Emma! Sorry, I cut you off . . .'

'Did I wake you?'

'No, no, I was up, I . . .' Tess rubbed her hand over her mouth. Her tongue was glued to her palate. 'Sorry. I'll start again: you can probably tell I'm a little disorganized this morning.'

'Haven't you had any sleep?' Emma asked without a hint of accusation.

'A few hours. Been working.' She stood, a little unsteady on her feet, in the damp T-shirt and boxers she'd gone to bed in.

'I got your text, but I'm sorry, I only checked my phone a few minutes ago. I hope you haven't been waiting for me to call back all night.'

'No. I expected you'd be asleep. Now's good, Emma. Thanks for getting back to me.' Tess had found her way out of the bedroom and into the bathroom. She desperately needed to relieve herself, but not while she was on the phone to her employer. She turned on the cold faucet and filled a glass.

'You said to call you urgently,' Emma pointed out.

'Yes. But I meant at your convenience.' Tess quickly took a mouthful of water and swilled out her mouth. She held the phone aside as she spat into the sink. Her mouth tasted foul, and she was so relieved she hadn't given into temptation and eaten any of the pizza Po had gorged on.

'Are you OK, Tess?' Emma asked.

'Yes, I'm fine.' She slugged more water, and her tongue was more manageable. 'You asked me to find more proof that there's a serial predator . . .'

'Carrie Mae Borger,' Emma stated to Tess's surprise. 'Yes. She was one of the women you listed as a possible abductee. After we spoke, I did a bit digging of my own, and I placed her name – and the others you mentioned – on a watch list. I saw the police report of her discovery.'

'Is it enough to get the FBI in on the case?'

'We have to be cautious of extrapolation. One murder doesn't indicate a serial killer. The connection you made between those missing women is interesting, but it's also convenient. The tattoos, the scars, the athletic builds, they're interesting coincidences, but there are probably dozens of other markers we're missing that differentiate those women too.'

'I know what you're saying,' Tess admitted. 'There's a danger in forming recognizable patterns in the randomness of chaos. It's a human trait, where we look for something familiar in the mundane. But you know I'm on to something, Emma, otherwise it wouldn't have piqued your interest enough to check for yourself.'

'I didn't say that I doubted you, only that the FBI are less likely to take you seriously.'

Tess sighed.

Emma forestalled any further disappointment. 'I've sent over copies of the missing-persons reports of the other women to the lead detective on the investigative team at Belchertown PD. What Detective Ratcliffe does with them is open to conjecture, but I will follow up with a call once I'm in my office. There's no evidence to show that Jasmine Reed was anywhere near Massachusetts when she disappeared, don't forget.'

'Even if I'm wrong about her, I'm still confident that the other girls are in danger. Lucy and Elsa were both last seen in the area.'

'And I'll make that clear when I speak with the detective. In the meantime, there's not a lot we can do.'

'I've still some ideas,' Tess replied, but if she were pressed for details she'd be hard pushed to come up with something convincing.

'Good. Keep digging. I'll do what I can from my end.'

Tess thought about telling Emma about the tentative connection she'd made between Daryl Bruin and Calvin Hopewell. But Emma had just warned her against extrapolating without solid proof. Maybe she was forming a pattern in her mind that had no basis in truth. Until she knew better, it would be best to keep her suspicions to herself concerning Bruin at the very least.

'Any news on Calvin Hopewell?' she asked instead.

'Nothing,' Emma replied.

'OK.'

'Once I've spoken with Detective Ratcliffe I'll be in touch.'

'Thanks, Emma,' Tess said, but Clancy had already ended the call.

Back in her bedroom, Tess straightened her bed covers, then as an afterthought dug under the pillow alongside hers. As she'd promised to Po she'd kept her grandfather's Service Six close to hand. She was only relieved that during the nightmares she hadn't given in to fear, grabbed for the gun and started blasting the shadows. She set the gun on the cabinet alongside her cellphone and returned to the bathroom where she gratefully relieved herself, then brushed her teeth vigorously. Showered, and her hair dried, and dressed in fresh clothing, she felt much better than during her talk with Emma. She was thinking more clearly too.

She returned to her work station, hitting a key to waken the screen on her iMac. This time she altered her search parameters, searching sex-offender records, and included the tags 'Tattoos' and 'Scars'.

Most of what was returned was unhelpful, the rest a complete waste of time. She changed her search to check for unsolved sexual assaults and sexually motivated murders in Massachusetts, but the list was far too long to pick anything pertinent from as it included everything on record, so she pinpointed the search to focus on the area radiating twenty miles from the I-90 and I-91 interchange near Springfield.

The list still made for depressing reading, and was far too random to be of any help. She searched the same region for registered sex offenders and the list was more manageable. She filtered out those in prison or a state institute, were aged and frail, and the deceased, and the list held only five individuals, three from Springfield, one from neighbouring Holyoke, and one whose last known address was on a trailer park outside Amherst.

She formed a rogues' gallery of their mugshots, staring at each in turn, as if she could read something of their depravity behind their flat expressions and soulless gazes. In varying degrees, every one of them had committed crimes against women, but time and again her attention was drawn back to the guy from the trailer park, and she could say why: of the five he was the only one who, as a sexually-frustrated teenager, had held his victims prisoner – shockingly his own sister and an aunt – dominating them sexually and physically for a period of days in his Josef Fritzl-style basement dungeon before the alarm was raised by a neighbour and he was brought to justice. All five were abhorrent individuals, any of them capable of reoffending, but there was one major point that set him apart. He was the only one tattooed, and scarred.

She fetched her cellphone from her bedroom and called Po. 'On my way to yours,' he told her as soon as he answered.

'Is Pinky with you?'

'Right here, Sweet Cheeks,' Pinky answered. 'I hope you've only good things to say about me 'cause Nicolas has his volume turned to the max.'

'Good,' she answered. 'Are you guys up for a road trip?'

'Where are we going?' Po asked.

'Springfield,' Tess announced.

'Where the Simpsons live?' Pinky said excitedly.

'Springfield, Massachusetts.'

'What's in Springfield?' Po asked.

'Only a jumping off point,' she said.

'How far is that, about two hundred miles?' Po wondered.

Tess had no clue.

'I'll have to fuel up,' Po explained his reasoning behind the question. 'Be with you soon.'

He ended the call, and Tess went through her rooms, pulling a few necessary items together for the trip. She also bagged her iPad, and as an afterthought her grandfather's revolver and the charger for her cell. The phone she pushed in her back pocket. While she waited for Po and Pinky to arrive she brewed coffee and ate a bowl of cereal at her kitchen counter. She dumped the empty bowl and spoon in her sink, and took her coffee with her to her living-room window overlooking the street. Down below she spotted Mrs Ridgeway arriving for work, but the woman was distracted and didn't look up. Tess was thankful, she'd no wish to have to spend time explaining what had gone on yesterday afternoon, though she would have to do so at some point. She stepped back a pace so that she was out of sight, and peered instead along Cumberland Avenue in the direction she believed Po would arrive. There was a parked car on the opposite side, and a man sitting inside, but he was far enough away that she couldn't make out his features, only that his head was angled so that he could watch her house. But she knew who it was.

Without warning, the car reversed quickly and took a turn into the next available space, then swung around and sped off. It passed Po's Mustang coming the other way.

It was a shame John Trojak had sped off. Perhaps he wasn't a total nuisance, she thought, because maybe he could help after all. Not in finding Jasmine Reed, but in confirming her suspicions regarding Bruin and Hopewell. He might do Bruin's bidding with the eagerness of a puppy thrown a treat, but he'd no loyalty to Hopewell, and owed the man who'd almost crushed his skull with a tyre iron. Once informed of his attacker's identity, he might have a different take on where his allegiances lay. Speaking with Trojak could wait, she decided, and bringing down his cousin. She hurried out to meet Po at the kerbside. He stepped out, and gave her a brief hug, before bending and levering down his seat so she could climb into the rear seat. She didn't mind vacating her usual perch alongside him, because Pinky required the extra legroom afforded in the front. She tucked her knees up, seating herself sideways on the bench seat: she might as well make herself as comfortable as possible because it would be a few hours before they would reach their destination.

# TWENTY-NINE

J ohn Trojak thought back to the first time he watched a kung fu movie, in the 1970s, and how cool Bruce Lee had looked sporting an array of bleeding cuts on his face during the final showdown with the steel-clawed bad guy, Mr Han. Trojak wore similar cuts now. They were anything but cool as he studied them in his rear-view mirror, but every bit as vivid as those carried by the Little Dragon. They were shameful, and unnecessary, and he rued the day he swore he'd never lift a hand to protect himself from Vero's vicious attacks. She was unwell, to be pitied, not to be manhandled into submission. He'd raised her ire, unfortunately an easy thing to do lately, and she'd gone for his eyes with her fingernails, for no other reason than he'd attempted to explain that he'd a job to do. He'd managed to avert his face enough to save his vision, but her right hand had raked him from his left eye-socket to his chin. Her other hand clawed at the side of his head, nicking his ear, but most of those weeping wounds were under his hair and not as visible.

Dabbing at them with a tissue, he'd almost missed when Tess Grey came to her window and spied directly at him. Flummoxed, he made a stupid mistake, ramming his car into reverse like that, and spinning away, when he'd been building his courage to go and speak with the private detective anyway. But his panicked escape had proved fortunate, because he'd almost run into Po Villere, and he knew once that lout was on the scene he'd have no way of engaging Tess in a frank and reasonable discussion. He needed her alone, without her posturing bodyguard looking for a reason for a fight. Trojak would happily oblige him on another occasion, and would gladly take out the frustration he felt at Vero on the Cajun's face. But right now he didn't need an enemy, he needed an ally, and fighting Po would only alienate his girlfriend.

Last night Daryl crossed a line and Trojak wasn't sure he could forgive him.

'*Who employs you, Johnny?*' Daryl had demanded. '*Who signs your damn pay cheque? Who keeps Vero in all the fine things she demands? You? Are you responsible for all those things?*'

Daryl claimed he made all the right decisions, but he was wrong.

'*You'd be nothing without me. Look at what I've given you: a job, a home,* stability. *Where would you be if I hadn't given you all those things? Stacking goddamn shelves at Walmart!*'

He was so, soooo wrong; he was so blinded by his own self-importance that he couldn't see it. But Trojak had a moment of epiphany. He realized that he owed Daryl nothing except for his enmity and it had been a struggle to play along as his obedient lapdog until he could leave.

Daryl thought Trojak was stupid, and maybe he could make a poor argument to the contrary considering he'd allowed his conniving cousin to manipulate him all these years. Daryl had employed him, given him a regular pay cheque with which he supported his unappreciative wife, but it wasn't from altruism. Daryl paid for his services, but more for his silence. Those *right decisions* Daryl was so proud of would be his undoing if they ever came to light, and more than anybody Trojak was the keeper of their secrets. Daryl paid him because without Trojak *he'd* be nothing. He'd be finished, his business would be finished, and the scumbag he was protecting would be finished too.

He'd told Vero what happened all those years ago. In her madness she hadn't realized that Trojak was opening his soul to her, hoping that she'd understand why he must help bring home Jasmine Reed unharmed and safe from persecution. He'd a job to do, one that was more honourable than any he'd ever completed for Daryl, but Vero hadn't seen things his way. She was terrified of losing a regular income, had laughed scornfully when he said he'd happily stack shelves at a convenience store instead, and had gone for his eyes when he had dared reason with her. He'd made excuses for Daryl for too long, and it took this latest unprovoked attack to assure him he'd made excuses for Veronica for far too long as well. Her madness was self-induced and without paying to feed her alcohol and drugs dependencies he could get by on an honest wage. It was a time for epiphanies, he understood, and for a change he believed he'd made the *right decisions.* He'd walked out on Vero. Daryl would learn soon enough that he'd walked out on him too, though he owed his cousin for one pearl of wisdom from last night.

'*You have to make your own luck,*' Daryl had said. '*Take the fucking initiative, why don't you?*'

Well, Daryl, he thought, I'm taking the initiative by both hands, but I doubt it will make you happy.

After driving away, he'd stopped a short distance up the road, watching as Tess joined her friends in the muscle car and took off in the opposite direction. He was tempted to follow, but knew he'd be spotted in no time. Po would come swinging, and he would respond with like mind. Instead he parked behind the Prius on the drive and went up the steps to Tess's door. He knew nobody was home, but it paid to be cautious. He knocked and waited. The only sounds he heard were the dripping of water from the eaves. A quick glance around, and he dipped his hand in his pocket and withdrew his lock knife. He snicked it open, and inserted it between the jamb and lock. He levered, pushing his shoulder into the centre of the door. The lock popped open and he stepped inside. Before committing to the house-breaking, he leaned back out the door and checked he hadn't alerted any noisy neighbour. The woman in the antiques shop could prove a problem. She didn't show, which was good enough for him.

He pushed the door shut with the tip of his knife, but the snib was in its locked position, so only sat against the slightly warped retainer. When Tess returned it would be obvious someone had forced entry, but he was confident that anyone glancing at the door from the bottom of the steps wouldn't spot that the door was open.

The rooms were neat, comfortable, and just barely large enough for one occupant. He went through the space quickly, unsure what he was seeking, but happy he'd know it if he found it. He took only cursory glances in the bedroom and bathroom, then went into the kitchen. An empty cereal bowl and spoon sat unwashed in the sink, and a cup containing the dregs of coffee had been placed on the table. Even if he hadn't watched her leave, he could have deduced that she left in a hurry. He returned to the living room, instantly spotting Tess's work station, and a fan of discarded notes and printed documents on the desk.

He was careful not to touch anything; leaving fingerprints would be foolish. He lifted the ends of the papers on the edge of his blade, then slipped the full stack on to the palm of his hand, then decided juggling like that would be awkward, so decided he'd take the lot with him. First though he began flicking through, and saw that Tess had been making progress in her search for Jazz. There was a printed map, and at first he couldn't decide where it showed, but a quick perusal of the town names told him he was looking at an area in Massachusetts. A small community called Amherst was circled in ink, and also a cross was noted on the western bank of a huge lake.

With the tip of his knife he touched the space bar on the keyboard, and was delighted when the screen of Tess's computer flashed to life: for an ex-cop her security protocols were shockingly lax. To be fair, she'd left in a hurry, but he was surprised that the computer wasn't password-protected at the very least. He wasn't particularly tech-savvy, but he could still find his way around by trial and error. It didn't take him long to bring up the most recent searches and he saw that Tess had been checking the details of sex offenders around the area of Springfield, Mass. One resided in a trailer park near Amherst.

Who needed to follow close on their tail, when he knew now exactly where Tess and Po had gone?

'*You have to make your own luck.*'

He double-checked the photo of the creep on the screen, then shuffled through the stack of papers and found a corresponding image, plus the man's details and address.

'Ugly son of a gun, aren't you?' Trojak whispered at the photo, before he folded it over and jammed it in an inside jacket pocket.

More of flicking through Tess's recent searches highlighted that she'd been plotting the disappearances of several young women in the near vicinity of Springfield, and subsequently one of them, Carrie Mae Borger, had turned up dead near

Quabbin Reservoir – the 'X marks the spot' indicator on the map. He smiled to himself. He recalled moaning at Daryl that he wasn't a detective; well, perhaps he had an aptitude for this stuff after all. He folded the map and shoved it in his pocket alongside the creep's image. The rest of the papers he rolled and stuffed into his trouser pocket. Those he'd dump once he was on the road. He sent the computer to sleep, then wiped down the mouse and keyboard with a tissue he returned to his pocket.

He looked around.

There was nothing else he could see that might prove helpful. Done with his snooping, he paced to the door and drew it open with his knife tip, turned and took one last lingering look over his shoulder. If not for his pilfering of the papers, and the slight damage to the lock, nobody would have another clue he'd been there. He smiled to himself, turned to leave.

The barrel of a gun touched his forehead, and his smile flickered and dissolved as Daryl's words trickled through his memory.

*'That sick-minded son of a bitch never could keep his dick in his pants. From what I hear he's got a boner for Tess Grey. You watch her, he'll turn up sooner or later for her.'*

# THIRTY

'Well, this sure ain't Disney World, you ax me,' Pinky said as he eyed the entrance to the trailer park disdainfully. 'I guess poor white trash gotta vacation somewheres, though.'

In the back, sitting crosswise, Tess rested an elbow on the back of his seat so she could see past him. On her knees she'd perched her iPad, using its GPS app to guide them into the residential site. There were many hiking trails around the nearby reservoir, and campsites to accommodate holidaymakers, but this wasn't one of them. This was the kind of place people came to lose themselves, to hide from the rest of the world, and where nosy visitors weren't welcomed with open arms. 'I can't be positive Randall's even here, but we have to check.'

Jesse Randall. As a requirement of his parole conditions he had to register as a convicted sex offender, and to supply a current permanent address where his parole officer could pay him unscheduled visits. But Tess was under no illusion: parole violations occurred all the time, so there was a real possibility that he wouldn't be home. Often, parolees registered transient addresses such as a trailer on a park such as this, enough to appease the rule makers, but it wasn't where they actually spent any time. She guessed that many of the scruffy mobile homes clustered in the field supposedly housed criminals with no intention of going straight. Then there'd be other people who were simply down on their luck: she shouldn't judge, though the fact she hadn't commented on Pinky's poor white trash comment said that subconsciously she already had.

'Doesn't look too bad to me,' Po interjected. 'They have a stunning view of the water-treatment works over there.'

'Is that what the smell is?' Pinky wafted a hand under his nose.

On a plot on the opposite side of the road, hemmed in with tall wire fences, stood a series of circular pits and turbines. The atmosphere was redolent with the stench of stirred-up effluent.

'Either the good folks here are used to the stench, or their trailers smell worse,' Po suggested. 'You sure you want to go visit?'

'I need to get a sense of this guy,' Tess replied.

'The sense I get is he's a sick motherfucker who'd be better living in that cesspit over there,' growled Po.

Pinky concurred with a snake-like hiss. Convicts' hatred of sex offenders was legendary, and they'd just proven their point. Tess couldn't find an iota of argument to fire back at them: cops equally despised rapists.

'Remember, I've no proof that Randall is our man. He could be totally innocent of any involvement, so tread easy on this one.' She tapped Po on his ear for emphasis. 'Now, seeing as there's been the body of a woman found nearby, the cops will have spoken to Randall already – or he's on their list to speak to. We can't spook him in any way.'

'I vote we waterboard him, using some of that crap from the sewage plant,' Po muttered. 'He'll give us the answers you're looking for then.'

'He served his time. He shouldn't automatically be treated as if he's going to reoffend.' Tess paused. She recalled a conversation where Po had posed a question regarding ex-cons and ex-cops: were they ever anything but? 'But if he is our man, you have my permission to bury him headfirst in that crud. I'll help.'

Po drove the Mustang between the gateposts. An asphalt strip led towards the central hub of the site. It was potholed, crumbling at its edges, and in more than one place the parched grass of the verges was rutted with deep tyre troughs. The storm that had raged over New England had touched this area of Massachusetts too, and most of the ruts were full of muddy water. Po stayed to the middle of the road.

'There has to be a site manager's office,' he said, as he peered for a likely structure.

'There.' Tess pointed at a huge square trailer, permanently parked against an adjoining raised deck made of planks. Some attempt had been made at making the place look homely with a few potted plants, but the windows were almost opaque with orange dust, and the roof and one corner were decorated with a montage of bird droppings. The thing that singled this trailer out from dozens of similarly dilapidated mobile homes was the hand-painted sign driven into the earth at the bottom of the steps to the deck. OFFICE. PLEASE RING BELL. A poorly drawn diagram of a pointing finger aimed at a post on the opposite side of the steps on which was a cheap battery powered doorbell.

Po brought the car to a stop.

'Going to step out and stretch my legs, me,' Pinky announced. 'Now as much as I love the throb of American muscle, it does chafe my butt.'

Tess slapped him playfully on the shoulder.

'I only meant sitting in this teeny seat all this way,' Pinky croaked.

'I know *exactly* what you meant, you shameless creature,' Tess said in a mock-scalding tone.

Pinky eased out, stood knuckling the small of his back. It allowed Tess to clamber out from behind him. Po stayed behind the wheel. Tess hit the buzzer.

From nearby there was a shout followed by raucous alcohol-fuelled laughter. A dog barked. An engine started with a throaty roar and belch of diesel fumes. But there was no reply from the trailer. Tess hadn't heard the bell ring either; the battery had probably died with the pot plants. She went up the steps and rapped the back of her knuckles alongside the door.

'Sorry, we ain't got no vacancies,' a voice hollered from somewhere behind her. Tess turned and peered over the Mustang at an old man emerging from between two caravans. He reminded Tess of an old-time miner, bent and bow-legged from shuffling through cramped tunnels. His hair was long at the sides, non-existent on top, and stained yellow over both ears; the hand-rolled cigarette hanging from the corner of his mouth hinted how it had got its tint. He wore dungarees with suspenders, over a plaid shirt. The sleeves were rolled to his bony elbows, and he wore dirt-crusted gardening gloves. They'd disturbed him doing some much-needed grounds maintenance, but he didn't look sorely disappointed. 'But that isn't what you're looking for. What can I do fer you, ma'am?'

Tess considered lying, telling him they were friends of Jesse

Randall, but the old guy was no fool. He'd flicked a glance over the Mustang, deemed it a chariot of the likes none of his usual customers could afford, and made up his mind about them. Not from these parts, and up to no good.

Tess came down the steps and round the car, watched by Pinky, who was dying to make a flippant comment about the old manager's appearance.

'We intend causing you no inconvenience, sir,' Tess said as she approached. 'We're looking for Jesse Randall. Can you show us which is his trailer?'

'Randall, huh?' The manager scratched his chin with a muck-encrusted glove finger. 'What do you want with him?'

'I'm not at liberty to say, I'm afraid.'

'Is that right? Then I might not be at liberty to point you in the right direction.'

Tess squeezed him a touché smile.

'I just need to ask him a couple of questions. Once he clears up a few points we'll hopefully be on our way.'

'No mess and no fuss, huh?' asked the old man, and nodded to himself. 'This about his old problems?'

'I'm not at liberty to say.' Tess's smile this time was more open, and she forced a similar response from the manager. 'Have you been following the news, sir?'

'Don't have much time for the news these days. There's only me to look after this place, and as you can probably tell there ain't enough hours in the day fer one man to keep on top of it.'

'And I don't intend taking up any more of it than necessary. Can you save us both some time, and just point out where he lives?'

'I can show you, but he ain't home.'

'You know that for certain?'

'He used to work, only came back here to sleep now an' again. But then he got laid off his job. Hung around here, mostly pumpin' weights, 'til he got himself a truck. Spends as little time here as he can these days. I know he's not home, 'cause his truck's not here.' The manager thumbed behind him. 'That's Randall's trailer right there. Now, I'm guessing you want to take a look inside.'

'Can I?'

'Not without a warrant, ma'am.' The manager's eyelids crinkled.

'I'm not a cop.'

'I'm not stupid.'

Pinky, who'd been following their conversation, bristled. 'Yo, you sayin' I look like freakin' Five-O, too?'

'Son,' answered the manager with a brief sniff, 'I couldn't rightly say what the hell you look like.'

'String-bean-Ebenezer-Scrooge-looking fool!' Pinky called him. 'I don't care how long you been drawing a pension, you could be Methuselah and I'll still kick your ass for that wise mouth of yours!'

'Chill, Pinky,' Po drawled from inside the car. 'The guy's got responsibilities he has to protect.'

'I have a responsibility to protect my honour, me. What, Old Timer? You don't get many black gay boys roun' this goddamn shanty town?'

The manager didn't appear ruffled by Pinky's bluster. He cackled out rough laughter. 'All I meant was I can't see to spit beyond the length of my arm.'

'You blind?'

'As near as dammit,' said the old man.

'Yet, you don't seem to miss much,' said Tess, getting things back on track. 'When was Randall last home?'

'That's the thing – he was back fer a coupla nights. But then he lit outta here again yesterday.'

'No idea where he went?'

'He doesn't say much, least of all about his business.'

'He didn't return last night?'

'Nope. I'd'a heard that ol' truck of his if he had. Nothin' wrong with my ears,' he added for Pinky's benefit.

'Do you know what kind of truck he drives?' Tess prompted.

'Flatbed, old Ford,' said the manager. 'Bottle green I'd say. Has one of them rigid canopies he can put on the back. If it ain't lying there by his weight bench, then it's on the truck now.'

Pinky angled for a look. 'I see a bench and some free weights, but no canopy, me.'

The manager raised his eyebrows, and plucked out his

cigarette. It was unfiltered, unlit and damp where his lips had worked on it. 'Can't let you inside his trailer,' he said, with a wink, 'but there'll be no harm done if you happen to take a peek in through the windows. I'm blind enough I won't notice if you snoop around for a bit. Got no love of reformed rapists, y'know what I mean?'

Tess was about to decline the offer. She doubted she'd find any abducted women secreted in the trailer when it was so close to the manager's office, and there was no hint that Randall had dug a secret bunker beneath it either, similar to the one where he was known to have sexually abused his sister and aunt seventeen years earlier. If he was responsible for snatching women, he was keeping them elsewhere. A look inside might have turned up a clue or two as to where, but the blinds were dropped. Right now she'd rather check out the flatbed of Randall's truck, under that rigid canopy. She wondered if it only got erected when he was transporting his latest abductee. But she'd be a fool to pass up the opportunity. She thanked the old man, then nodded at Pinky to get back in the car. Tess headed for Randall's trailer, but ignored the front. She went around the back, and saw where the manager had been digging a drainage trench. If she'd arrived later and found it back-filled she might have jumped to the wrong conclusion.

There were sundry items of junk stacked against the side of the trailer. Nothing that suggested it was the home of a sexual predator, but handy to climb on so she could spy through the windows. Through chinks between the blinds she saw a scruffy, unremarkable home, but nothing to indicate any of the missing women had spent time there.

She took out her cellphone, and was relieved to find that even out here in the sticks she had good 4G coverage, so remotely logged into a DMV database via Emma Clancy's office, and input Jesse Randall's details. Seconds later she had full details on the make and model of his truck.

But it wouldn't help her find him if he didn't drive by.

# THIRTY-ONE

Fashioning a mallet and awl from a hunk of rusty chain and the twisted rim of a bucket proved impossible. Elsa slipped the edge of the folded tin she'd finally broken from the bucket under the top of one hinge-pin. But it buckled without budging the pin a hair's width because brass was tougher than tin. It didn't stop her trying to lever the pin again, and when that failed she moved to the pin in the second hinge: that was even more resolute. She required something sharper and stronger, which she could hammer with a bunch of links, but there was nothing. She checked the engine block, but it was a single solid hunk of rusted iron. On hands and knees she scraped up pebbles from the dirt's cloying embrace, but all were rounded. Even the padlock her captor had failed to lock proved useless as a lever, the edges being beveled, too thick to get under the head of the pins. She wouldn't give up, she promised, but she'd gone beyond hope to futility by the time she heard the monster return to the hallway.

After laying the chain over the block, as if it was still secured beneath the rusting weight, she scurried back to her usual position, placing her back to the door. Head bowed. Cupping the wedge of broken tin against her abdomen.

The flap covering the slot in the door clanked open, followed by a thud on the dirt floor.

The slot was sealed again as equally briskly, and the monster moved on. Twice she heard flaps open and close, as the other captives were briefly visited. Elsa waited, expecting him to return, but all she detected was the faint tapping of his boots in the corridor as he followed other unknown errands. Uncurling, Elsa peered through the dimness and her lips cracked in a feverish grin as she spotted the bottle of water dumped through the slot. She scrambled for it and snatched up the crinkling recycled bottle, barking her palms in her haste to twist off the cap. There was no Evian for her, only flat tap water, but her thirst was so desperate she sucked on the bottle to extract the last drop. She felt heady, and for a second feared he'd drugged the water, and sat down dully on her backside. But it was only the reaction to the sustenance she had craved for so long. Her stomach cramped, but she was never so thankful to experience nausea.

The pint of water wasn't enough, but it took the edge off her desperate thirst, and, once the euphoria had subsided, she could think a little straighter. It was a waste of time attempting to prise out the hinge-pins. She saw that now, but all of her efforts hadn't been for nothing. She gathered in her chain. Her hands were still shackled, but looping it around the links between her wrists, she folded it into three-feet lengths and knotted the free end to the shackle. The hunk of tin she kept cupped in her palms, as she squatted and waited.

She had no way to measure time passing but for the light through the chinks in the ceiling. She watched the spear point tips of greyness move down the walls, lengthening, then across the dirt floor, longer and fainter still, until they began to retract and supposed it was past midday. Periodically she eased up, chewing her lips against the moans she wanted to emit, as she worked out the kinks in her muscles. After the beating she'd sustained she was surprised to be moving at all, and thought that her earlier efforts had served purpose beyond offering her some base weapons.

She waited some more. Her body must have absorbed every drop of moisture from the bottle, because she felt no urgency to relieve herself. Her skin felt brittle and slack where it wasn't swollen or scratched. The older scars on her left hand and throat felt as if they hung from her in loose folds. She remembered the scalding with hot oil she'd endured as a child, and how she'd believed there could be no greater agony; well, she'd nothing to compare to then. The aching within her chest and the fierce pulsing of blood through her skull was enough to want to explode. And that was the plan.

He came back as the light began to track back up the cell wall, when her vision had hazed out while watching dancing motes of dust, and she was about to fold. She hadn't heard his shuffling progress through the tunnels, so she might have dozed.

The flap over the slot clanked open without warning. A flashlight flared inside the cell, and her shadow was cast on the wall, a squat, ugly toad-like presence amid a halo of yellowish light. The muscles tensed in her thighs, and she shivered.

His orders were explicit, though whispered in barely audible sibilance.

'Do not look at me.'

Elsa didn't look.

'Do not speak to me.'

She didn't speak.

The locks and bolts rattled and clicked, and the door swung wide on the hinges that had thwarted her.

'Put that on.'

A familiar contraption rattled on the dirt beside her: a buckled leather strap, and heavy rubber ball.

Elsa didn't move.

'Put it on. *Now.*'

Elsa nipped the folded metal between her knees, and reached tentatively for the gag. The beam of his flashlight remained centred on her back, and she hoped it would stay there, and not track back to the engine block. She pulled up the gag, and inserted the rubber ball between her teeth, her lips cracking as they stretched wide, then halted.

'Buckle it!' His voice had risen, and she knew she was courting a vicious attack, but to buckle the strap behind her head she'd have to lift her shackled hands over her head and he'd spot the bunched links of chain.

She spat out the ball, and it fell at her feet.

'I . . . I can't lift my arms,' she croaked. 'You . . . you broke them, I think.'

'What did I tell you? What are the fucking rules?'

'I can't obey your rules *and* answer you,' Elsa reasoned as she fed her hands between her knees and clasped the twisted metal.

The flashlight beam snapped up and down, and Elsa knew he was coming. She'd dared defy him again. And that ensured swift retaliation. In her mind she urged him forward, because if he even glanced at the engine block, she was done for.

She uncurled.

In the moment she experienced the twisting and pulling of her tormented muscles, and it was as if she moved through thick sludge. An age must have passed before she turned, but apparently not. As she whipped around he was still mid-stride a couple of arm lengths away, with his flashlight held aloft in his right hand, and his left trailing the rubber hood he would have next forced over her skull. As his foot came down, and his momentum brought him forward, her arms followed the swing of her torso, and arcing behind them the flailing chain.

He was backlit, his muscular body in silhouette, but the backwash from his flashlight lit his features. It was the first time she'd glimpsed his face, and she understood why he demanded his slaves never looked upon it. His face was horribly scarred, a deep and poorly healed furrow splitting him from brow to chin, intersecting the bridge of his broken nose, and the right corner of his mouth. His right eye was milky, the eyelid warped. His other eye, bright with surprise, opened wide and he jerked to a halt as Elsa's screech split the air.

The chains slashed into him.

His upraised arm saved him a crushing blow to the face, but not all injury. His arm was battered against him, the flashlight knocked from his hand, and the loose ends of the chain flayed his shoulder and neck. He staggered sideways, a gasp of pain hissing from him.

Elsa saw the open portal.

But he was still between her and freedom.

She yanked free the chains, but his arm whipped after them and grabbed at the final few links. He shouted wordlessly as he snatched her off her feet. She was weightless. Borne aloft, and into him. He snapped fingers at her hair, but the rubber hood encumbered him. It slapped her face, momentarily blinding her. Elsa tried to duck below his arms, to flee, but a snap down on the chains he gripped sent her to her knees. His body rode over her, and a boot heel drove down her thigh, scoring the skin. Off balance he stumbled past, but he wouldn't release the chain and Elsa was tugged after him. She fought to stand as he fought for stability.

Elsa could feel the tightness in her face, hear the hiss of wildcat defiance between her lips, as he rebounded from the wall and spun to confront her. Her knees almost exploded as she pushed up and at him. He helped, yanking her tether, and she spearheaded the catapulting force with her hands thrusting at his throat. The hunk of twisted metal in her hands furrowed his collarbone, bending, but still formidable as it raked under his chin, springing clear below his right earlobe.

He howled, his disfigured face more distorted by terror. Blood poured from his new wounds, and he dropped the chain to clasp both hands over his opened throat. Elsa fell down, kicked backwards on her butt. His hands fluttered and danced, and his mouth hung open at one side, streaming saliva. Elsa had seconds before he realized he wasn't in mortal peril. She'd failed to cut a vein or artery, his cuts were painful but super-ficial. She grabbed the flashlight. It was two feet long, tubular steel, and as he bent at the waist, checking his hands for sign of his ebbing life, she rose up. His gaze went from his palms, rose up to meet hers, and she brought down the flashlight in a blur from behind her right shoulder.

The first blow sent him to one knee.

The second face down in the dirt.

Screeching in combined hatred and terror, Elsa smashed him a third time.

She stood over the downed brute, the flashlight ready again, but he wasn't moving. His arms were splayed, his face pressed into the slimy muck. There was nothing more she wanted than to keep hitting him, to pulp his skull into the filth, except one thing. Get out, get out, get out! Before he gets up again and kills you!

She dropped the flashlight and ran, naked and terrified, her chains now flailing behind her with every step, no sense of direction other than away.

Behind her the other captives screamed, banging at their cell doors, but in her frantic haste to escape, those inside her head buried their cries. Elsa simply ran, caroming off walls, tripping up steps, taking corners at random, as long as it was away from the scarred man, the whispering devil of her nightmares.

She fell, tripped by her chains. She fought loose of the links wound round her ankle, but stayed shackled at the wrists. Finally her thoughts began to crystalize, and she pulled the chain into her embrace as she ran again. She was in a narrow passage, walls dotted with black mould and flaking paint encroaching on her. Overhead lights were dim, their covers thick with dust and grime. In the distance there was a brighter glow. She ran for it as if it was a gate to sanctuary.

She smashed into stacked tin sheets. The glow was a reflection from her right. As the sheets collapsed, an edge cutting viciously at her feet, she stamped over them and fell through a door into an echoing space. Again she forced up from her knees as she searched for a way out. She was in a cavernous room, dimly lit by overhead striplights, most of which had long burned out, some flickering madly, her mind unable to make any sense of the ancient machinery on all sides. Electrical conduit and metal pipes were strung from the ceiling and angled for the floor, some adjoining one machine to another, forming cages between others. There was no obvious path through the maze of rusting machinery, so she took the first direction that beckoned. Her bare feet slapped on crumbling concrete.

On more than one occasion during her captivity she'd fancied she was stuck in a labyrinth, like the one through which the Minotaur once stalked its prey. She twisted and turned, sometimes having to turn back and retrace her frantic steps, before finally she spilled out on to a wide concrete platform, tripped over its edge and fell four feet on to a worm-eaten wood trestle that collapsed beneath her. As she struggled to rise, she was almost consumed by despair. She had run the wrong way. She had descended lower into the bowels of some ancient, decommissioned factory, and now stood at the edge of a huge space in which there were deep trenches. Dark, filthy water filled the trenches almost to their rims.

'Where in hell am I?' she moaned.

There was a faint cry from her left.

Was it the voice of one of the other captives? Had she run almost full circle? In her blind panic she had no idea of the number of turns or directions she'd taken. For all she knew a single wall separated her from where she'd once been imprisoned, though she was down a level at least.

She peered around, seeking exit from the cavernous space,

and her gaze fixed on an old green pickup truck, and beyond it a huge roller shutter door. Without hesitation she sprang towards them, skirting the nearest pit. Chips of perished concrete dug painfully into her soles, but she ignored the gnat-bite stings: compared to what she'd suffered her latest injuries were nothing. Ignoring the truck, she crashed up against the steel shutters, and rebounded. She stooped, got her hands under its lower edge and tried to lift, but she'd have had more chance of over-turning a mountain. The doors were of industrial size and required motors to shift them. A man-sized portal was to her left, but it was padlocked shut. Futilely she slapped her palms on the door. The thrum echoed through the vast room.

Another faint cry.

Elsa turned around, gawping in the dimness.

'Elsa! Over here!' called the voice from somewhere beyond the truck. 'It's me! Jasmine! Help me!'

Disbelief caused Elsa to walk in faltering steps towards the voice. As she approached its source she began to speed up and she fell against the door, panting out in a mixture of shock and joy. She had truly believed Jasmine had been murdered, her tongue sliced out and her body fed into the furnace she'd conjured from her imagination. Yet Jazz was alive!

'I . . . I'll get you out,' she croaked.

But she couldn't. Not immediately. The door was secured as formidably as her cell had ever been. Padlocked bolts, and a huge steel bar were locked across the door. A small slot in the door allowed her to feed in her fingers, and Jasmine held on to them like a lifeline.

'I'll get you out,' Elsa said again, the promise heartfelt, but impossible.

'You can't.' Jasmine bent so she could lock eyes with Elsa through the slot. 'Not without keys or tools. So don't even try.' Her hand pushed through the slot, flicking to the right. 'There, that door. It's where he first brought me after I was snatched. He stripped me there, took my belongings from me. My cellphone, Elsa, find it and call for help.'

Elsa craned to look at the door Jasmine indicated.

'Hurry, Elsa, before he comes.'

'I . . . I killed him,' she croaked. 'I hit him, again and again.'

'Are you certain he's dead?'

'Yes. N-no. I'm not sure.' Elsa clawed at her own face. 'He could still be alive . . .'

'Then hurry!''

She turned for the door, her chain again loose and rasping along the floor behind her. The door was unlocked but she was afraid to enter.

'Elsa! For God's sake!'

She pushed inside.

It was an old office. There was a desk and a collapsed wooden chair. A table, on which were stacked clothes. She knew hers were on the table, mixed among the clothing of the monster's other victims. Handbags. She couldn't see hers, so grabbed for the first she came to and upended it. No phone. She ignored the others and instead pulled open the desk drawers. There were sundry items, stripped from the girls, jewellery, credit cards, and parts to phones. A mix and match potpourri from different models, batteries and SIM cards scattered in the bottom of the drawer. She stared at the parts forlornly. Ordinarily she wouldn't be fazed by the puzzle presented to her, but in her overwrought state the individual bits looked like alien technology.

'Elsa! Hurry!'

Jasmine's frantic warning made her jump. She grabbed pieces, pulling them from the drawer, and dumping them on the desk. Scanning, she saw two as parts she recognized as belonging to a Blackberry. Her hands felt numb and useless, as if she wore boxing gloves, but she scrabbled about and hooked a SIM card with her nail, and by more luck than design slotted it into its holder. It took more tries to get the battery to slide in place, but then she had an entire phone. Please, please, please work . . .

She depressed the power button, holding it down and to her relief saw a red light flash on the phone, but the screen remained dull matt black. Please, please, please. She held down the button, and the Blackberry logo sparked to life.

'Thank you, God. Thank you. Thank you.'

The logo blinked off, and Elsa gawped at the screen.

But in its place a rounded square appeared and a pale blue serpent began eating its way around the perimeter as the phone began to initialize.

.

'Elsa!' Jasmine shrieked. 'Look out!'

The door behind her crashed shut, and Elsa knew she was too late to summon help. She dropped the phone, and ran screeching at the scar-faced brute in one final desperate attempt at killing him.

His powering fist met her jaw.

She must have been knocked unconscious, because her next lucid impression was a worm's eye view from flat on her back. She blinked as a shadowy form crouched and snatched something from the ground, and peered at it quizzically. Cognisance swam in and out of focus, but she knew it was *him* and that he was checking the Blackberry's screen. He snorted, looked down at her and his ugly mouth twisted up at one side.

'So you didn't get to ring nine-one-one, huh?' he whispered. 'Too bad.'

He dropped the phone and it clattered by her face.

Feebly she reached for it, but in the next instant it was buried beneath his foot as he stamped it into tinkling components.

# THIRTY-TWO

'If he has touched her, I'm going to kill the bastard,' Cal Hopewell announced. He was sitting directly behind the driver's seat, with a gun taken from Maxwell Carter's office at Bar-Lesque aimed at Trojak's lower spine.

Trojak felt his scalp creep over his skull, his injuries itching as the poorly knitted flesh crinkled. 'Considering what you have in mind, I'd have thought Randall might be your new best friend.'

'Don't associate me with the likes of that ugly piece of crap,' Hopewell warned. He raised the muzzle of the gun and pressed it to the back of Trojak's neck. 'Don't forget: I can get by without a driver now if it comes to it.'

Hopewell had forced cooperation from Trojak at the end of his gun, pressing him into service to drive him to the trailer park near Amherst after realizing the importance of the documents Trojak had filched from Tess Grey's house. For Trojak the three hours' journey had felt like an eternity. Twice already Hopewell had come close to pulling the trigger. It was only because they were driving at speed that he hadn't, but now they were parked in the entrance to a water-treatment works. Having gotten eyes on the Mustang, Hopewell didn't need him any longer: the promise of a bullet was no longer a mere threat.

Trojak's only hope of survival was to keep Hopewell talking, reminding him that – partly – they were in this together, even if their reasons were at polar opposites.

'I don't get you, Cal. Why go to all this trouble to get your hands on Jazz? Going after her like this, it only ensures that her story gets out.'

'Not if I shut her up.'

'But others know what happened. Max, Daryl, her grandmother, even your own father.'

'I'm happy to shut them up too. I'm pretty certain the detective has figured it out too, but I've enough bullets to include her,'

Hopewell tapped the gun on the back of Trojak's head. 'You know what happened too.'

Sadly, Hopewell's statement was true. He'd only learned sketchy details from Bruin, but Hopewell had regaled Trojak with the tale in all its sordid detail on the drive over.

'Jasmine ran away,' Trojak reminded him. 'You ask me, she had no intention of telling anyone what happened. If you'd left well and good alone, she'd have stayed hidden, and you and the others would've been safe. But now?'

'She only ran because someone told her I was getting out of prison. I wonder who that was?' He screwed the barrel into the back of Trojak's skull, forcing his head down. 'I know now it wasn't Daryl or Maxwell; who else was in their little inner circle, Johnny?'

Trojak didn't answer.

The pressure went from the back of his head, but the gun was still an immediate threat. He straightened marginally.

'You do understand that Daryl is using you the way he has me for years,' he said.

'I'm not stupid. Of course he is, but what he doesn't realize is that after I finish with Jasmine, I'm going back for him. Who will be using who then?'

'You're confident you'll make it back to him?'

'Nobody has stopped me yet.'

Trojak thought about Po Villere. He thought about Tess Grey. He thought about himself.

'What about this Randall character?'

'He sounds like a mommy's boy to me,' Hopewell sneered. 'You know why he has to snatch girls, right? He's too fucking ugly to attract one and knows it. Bet you he puts a bag over his head when he screws them.'

'If Tess Grey's deduction is to be trusted, he's been at this for some time. He might be good at what he does.'

'You admire her, huh? The detective?'

Trojak shrugged. 'I've nothing against her.'

'Bet you wish your body was. Tell the truth, Johnny, if you could get in her pants you would. I got close the other day, wouldn't mind another go.'

'I'm not into that kind of dirty talk,' Trojak said.

'You always were a prude. That's why you weren't invited to the party that night. We knew you'd make a fuss.'

Trojak nodded. He would have. It was Daryl and his seedy pal, Maxwell Carter, who'd coaxed Jasmine, a young impressionable girl with a bit of a wild streak, into Calvin Hopewell's bedroom. Gave her alcohol, and set her up for Cal to have his way with her. Daryl had always intended going second on her, Max third, but Jasmine – even drunk – had resisted. The younger boys had helped hold her down while Cal attempted to take her virginity. She'd fought, and Cal had resorted to threatening her with a knife. Still unbowed, she'd required further warning and Cal had found that he was enjoying the fight more than the sex, especially after drawing first blood.

'I'd have taken that knife from you and put it in your eye,' Trojak assured him.

Hopewell laughed at him. 'Maybe we're not so unalike, eh?'

'We're a gulf apart, Cal.'

'That time you followed me, and spotted me burning my car, I could have killed you then. I didn't realize it was you until after, but I didn't feel bad about hurting you, and I won't now. Maybe I should've kept smashing your stupid head in, saved myself the trouble later.'

'We're all wise in hindsight.'

Hopewell laughed again, but this time without humour.

'Are you saying you want to stick a knife in my eye now, Johnny?'

'Do you want to put a bullet through mine?'

Neither man spoke.

Finally it was Trojak who broke the prickly quiet. 'So your daddy made everything go away, huh? Paid off Margaret Norris to keep Jasmine quiet. Paid off Daryl and Max, too.'

'Max didn't get a brown cent. Daryl more than his fair share. How'd you think he got started in business?'

'I knew it wasn't through an honest day's labour.'

'He's been blackmailing my father for years. He isn't afraid of being named in an attempted rape case, not when he can argue he was just a stupid boy who was drunk and being manipulated by me. Fucker would probably earn some sympathy instead of punishment. No, what Daryl fears is the story going public, because then he'll have nothing left to lever more cash out of my dad.'

'Whatever happens now, the story will come out. You've been lucky 'til now, Cal. The police haven't been looking for you as a rape suspect, only for the violent assaults you've made on Max and me, and your aborted attack on Tess Grey. You're not going to get away with this.'

'I know that. But that's why I want some fun before they get me. You've heard the expression "you may as well be hung for stealing a sheep as for a lamb", right?'

'That's what all this is about? You want to finish what you started with Jazz?'

'You've never done time, have you, Johnny? When you're locked in a cell twenty-three hours a day you get a lot of thinking time. I'd had my way with a few women by then, but they were conquests, not fantasy any more. I thought about them occasionally, but most of my time was spent dreaming about my first victim; the one that got away.' He snorted. 'If I'm going back to prison, I'm going to take some pleasant memories of Jasmine back inside with me.'

'You do know she might already be dead? They found another of Randall's victims; Jazz could also be in a shallow grave out there somewhere.'

'If that's the case, Randall will suffer. Jasmine's mine, she was always mine, and if he's harmed her I'll peel off his ugly face and feed it back to him.'

'Cal, you do know how crazy you sound, right?'

'All a matter of opinion, Johnny.'

'I couldn't agree with you more. To me women are to be protected, not to be used and abused.'

'That's why you've been treated as a doormat all your life, Johnny. Look at your face, all scratched up. I bet your wife did that to you: if you'd showed her the back of your hand years ago, she'd have known her place.'

'But that would make me just like you, Cal, and I'm sorry to say but you're everything I hate. A man who hurts women and children is the lowest of the low.'

'Like I give a fuck what you think about me?' Hopewell jabbed the gun under Trojak's left ear. 'All you need think about is that there's a bullet with your name on it if you insult me again.'

'I was stating fact.'

'I don't hurt children,' Hopewell growled.

'Jasmine was a child when you first hurt her.'

'She was old *enough*,' Hopewell snapped. 'Haven't you heard, Johnny, if they're old enough to bleed, they're old enough to breed.'

Trojak didn't respond, except to slide shut his eyes in disgust.

'Hey! Hey goddamnit!' Hopewell shoved his shoulder. 'Get with it, Johnny. They're on the move.'

As Trojak stirred, he spotted Po Villere's Mustang come roaring from the trailer park. It barely paused as it met the junction, and turned to speed away from them, kicking up a spray of gritty water from a dip in the road.

'Where are they off to in such a hurry?' Hopewell demanded. 'After them, Johnny, and don't spare the horses.'

# THIRTY-THREE

Only moments earlier, Tess was running for the car before she had fully absorbed what she was looking at, her cellphone held before her like an Olympic relay baton.

'I've got a hit!' she announced as Po jumped out to throw forward his seat so she could get in.

'A hit? What?' Po glanced over at the old site manager, who was frowning back at him, equally perplexed.

'Get in, Po,' Tess hollered before she was fully in. 'Get moving!'

'Where?' Po demanded as he jumped back inside, and fired up the engine.

'Wait up. I'm looking now. But get us out of here!'

Po spun the car around, spraying dirt as the back wheels clipped the verge near the old man's feet. He jumped back, exclaiming loudly, his unlit cigarette flying from between his lips.

'Good job he's got good ears, him,' Pinky announced with a laugh. 'You almost took off his toes!'

Neither Tess nor Po paid him any mind, Tess working frantically on her phone while Po took the serpentine, rutted track with the skill of a seasoned rally driver.

'Left, left, left,' Tess barked from the back seat as they reached the exit and met the road. She watched for traffic on Po's behalf. The sewage-treatment plant was slightly to their right, and there was a car parked in its entrance, but the road was clear. 'Go, go, go,' she hollered, slapping a hand on the back of Po's seat.

'What's going on?' Pinky now wondered as the Mustang powered forward, giving sound to the unspoken question on Po's creased face.

'I got an alert through on my phone. From the programs I've been running? One of them just got a ping from Jasmine Reed's cell!'

'Where from?' Po asked, as he concentrated on covering

ground. There was no turn off in sight, so he merely hit the gas, aiming for the near horizon.

Tess scrabbled about in the back, bringing her iPad to life. 'I'm bringing up a map, can't see for shit on my phone. But her cell made a brief connection out by Quabbin Reservoir.'

'Where the other girl was found?'

'No. A lot further north.' Tess flicked and swiped the screen on her tablet. She had her phone, her tablet and even her iMac back home synchronized on the same network. 'Got it, now just hold on and I'll . . .' She enlarged the map. A red cursor blinked but the area looked featureless, woodland and scrub on the western shore of the man-made lake. Finding Jasmine in that trackless area would take for ever. She switched to a satellite view, zoomed in on a series of rooftops, indistinct beneath the forest canopy. 'I can see a derelict factory or something. Stay on this road, Po. We're about ten minutes away.'

Po gave the engine more fuel. 'Make that eight minutes,' he said.

Tess shoved the iPad into Pinky's hands. 'Make yourself useful, Pinky. Tell Po when he needs to make a turn.'

'Eh, uh, yeah,' Pinky said staring at the screen, 'I would, but where the hell are we now?'

Tess almost clambered into the front to tap on the screen. 'Right there,' she said, indicating their position on the road. 'You got it?'

'I got it.'

Tess called Emma Clancy.

'Emma, I haven't time to explain, but I need something from you.'

'What is it?'

'You said you were going to talk with the lead investigator on Carrie Mae Borger's case? Can you give me his name and cell number?'

'It's not a he, it's a she: Detective Karen Ratcliffe.' Emma scratched around a few seconds, each of them ticking down like the doomsday clock in Tess's mind. 'I've got the number right here.'

She read it out, and Tess repeated it to her.

'Right, thanks, Emma.'

'Tess, what's going on?'

'Sorry. No time. Gotta go!' She ended the call and punched in the number for the lead detective on the Homicide investigative team at Belchertown PD.

Po hit a hump in the road and the car sailed. Bouncing around on the bench seat, she fought to keep her phone next to her ear.

'Detective Ratcliffe,' a female voice announced.

'Hello, Detective Ratcliffe, my name is Teresa Grey, I work for Emma Clancy in Portland, Maine. I believe you've already spoken to my boss?' Tess realized she was rattling out her words, and made a conscious effort to slow down.

'Hello. Yes. This is Tess, right? Mrs Clancy told me I should expect you to call.'

'She sent you my report on the other missing persons?'

'The missing girls? Yes. I have to admit that the coincidences between their disappearances were remarkable but . . .'

'I think I've found another of them,' Tess announced, though she'd no real proof. All she had was evidence that Jasmine's phone had been briefly switched on and off again – that didn't say Jasmine was present. She could have been murdered weeks ago, her phone could have changed hands a half-dozen times. Who knew? Except why the hell would it have been turned on at such a remote location? She was certain it was where the abducted girls were being kept. The abandoned factory sat firmly within the wedge of countryside between the two interstates from which some of the girls had gone missing. 'We've had a hit on one of the missing women's cellphones, from an abandoned plant north-east of Amherst, up near the reservoir.'

'It could mean anything,' Ratcliffe cautioned her.

'But it needs checking out.'

'Where are you, Tess? You aren't calling from Portland, are you?'

'I'm north of Amherst, on my way to the location now.'

Ratcliffe hissed a curse. 'Stop. Stop now, Tess.'

'Sorry, Detective, but I can't do that. I made her grandmother a promise I'd bring Jasmine Reed home. If this is the only opportunity I get . . .'

'Stand down,' Ratcliffe warned her. 'I'll have a patrol dispatched to the scene. Do not interfere.'

'One patrol car isn't enough,' Tess replied. 'Send everyone you've got. I called you out of professional courtesy, Detective. But if you aren't going to take this seriously, then someone has to.'

'I am taking it seriously, goddamnit, but I need more proof before I mobilize my department.'

'You've studied the files, studied the girls. They're all similar-looking. They all have tattoos and scars. OK. Now check out Jesse Randall on your sex offenders' register. Tattooed. Scarred. And living right here near Amherst. I just bet he knows about that old factory and is there right now. With those missing girls.' Again Tess realized she was rattling out her words, but she no longer cared. Ratcliffe would send back up, or she wouldn't. Tess had done her bit to keep the cops in the loop, and it would have to do. She ended the call, just as Pinky waved frantically at an upcoming hairpin bend.

'I've got it,' Po reassured him, and barely slowed as he drifted the muscle car around the tight bend. Ahead was a straight stretch of road that paralleled a stream. The hills on either side were rounded, only sparsely dotted with vegetation, but to the front and to the right, Tess made out a dark band she assumed was the woodland in which the abandoned factory was located.

'We've somebody following us,' Po announced after flicking a look in his mirrors.

Tess twisted round, peering out the tiny window, and coming out of that last bend she spotted another car. The driver wasn't as accomplished as Po and almost lost control of the vehicle. Tess's first thought was that it was an unmarked cop car, one they'd sped past and who was now giving chase. But it wasn't displaying lights or sirens.

'They aren't gaining on us,' she said.

'And they won't,' Po responded, and flattened the gas pedal to the boards.

The muscle car rocketed on, bouncing over the small humps in the road, as Po pushed it for the distant forest.

Behind them the car dwindled, and was hidden from sight by the intervening contours of the land.

Another few minutes later, Tess had disregarded their tail as the Mustang followed a number of switchbacks down a hillside.

Trees filled the broad valley below, and beyond them was the vast expanse of water that was Quabbin Reservoir. Pinky passed back the iPad to her and she directed Po along the edge of the woodland.

'Watch for service trails. I'm not sure this place is still in use, but there's still bound to be a noticeable road in.' She zoomed the map out so she could keep track on their location in relation to the factory. 'OK. We can't be far away now. Slow down, Po. There. There!' She was now viewing the road ahead over Po's shoulder. There was a definite gap between the trees, and as Po began to brake she spotted an old mesh-link fence on which were hung faded old signs. She couldn't make out much of what they said, expect for one that warned of danger, and prohibited entry. Po took the turning and a chain-link gate out in one manoeuvre, blasting the gates wide and leaving one hanging on a broken hinge. He kept the car moving at speed, though nowhere as fast as earlier, because the road was narrow and in severe disrepair. Tess again checked the satellite imagery on her tablet. The red cursor blinked, beckoning them to find it. 'We're about a quarter-mile out,' she told Po, 'maybe you should take things a little easier. If Randall's here we don't want to warn him we're coming.'

Po took some weight off the gas pedal.

'Thank God for that,' Pinky declared, and wiped at a film of sweat on his forehead. 'I've been thrown around like dirty laundry in a washer, me. You didn't think to add air-ride suspension to this ol' hunk of scrap metal when you customized it?'

'Didn't ever expect to have an ol' hunk like you riding shotgun,' Po told him with a grin. 'Those shock absorbers weren't made to handle someone like you, Pinky.'

'I think "shock absorbers" is a real stretch of the definition,' Pinky replied archly. 'The only shock absorber is my head on the damn roof!' Their banter was an indicator of anxiety. Despite their jokes, they were as tense as Tess was, perhaps for different reasons. She was nervous in case she'd called it all wrong, whereas Po and Pinky were girding themselves for trouble. On that note, she reached in her purse, and felt for the butt of her grandfather's Service Six.

# THIRTY-FOUR

Elsa's imagination had conjured a roaring furnace from noises she'd heard in the distance, and throughout her incarceration had expected that immolation was the end game for all of the girls in the whispering devil's harem. She'd called it wrong. The noise she'd listened to, filtered and distorted by the many walls and echoing rooms, was the opening and closing of the massive roller shutter whenever the brute came or went with his truck. The site appeared derelict, decommissioned, but her abuser had rigged some kind of power supply to feed the lights and the motor on the shutter. She knew that now because as he dragged her past the nearest trough she spotted the roof of a car submerged in the filth below. He'd been bringing not only the abductees to this place, but their vehicles too and burying them from sight in the sludgy depths. She wondered fleetingly into which trough her own car had been pushed.

After gloating how he'd foiled her attempt to ring the police, he remained silent. His commands were given in wrenches of her hair, of knuckles in her spine, of fingers at her throat. He forced her past Jasmine's cell, from which the young woman reached futilely to grab hold of her, to foil what he had in mind. He'd fetched with him the flashlight Elsa had used to knock him cold, and used it similarly as he whacked Jasmine's arms and she withdrew them with a cry of agony.

'I'll come back,' Elsa screeched at the imprisoned woman. 'I promise you, I'll come back.'

Her captor grunted at the absurdity of her pledge, and almost lifted her off her feet with his fingers clenched either side of her jaw. Roughly he spun her, and kicked at the backs of her legs to get going. He snatched up the chain trailing behind her, whipping it as if mushing a dogsled team. Elsa tripped and stumbled, with no idea where he was taking her. Would he make her retrace her steps back to her cell, or take her elsewhere? Wherever it was, it wasn't going to be good.

She'd seen his face, could identify him. There was no way a person with such a horrible deformation to his features could hide in normal society. But even without seeing his face she was positive she could identify him in a line-up, and not because of his stature and overblown muscles. He wore jeans and a work shirt with the sleeves torn off. Every inch of visible skin from his chin down was covered with a hotchpotch array of tattoos. They were as grotesque as his face, random shapes and letters that were blue and blotchy, the ink feathering into the surrounding skin. In an attempt at drawing an observer's eye from her crinkly burn marks, Elsa had gone under the tattooist's gun. She wondered if he'd made a similar attempt to pull attention from his face by making his body as equally ugly. There was no artistry in his tattoos, and she suspected they were the product of a drunken friend or cellmate with a needle and ink, or even by his own poorly guided hand. Ordinarily she would pity someone so horrifically deformed, but not in his case. His outward appearance was every bit as warped as he was inside.

When Jasmine had thrust out her arms to hold on to her, they had been tattooed. Were their tattoos the reason the monster had snatched them? Did he somehow believe that their body art intimately connected them? It was a possibility, but for one thing – he could not have known of Elsa's tattoos before ramming her car off the road.

There was a flight of steps at the edge of the platform she'd fallen from. She took them to the top, and paused, unsure where she should go next. He jabbed her in the left shoulder, and instinctively she moved right and faced a wall of shadows. She hadn't noticed the passage before. The entrance was hidden behind a curtain of plastic strips, filthy with decades of grime, and it was almost invisible against the surrounding darkness. She pushed through. He halted her with a tug of the chain while he edged inside. There was no light in the tunnel, so he flicked on the flashlight. Her shadow was cast before her in a pool of light that didn't reach far along the cramped passage.

He snapped the chain against her backside to get her moving, and Elsa fought to hold in her cry, denying him the satisfaction of hearing her in pain. She regretted wasting time on trying to phone the police now, when she should have grabbed some clothes. Naked, she was vulnerable and tempting. She could sense his greasy fascination as he fixated on the sway of her bare hips and thighs as he tried to bring a flush into them with the snapping chain. She halted.

'Keep moving,' he warned in his usual rasping whisper.

She took a few steps then halted again. She began to turn.

'Do not look at me.'

'I've already seen your face.'

'Do not talk,' he growled. 'You're beginning to try my patience, bitch. Don't you remember the rules?'

'Fuck you!'

'I won't warn you again, whore . . .'

'You're going to kill me anyway. So fuck you and your fucking rules, you ugly piece of shit!'

He yanked her towards him, the chain wrenching her wrists so that she bent at the waist. Defiantly she rose up, pushing out her chest as she eyed him.

'So have I to look at you or not?' she demanded.

He shone the flashlight directly in her face, and the sudden glare caused her eyelids to screw tight. She fought the urge to avert her face, and slowly peeled open her eyes to stare at him.

'I should kill you right now,' he said as he passed the flashlight into the hand clutching her tether.

'Do it. Death's preferable to spending another second in your stinking presence.'

His slap landed without warning, his knuckles battering her head sideways. She sagged, blackness edging her mind, but he shook her chain, bringing her back to her feet. Slowly she straightened up, and again stared him down.

'Is that it? Is that all you can do? Slap me like the bitch you are?' she goaded. 'You're so pathetic, you ugly . . .'

He struck her again, this time with the flashlight slashing across her left thigh. 'Keep going,' he warned. 'I can keep this up all day.'

'Ha!' said Elsa. 'Pity the same can't be said for your pecker. Those times you forced yourself on me, all I could think about was how I *soooo* wished you were a real man!'

He snarled, and his hand went for her throat.

Elsa ducked, then bobbed up inside his reach, her right knee battering at his groin.

He squeezed his thighs together, so that her knee merely glanced off him. He cupped the back of her skull, pulled her in tighter to him so she couldn't move. Blood from the cuts on his neck smeared her cheeks as he ground her against him. 'You think you're so smart,' he whispered harshly in her ear. 'You aren't. You're trying to force me into killing you cleanly; if you were so fucking smart you'd know you're doing the opposite. You're guaranteeing a slow and painful end, you stupid whore. Before I'm done you'll beg me to kill you.'

His fingers entwined her hair, and he yanked back her head. 'Look at me now!'

She looked, her pupils shuddering as they took in the enormity of his savage deformity.

'You'll wish your face was as pretty as mine before I'm finished with you.'

'I'll . . . I'll never beg . . .'

'Perhaps not out loud,' he acquiesced, 'because first thing I'm going to do is rip that disobedient tongue out of your stupid fucking head.'

Elsa suddenly wrenched against him, and when he grappled her again, she clamped her teeth on his lower jaw. She bit with every ounce of outrage left in her, the muscles in her own jaws cramping with the effort. He had no option but release his hold on her, both on the chain and her hair, and he got his hands under her chin to prise her away. He screamed deep in his chest at the effort, but equally at the thought of being further disfigured. The flashlight fell, bounced off the wall and spun away. Elsa's teeth snapped open, and she took flight, tasting his blood in her mouth.

She made it ten feet before his boot stamped down on her trailing chain. The sudden yank spun her and she fell on her back.

He grasped the chain, and came up, and in the lambent glow of the flashlight she would swear his one good eye was as red as the fresh wound on his face. He touched the torn flesh on his jaw, held his fingers up to inspect them, and a change shuddered through him. Before his cruelty was epic, now it would be unquenchable. He roared, rushing at her with his bloody fingers like claws, as if he was about to literally tear out her tongue.

She'd tried so hard to fight him, to escape, to help save Jasmine, but now she had nothing left. She clamped her teeth, drew in her knees, and prayed her heart would give out before he laid his hands on her.

# THIRTY-FIVE

'I think we should split up, otherwise it will take for ever to search this place,' Tess suggested as she stood between Po and Pinky in front of the Mustang. They were on a turning circle in the forest, above a set of wide wooden steps leading down to a forested valley that met the edge of Quabbin Reservoir. The valley was filled with partly collapsed buildings and sheds, and a huge stack of rusting girders housing huge water wheels and turbines.

'You can't be serious,' Po said. 'If you're right about Jasmine being in there, you can bet your ass that Randall is too. No way am I letting you get within a mile of him alone.'

'Your concern for me is as touching as ever, Po,' she countered, 'and as inappropriate. I can look after myself, don't forget.'

He shook his head.

'And I'm the only one with a gun,' she added, and showed him the Ruger .38 revolver. 'So I should be more concerned about you guys. But I see no other way.'

'The cops are coming,' Pinky reminded her. 'You called them and they're sending someone, right?'

Detective Ratcliffe couldn't afford to ignore Tess's call. She was confident that the detective had dispatched a patrol to the location, but one or two cops weren't enough. To search an area as massive as the derelict factory would take dozens. She had to give the detective more proof that she wasn't crying wolf.

'We only need something solid to show the missing girls are here, or have even been here, and we'll get all the manpower we need.'

'I trust your instincts, Tess,' Po reassured her. 'But what if you're wrong? What if this has nothing to do with Jesse Randall?'

'If it's him or not, does it matter? Jasmine's phone was switched on at this location. If she hasn't been abducted, then there's still no good reason for her to be here. I have to find out.'

'I'll go ahead. I can cover more ground on my own,' Po finally said. 'But you and Pinky stay together. Look after each other.'

'Fine,' said Tess, 'but let's do this, shall we? The longer we wait here, then God knows what's happening inside.'

'You OK with this, Pinky?' Po asked.

'I make my living selling illegal guns, and here I am armed with nothing but my disarming smile.' He grinned. 'You go, Nicolas. I won't let any brute get his sticky hands on Tess, me.'

Po clapped a hand on his friend's shoulder. 'I trust you.'

'So what am I, chopped liver?' Tess asked.

'I trust you to keep Pinky safe, too,' Po reassured her.

'If you spot anything, and I mean anything, you call me. Right, Po?'

'F'sure.' He patted his pocket where he kept his cellphone, then dipped for his boot. He came up gripping the hilt of a knife. 'I'll do what I can.'

Before she could add anything more, Po took off, flitting down the steps with a fluid agility that belied his gangly frame. Tess watched him for a few seconds, then shifted to look at Pinky. 'Is it just me or is that man simply *infuriating*?'

'Nicolas lives for this kind of stuff, him.' Pinky nudged her. 'But I must admit, I'm enjoying the excitement, too. Like I said, there's never a dull moment around you guys.'

'I'd have never made you as an adrenalin junkie,' Tess said. 'You really ready for this?'

Pinky looked down the steep, rickety steps. 'They don't have a stair lift?'

His agility also belied his build. Although he carried excessive weight, he could move with the grace of a champion sumo wrestler when necessary, and he was as strong as one too. Po had disappeared within the nearest structure, so after descending the stairs Tess aimed down an overgrown trail towards the lakeside. 'We should start there and work back to meet him.'

'Ladies before gentlemen,' Pinky said with a flourish of his hand. 'But keep that gun handy, you. First time you spot pumpkinhead, put a bullet between his teeth. We can worry about ruining the rest of his day later.'

Tess led the way again.

'What is this goddamn place, anyway?' Pinky asked as they pushed through branches wielding wicked thorns. 'I'm sure I saw something like it on *Scooby Doo*.'

During her research Tess had glanced at a description of Quabbin Reservoir, the largest body of water in Massachusetts. When it was formed, swathes of land were submerged, some small towns were even evacuated to give way to the man-made lake. The reservoir was built to supply water to as far away as Boston on the coast and all points between, and was an incredible undertaking back in the 1930s. How many people had been dispossessed? She suspected there might have been many homes and businesses abandoned along the emerging shoreline, too, this old factory being one of the casualties of progress. She'd spotted the stack and the water wheels and thought that this was a precursor to the newer hydro-electricity plants fed by the lake, but Pinky's description suited it better. It was like a creepy haunted building in her mind too. Sadly, she hoped the ghosts of Jasmine and the other abducted girls weren't its resident spooks.

The path sloped downward, and over the decades the walls of the buildings nearest them had borne the brunt of the minor slippage of the landscape and the constant assault of the elements. Some had cracked, others collapsed, and tin-sheet roofing had spilled down to fill lots piled with crumbling masonry and rotting timber. They were still a good hundred and fifty yards from the shoreline when the heavens opened and rain lashed the foliage.

'Let's try to find a way inside here,' Tess suggested, indicating a gap in the shrubbery. The undergrowth appeared beaten down by the local wildlife, and offered passage to an entrance into a larger structure that looked less weather-beaten than the rest.

Pinky didn't look keen, but he followed, cursing under his breath at the branches that snagged round his feet, and at the rain now invading his clothing. Tess reached the door. It was wooden, and crumbling with rot. It had become skewed in the frame, only held in place by a chain so ancient it had rusted to a single solid lump. 'Crap!' said Tess.

'Stand aside,' said Pinky. He grasped the chain in his hands.

'You won't break that,' Tess told him.

'Don't have to,' he replied as he yanked the chain and the handle it was fixed to from the rotted door.

'I stand corrected.' Tess smiled at him, as he pulled the rest of the broken door out of its frame and let it fall on the nearest bushes.

'Ladies first,' he said again, and wiped rust and splinters from his palms.

Tess peeked inside the open portal. Then followed it by quickly stepping inside and sweeping the area with her gun. 'Clear,' she said.

'You call this clear?' Pinky eyed the mounds of junk that had fallen from an upper floor when the floorboards gave out. 'How'd you suggest we get over that death trap?'

'If we stick close to the walls there should be a way through. C'mon. What's the worst that can happen?'

Pinky blinked up at the yawning hole in the ceiling above. 'I don't even want to think about it, me.'

Tess picked a way around the mound of rubble and shattered furniture. Pinky followed, one eye on the ceiling as if he expected it to collapse at any second. He wasn't happy until they were through the next door and he had a solid ceiling overhead again. He bumped into Tess, who'd halted. She lifted her left hand for silence.

'Did you hear that?'

'All I hear is my heart in my mouth,' Pinky admitted.

'There!'

This time the faint sound couldn't be denied.

'That was a woman's scream,' Pinky announced.

'They're here.' Tess looked at Pinky wide-eyed. 'They're really here, Pinky.'

'So let's go get them, us,' he said, and she felt a wave of gratitude pass through her at his selfless bravery.

'I've something to do first.' She dug out her cell and hit the last number on her call list.

'Detective Ratcliffe,' she said without preamble. 'Please tell me the cavalry are on the way. I'm inside the factory I told you about and just heard the scream of a woman. Somebody is being hurt, right now!'

'Tess, I warned you to stand down, damn it!' the detective replied harshly, but behind her voice Tess was relieved to hear the wail of a siren. 'But I guess you're there now, and I'm still on my way. What have you got?'

'First you should know I'm here with two male colleagues, so please don't come in shooting. We've gained entry to the old water plant and just heard a woman screaming from somewhere further inside. She sounds like she's being beaten. We're going to look for her now.'

'We're only fifteen minutes out. Stay where you are and leave it to us.'

Distantly a woman's shriek echoed again.

'Fifteen minutes is way too long,' Tess croaked. 'I have to do something now. Just get here, Detective, as quickly as possible.'

Tess ended the call.

'Maybe we should do as she said,' Pinky counselled. 'We don't know if Randall's armed.'

'I'm armed,' Tess replied and held up the gun in emphasis.

Pinky looked at the old gun with some doubt. 'I meant if he spots us coming he might kill the girl before we can help.'

'Pinky, can't you hear? He's killing her now.'

'I hear. Let's go.'

Their feet clattered through debris as they charged along a corridor. Another door barred progress but Tess took a leaf out of Pinky's book and used brute force to make a way through with a jumping kick that knocked it off its hinges. The crash echoed through the ancient building, and the screaming stopped. But nearer by fresh voices were raised in frantic calls for help. Two voices, Tess realized. 'We have to free them first,' she decided, and ran in their direction, Pinky following. She hoped Po had also heard the original screeches and gone to their source. She could only pray that the cessation of the woman's agonized squeals meant Po had stopped her abuse; the alternative was that she was too late to be saved.

# THIRTY-SIX

Rain pelted the windshield and the hood steamed as John Trojak brought his car to a halt fifty yards short of the Mustang. He peered through the smeared screen, wondering if Po or any of the others were still inside the muscle car, sheltering from the latest downpour. They would have to be nuts to go poking around in this weather, unless urgency forced them.

'Drive closer.' Cal Hopewell shoved the gun against the back of Trojak's head.

'You want them to see us?'

'I don't care if they see us. I'm confident I can handle a bunch of amateurs. Don't forget I'm a highly trained Marine.'

'Hooah,' Trojak replied sarcastically.

'That's "Oorah", asshole. If you're trying to be snarky, at least get your fucking facts right.' Hopewell leaned forward for a better look. 'They aren't even in the car. They've already gone inside those buildings down there.'

Trojak drove the car forward and parked alongside the Mustang. He kept the engine running.

'Hoping for an early finish?' Hopewell asked sarcastically. 'Turn off the engine and pass back the keys.'

Trojak complied without comment.

'Hands on the wheel, buddy,' Hopewell reminded him.

Trojak gripped the steering wheel.

'Don't move until I tell you.'

'We're getting out?'

'Not afraid of a little rain, are you? The detective and her buddies have gone inside for one reason. They're looking for someone. If it's Jasmine, then great, I'll take her off them. If it's that sicko Jesse Randall, I need to speak with him before they hand him over to the cops.' The back door clunked open, and Hopewell slid out. The gun was an ever-present threat alongside Trojak's head, even for the brief moment before

Hopewell pulled open the driver's door. 'OK. Out, with your hands behind your ears.'

Rain stung his features as Trojak struggled out of the car: it wasn't easy without the assistance of his hands.

'Clasp your fingers together,' Hopewell ordered.

As soon as his fingers were knitted, Hopewell stepped behind Trojak and grabbed them. He pushed the car doors shut with his knee. He never once lowered the gun. 'Walk. Take those steps down, but one at a time. Try to pull free, I'll shoot you where you stand.'

'What if I slip and you let go?'

'Simple answer: don't slip.'

The warped boards that formed the steps were slick with wet moss. Trojak negotiated them as warned, taking single tentative steps then settling his stance, before moving down again. 'Jesus, you move like a geriatric,' Hopewell growled.

'Just ensuring I don't trip as advised.'

'You know, Johnny, I can't make up my mind if you're incredibly stupid or incredibly brave. Brave I can deal with, stupidity not so much. Whatever, don't fucking try me.'

Trojak picked up a little speed.

Hopewell descended behind him, still gripping his clasped hands, but his attention was straying. He checked out the nearest structure for any sign of movement. Rain in the treetops and on the nearby tin roofs made hearing anything else impossible. They reached the bottom and stood on a platform of poured concrete. The concrete had crumbled at three corners and bushes had invaded the cracks. To the left was a ten-foot drop to the sloping hillside that was overgrown with shrubs, to the right a set of concrete stairs allowed foot passage to a cinder track that ran around the nearest building. Ahead was an entrance to a foyer area, the doors hanging askew in the frame. 'I guess that's the way inside,' Hopewell said.

Trojak took a step, but Hopewell jerked back on his captured hands. Trojak grunted, and struggled to find his footing.

'End of the line for you, Johnny.'

His fingers were released, but Trojak didn't move. He knew the gun still threatened him.

'Turn around,' Hopewell commanded.

Trojak did, and the rain was in his face again. He squinted through the droplets on his lashes, as he slowly lowered his arms.

'So what happens now, Cal?' he asked.

'Can't have you slowing me down; can't let you go.'

'So you're going to shoot me?'

'I don't have any other option,' Hopewell said glibly.

'I'll go and wait in the car,' Trojak offered. 'Not as if I can go anywhere seeing as you've got the keys.'

'I won't need a driver for the return trip.'

'So old times don't account for anything?'

'We were never friends.' Hopewell lowered the gun so it was centred on Trojak's heart. 'And speaking of old times, you said earlier if you'd been at the party that night you'd have taken my knife and stuck it in my eye.'

'Still would, given a chance,' Trojak admitted. 'Shame you took my knife off me back at Tess's place or I'd have tried now.'

'That's why I can't give you a chance. I've made up my mind about you. You're brave *and* stupid. But stupidity has the edge: you do realize you just talked me into killing you, right?'

'You didn't require convincing,' Trojak said.

'Not really,' Hopewell smirked.

Without warning Trojak lunged away.

For the briefest moment, Hopewell was slow to react, his mind still working on where best to shoot Trojak. Now his options were limited, as Trojak raced to the edge of the platform. Hopewell fired, and blood puffed on the air. Trojak twisted, his arms outstretched as his feet swept from beneath him and he pitched over the ten-foot drop. From where he was in a shooter's crouch on the platform, Hopewell heard Trojak pound the earth on the downslope, and the rattle and crackle of him breaking twigs as he rolled. He stalked to the edge of the platform, the gun held in both hands. He aimed below, but there was no sign of Trojak. If he hadn't seen proof that he'd hit his target, the blood on the platform and glistening on leaves below, he'd have been more concerned. If Trojak wasn't dead, he was mortally wounded, and had rolled into the damp space beneath the platform to die.

Hopewell stared for a moment longer, then shrugged and

turned towards the foyer. He had more important targets than
trying to root out a man already beyond help. He'd shot a man,
most probably killed him, and that meant he'd crossed a line
he hadn't even done while he was with the United States Marine
Corps. It was a line he couldn't retreat over and knew where
this new direction would lead him. He'd admitted to Trojak that
he saw Jasmine Reed as unfinished business, and he was determined to do to her what she fought against all those years
earlier. Holding his gun by his side, he dipped his other hand
in his jacket pocket and took out the lock-knife he'd liberated
from Trojak. He'd cut Jasmine when she'd defied him, he'd cut
her again, but only when he'd had his fill of her. He thought
about Jesse Randall, suspected of abducting women and keeping
them prisoner at this decrepit old factory. He felt no affinity
with the ugly son of a bitch, though he did experience a trickle
of respect for the man's audacity. Though not for a second did
it sway him: Randall had taken what was rightfully his and that
was unforgivable.

# THIRTY-SEVEN

I t was similar to trying to make her way through a funhouse, one dressed for Hallowe'en, Tess thought as she took the twisting passageways deeper inside the derelict structure. Many times she met blind ends and turns that led away from the girls' shrieking, and twice she and Pinky had to clamber over spilled rubble or kick through locked doors. Overhead the roof rattled and shook as the wind picked up, and the drumming of rain made hearing more difficult.

'Which way now, Tess?' Pinky asked, as they faced yet another dead end.

'The most direct,' Tess announced and approached the blockage in the passage. It was dark, but she brought up the flashlight app on her cellphone. She shone it over what was evidently a recent addition to the structure. Boards had been nailed to a framework of timber to block the passage. She wondered how long Jesse Randall had used the factory as his playground, and how many other adaptations he'd made to it to enjoy a self-contained space.

'Can you see anything we can use as a lever?' she asked Pinky.

'Shine your light this way,' said Pinky and moved back the direction they'd approached from.

Tess aimed the light after him and watched him root around in a pile of junk heaped against a wall. He came up with a length of steel pipe as long as her forearm, on the end of which was a coupling and some kind of valve. 'This should do,' he said, and tested the weight in his opposite palm. 'Stand aside, pretty Tess, this job requires brawn over brain.'

He went at the partition wall as if he was hewing down a tree with an axe, and with only a few hefty swings had smashed open a hole that Tess could peek through. The passage stretched on ahead. 'Go for it, Pinky,' she encouraged and he lay in again. Once he was satisfied that the boards were sufficiently weakened, he changed tactics, using his heels to kick a way through. As they passed through the barrier, he paused to wipe sweat from his brow. 'That manly stuff is rather liberating, hey?' he said with a grin.

'The next barricade's mine,' Tess told him with a wink.

They set off jogging, with Pinky puffing and panting now. Tess couldn't afford to slow. Their demolition of the wall must have been heard throughout the factory, and if Randall had given Po the slip, he might very well be on his way back to where they were heading.

'Hell . . . I haven't run like this . . . since trying to get . . . to the head of the chow line . . . at Angola, me . . .' Pinky wheezed behind her. 'Gotta stop soon . . . Tess . . . before I cough up a lung.'

'It can't be far now,' she said without slowing.

'Legs are burning . . .' he huffed.

'There's no gain without pain,' she replied.

'Actually, I managed . . . to gain all this weight . . . an' it was painless.'

Any other time, Tess would have welcomed humour, but right then couldn't help feel it was inappropriate. The pain those girls must have suffered was no laughing matter.

She slid to a halt.

Pinky almost flattened her, but at the last second proved he still retained some agility, by swerving around her and caroming off a corner in the wall. He spun around, hefting the pipe he'd carried with him like a club. His chest rose and fell as he gasped for air. 'Whassup?'

'There,' she replied and pointed to their right.

A dozen yards away somebody hammered against a door. Another ten yards further on a woman slapped another door, crying out because she'd recognized their voices as belonging to strangers. 'Over here! Over here! Please help me!'

Tess and Pinky moved closer, Tess's revolver leading the way.

Now the woman in the room nearest took up the caterwauling.

'It's OK,' Tess called out, 'we're here to help.'

She'd put away her cell after Pinky knocked down the

partition, but she pulled it now, but only so she could switch on the flashlight app.

She shone it on the nearest door, then flicked it at the other. The backwash of the glow showed similar doors on the opposite side of the corridor. One stood open. She took a brief look inside. It was empty but for an old engine block, a flattened bucket, an empty plastic bottle and some smaller items of trash she couldn't identify. The ammonia stench from within raised her gorge, and she ducked out into the hall again. She turned to look at the nearest locked door, and was aware of Pinky gawping alongside her.

'Please, please get us out,' begged the nearest woman.

The other woman was overcome with emotion and now wept.

Pinky eyed the bolts and padlocks, then his pipe, but he stepped forward to attempt to wrench them loose.

Tess held on to his elbow. 'I told you the next barricade was mine.'

She had no intention of smashing the locks loose – she doubted either of them could – but she didn't need to. Affixed to the wall was an old wooden box, the door hanging open, keys on hooks inside. She passed them to Pinky while she covered the passageway with her gun. The doors took old-fashioned iron keys, while the padlocks were newer Yale locks. Pinky had to experiment before he found the correct ones, but soon had the first door open. He stood back, his lips stretched wide in an embarrassed grimace as he saw a naked girl standing before him. The girl seemed unaware of her state of undress, and held up her wrists to him. She was shackled to an oil drum filled with concrete.

Once he'd found the correct key, and unlocked her cuffs, the girl fell against Pinky. He sheltered her under his armpit and helped walk her from the cell. She blinked wildly, screwing her face as Tess shone the torch over her. The girl was dirty, tattooed, bruised and scratched, but recognizable.

'Lucy?' Tess asked her. 'Lucy Jo Colman?'

Lucy's mouth gaped, but then she nodded. 'I thought nobody would ever come,' she said, and tears flooded down her face.

'Hush now, honey,' Pinky soothed her. 'We're going to get you out of here.'

The other girl began banging on her door.

'We're coming,' Tess called to her. 'We'll be right there.'

Pinky slipped out of his coat and draped it around Lucy Colman's shoulders. Gratefully Lucy wrapped it around herself, as she made thanks under her breath to whatever god was looking out for her after all.

Tess wanted to check with Lucy about so many things. Where's Jasmine? How many other girls are here? Where's Jesse Randall? But she put her questions aside. She helped usher Lucy along the corridor while Pinky began sorting through keys again.

He opened the door in short time, and wasn't so abashed on seeing a second naked girl. He went to her, soothing her with a calm voice, and unclipped her from a length of chain that bound her to an enormous iron cog. The girl stepped tentatively into the hall before him, and this time it was Tess who shed her jacket and hung it over the girl's shoulders, but only after a brief inspection. As was Lucy, the girl had been bruised and cut, but there the similarity ended. This girl was neither tattooed nor carried old wounds. Unsurprisingly Tess didn't recognize her, as she wasn't one of the women she'd originally listed. Emma Clancy had warned her about looking for patterns in chaos, and she was ashamed to admit she had done so, and had missed this victim entirely through her short-sightedness. The tattoos and especially the scars might have had nothing to do with Randall's process of selecting victims. In hindsight, the scarring was probably about Tess projecting her personal insecurities on the victims. She thought she was over the trauma of almost losing a hand, but apparently not: it was still there lurking in the back of her mind. But it didn't matter, she'd still identified that girls were being taken, where nobody else had. For that she wasn't smug, only thankful that she'd followed her hunch.

'I'm Tess Grey,' she told the young woman. 'I'm a private investigator and I've been looking for you all. What's your name?'

'Maria,' the girl whispered. 'I'm Maria Belfort.'

'Well, Maria, you're safe now. You and Lucy are both safe.'

The two girls shared a look, and there was some confusion on their faces. Tess realized this was possibly the first time they'd laid eyes on each other, and possibly learned their fellow captive's name. It didn't matter because they were bonded by experience. The two girls went to each other and hugged, weeping silently. Tess allowed them a few seconds, but none of them were safe where they stood.

'The one who held you?' Tess prompted.

'He's a monster,' said Lucy.

'Who is he?' Tess went on.

'I never heard his name,' Lucy said. Maria also shook her head.

'Is he a big guy,' Tess went on, and traced her hand down the side of her face, 'with a huge scar down here?'

Lucy looked at Maria. 'I never saw his face. He always made us turn our backs to him, then he hooded and gagged us.' Maria nodded to agree that was what she'd experienced of their captor too. 'But,' Lucy went on, 'he was big. Muscular. Very strong. A monster.'

Pinky exhaled loudly, and went to fetch his pipe. 'Let's see how strong the bastard is,' he said under his breath.

'There were other girls . . .' Tess prompted.

'Yes,' Lucy said, the more talkative of the two. 'There were three others.' She stopped, swallowed hard, and Tess saw regret wash over her features.

'The bastard murdered a girl the first day I was here,' Maria announced. 'But I don't know who she was; I only heard.'

Carrie Mae Borger. Tess could have spoken her name, but decided to keep it to herself for now. She didn't want either woman to dwell on who had failed to escape this hellish prison, but on who now was safe.

'The other two?' she asked gently.

'Jasmine and Elsa,' Lucy nodded, and Maria joined in.

'We were forbidden to speak, but Elsa told us her name, and so did Jasmine. They were punished . . .'

'We heard somebody screaming earlier,' said Tess.

'That was Elsa,' said Maria. 'She escaped her cell and ran away. She was wasting her time. There's no way out of here and she was caught.'

'We're getting you out,' Pinky promised, and Tess thought she'd never seen him so adamant.

'What about Jasmine?' She felt a pang of guilt, because none of the girls was more important than another, and yet Tess had pledged she'd do everything to bring Jasmine safely home.

'He took her away,' said Lucy and pointed down the corridor, 'but that was yesterday, and she wasn't brought back.'

Tess slowly closed her eyes.

'OK,' she said, coming to a decision. She turned and looked up at Pinky. 'We have to split up. You take Lucy and Maria out to the car, I'm going to keep looking for the others.'

Pinky shook his head. 'Uh-nuh, Tess. Nicolas will never forgive me if I let anything happen to you.'

And I'll never forgive myself if I let anything happen to those girls, Tess thought. 'The police are coming, Pinky. They'll be here soon enough. Get Lucy and Maria safely to Detective Ratcliffe, I'm going to help Po bring out the others.'

Pinky searched the plaintive faces of the two girls, and finally nodded. 'I promised I'd get you out, and I'm a man of my word, me.' He turned to Tess with a scolding look. 'But don't you dare get yourself hurt, you, pretty Tess.'

She held up her gun, and tapped it against her head in salute. 'Brains win over brawn every time. Don't worry, I won't let the bastard get his hands on me.'

The looks Lucy and Maria aimed at her didn't do much for her confidence.

As Pinky ushered the girls before him, back the way they'd come, Tess turned and peered down the corridor Lucy had indicated. She could swear that the walls were closing in on her.

She glanced back, but Pinky and his wards had disappeared from sight. She shuddered out a breath.

'OK, Tess,' she said out loud, 'this was your idea.'

Before she could change her mind, she set off.

# THIRTY-EIGHT

The presence of an old Ford truck with a rigid plastic canopy on the back confirmed that although she might have been wrong about his process for selecting victims, Tess was spot on when she'd identified Jesse Randall as the likely perpetrator. The truck was rusty, at least fifteen years old, but was still a formidable beast. It had bull bars over the front grille, and when she peeked in the back there was a small motorbike lying on the flat bed. She assumed that Randall used the bike to get to the abduction sites so he could collect the vehicles of the women he'd snatched, and bring them here to dispose of them in the huge troughs. The bike was small enough that a man of Randall's strength could throw it into the back of a car for the return journey.

Finding her way to the cavernous room had been no mean feat. But once she'd negotiated a room crammed with ancient machinery, chock full of ducting and pipes, she'd discovered a passage unlike any other she'd walked since entering the ancient structure. It had largely been cleared of debris, and there were even weak bulbs strung along the ceiling, so it was a route that Randall must use regularly. Finally she'd found her way out on to a balcony-cum-platform of sorts and directly below her was a trestle table, recently collapsed if the fresh splinters that poked from the broken ends were anything to go by. She found some steps leading down, and almost missed the curtained doorway to her left. She considered taking a quick look inside, but her gaze was drawn to the distant truck, and she went towards it instead, comparing the licence number with the one she'd checked against Randall's ownership details.

She saw the submerged cars, and they numbered five in total, for which she was mildly relieved. In her search for a predator she had only missed Maria Belfort off the list of his possible victims.

There was a huge roller shutter at the lakeside end of the

room. She wondered what kinds of machinery were once housed in the troughs to require such a large door, but couldn't begin to picture them. Best she kept her mind on the task at hand.

With no idea where Randall was, she'd tried to be as quiet as possible. Stepping on grit and crunching it underfoot was unavoidable, but the noise from the teeming rain and the wind straining the shutter covered most sounds she made. But evidently she hadn't stayed undetected.

She was stunned when two hands suddenly thrust through a slot in a nearby door, and a female whispered, 'Help me, please.'

Tess stood still, her gun grasped in both hands, as she stared at the tattoos that extended all the way to the woman's knuckles.

'Jasmine?' she asked, barely above a whisper, because she could barely believe she'd almost passed by the girl she'd been seeking.

'Who are you?' Jasmine replied.

'I'm here for you,' Tess replied, and trotted forward.

'Who are you?' Jasmine asked again, but this time her voice shook with emotion.

'My name is Tess Grey. I'm here for you, Jasmine.' There was emotion in Tess's voice too.

'But how?'

'I've been looking for you.'

Tess touched Jasmine's fingers and the girl held on.

'H . . . how did you find me?'

'It doesn't matter; I'm here now and I'm going to take you home.' She gently extricated her fingers from the girl's hands, and tested the lock. There was no nearby handy key box. Could she shoot off the padlocks? She'd only six bullets, and a very dangerous sexual predator lurking nearby: could she spare even a single round?

'Are you chained up inside there?' she asked, recalling how Lucy and Maria had been secured within their cells.

'No, it's just the door keeping me in, but that bastard has the key.'

Tess glanced back at the truck.

'OK. Here's what I'm going to try to do,' said Tess and told Jasmine her plan.

'What if he has the key to the truck on him?'

'It's an old truck, I'm sure I can get it started.'

Back when she was a girl, her grandfather had an old Dodge pickup. He'd lost the keys, but bypassed the ignition with the help of a few extra bits of wire and a screwdriver. He'd taught Tess how to hotwire an engine, although, being a NYPD cop, had also warned of severe punishment if ever he caught her joyriding in someone else's car. She was positive he'd forgive her now.

She went to the cab and opened it. Randall had left the keys in the ignition. She ran back to the locked room, as she shoved her gun in a pocket. 'Jasmine, get as far back from the door as you can.'

'I don't hear the truck,' Jasmine answered.

'Give me a minute. Oh, and there's a change of plan, I'm not going to try to pull the door off its hinges.'

Returning to the truck she clambered inside, and twisted the ignition key. The engine roared. She threw the gear stick, let out the clutch and hit the gas. The truck responded with a lurch, and she fought the steering, having forgotten for a moment what it was like to drive an old truck without the luxury of power steering. She missed the nearest trench by a whisker, hauling down on the steering wheel and plunging directly at Jasmine's cell.

The bull bars smashed into the door. The locks couldn't withstand such force, and ripped loose as it was smashed inward, against the jamb. The truck's engine stalled, and Tess sank back in the seat, stunned by the violence of the collision. She shook to clear her head, and then reached for the ignition again. The engine turned over but didn't start, and for a second Tess feared she'd only placed another impenetrable barrier between her and Jasmine. She pulled the choke, tromped the gas a few times, tried again, and this time the engine roared to life. She tasted the fumes, found the reverse gear, and backed away. The bull bars were jammed in the ruined door, but they helped wrench it open. As Tess halted the truck, the door fell free and she was happy to have torn the entire thing out of its frame.

Jasmine, tattooed and scarred, but every bit alive, stepped out of the room towards her. Tess jumped out the idling truck, pulling at her shirt to offer to the girl, because she had a T-shirt beneath, but Jasmine shook her head. 'My clothes are in there,' she said, pointing at an adjacent room.

'Grab them quickly,' Tess urged her and took out her revolver. 'We're getting the hell out of here.'

Jasmine was only seconds inside the room, and emerged again clutching a bundle of clothing to her scarred abdomen.

'Get in the truck,' Tess said. 'You can dress inside.'

'I'm OK here,' Jasmine assured her and began to sort through the clothing.

'That's not what I meant. Quick, get in.' The noise of the rescue could bring Randall running.

Jasmine joined Tess in the truck and slipped into a pair of denims, while Tess checked over her shoulder and got the truck moving.

There was no way she was going to lead Jasmine all the way back through the old water works when a much closer exit beckoned. She reversed at speed into the corroded roller shutter, punching their way to freedom.

Tess would have preferred to drive them both back to the Mustang, but the road went in the wrong direction. If she'd had only Jasmine's welfare to worry about then she'd have taken it, but there were Pinky and the other girls, and most importantly of all, Po. She'd been so engaged in the hunt for Jasmine that she'd put the welfare of her lover to the back of her mind, but now she'd saved Jasmine, her concern for him avalanched through her.

'OK, now get out. We have to run,' she told Jasmine, who was still shocked by the way she'd been catapulted backwards from the factory into the middle of a storm.

Jasmine climbed out, started pulling on a T-shirt. She was soaked within seconds, her dark hair hanging loose around her face, but even one layer of clothing made her look less vulnerable.

Tess was about to join her, but if Randall had heard their dramatic escape and came running, she didn't want to leave behind anything he could use to aid his own escape. She rammed the truck into gear, released the brake and then jumped from the open door. The truck barrelled through the metal curtain it had so recently torn to pieces. Tess heard a satisfying splash as it went into the nearest scum-filled trench.

Jasmine was still barefoot, but she didn't care. When Tess urged her up the overgrown path alongside the derelict buildings, she ran exactly as one who'd dreamed to do so for too long. Tess jogged after her.

# THIRTY-NINE

S udden death didn't come to Elsa as she'd hoped. No massive coronary, or embolism to the brain, to save her from prolonged suffering. Dripping blood from his torn chin and throat, the monster knelt on her stomach, grinding her so hard she felt her innards were about to erupt from her orifices. His fingers dug at her face and throat as he repeatedly slammed the back of her skull into the ground. Starburst flashes scorched through her mind with each smack against the floor, but each time she remained cognizant and prone to further agony. Her strength had failed her, and she could do nothing to save herself except paw at him with her fingers, ineffectively.

After all the effort she'd put into fighting back and escaping, there was nothing left in her. No, that couldn't be true. Because lucidity was both a curse and a splinter of hope as he finally rose from her, and stood touching the freshest wounds on his face. Elsa lay still, feigning unconsciousness, and she was gratified to hear him moan as he traced the edges of her bite mark.

Where there's a will there's a way, Elsa thought. It was one of those old sayings that rolled glibly off people's tongues, and she was certain she'd used it in the past when referring to trivial problem-solving, but now she held on to the thought.

Unlike the brutish monster she'd once fancied he was, he wasn't unstoppable. He could be hurt, and not only through physical retaliation.

She snapped open her eyes and stared up at him.

His one good eye twitched as he returned the look.

'You thought you were ugly before? Think again, mister,' she said, and laughter bubbled from her.

Her burping giggles stopped him in his tracks.

'Look at you! You're so fucking pathetic!' Her giggles grew stronger, uncontainable. 'Not only can't you get a girl like a normal man' – she guffawed – 'you can't handle them when you take them by force. How freakin' ridiculous is that?'

He shook with rage, but there was also indecision – maybe even trepidation – in the stoop of his shoulders and the way his bottom lip trembled.

'You've beaten the crap out of me,' Elsa crowed, 'but what exactly have you achieved? Nothing, that's what! A big fat fucking zero . . . just like you are!'

'Shut up!'

'Shut up yourself. I'm sick of listening to your whining voice!'

Elsa pushed up on her elbows.

'Don't move or . . .'

'Or what? You'll hit me again? Ha! Like I'm afraid of you?'

'Bitch!'

'So now it's name-calling? Don't make me laugh, you momma's boy.'

'Shut up!' he bellowed, but he didn't advance. He stood bent at the waist, his fingers flexing in and out.

Elsa sat, drawing in her chain. Her manic laughter had faded, but not her disdain. 'Oh! So momma didn't like you either? That's why you have to hurt girls, right? 'Cause your momma didn't love you enough?'

He swung away from her, clubbing his knuckles into the wall. A depression was left in the crumbling boards. 'Shut up, shut up, *shuuuutttuuuuppp!*'

'And if I don't, what the hell are you going to do? *Whisper* me to death?'

When he rounded on her again, his teeth clenched, his deformed lips twisted in an agonized snarl, Elsa stood.

'Get out of my way,' she warned him.

His hair squirmed over his scalp as he tried to comprehend her command.

Before he could react further a boom went through the corridor, and Elsa could have sworn the ground shifted underfoot.

The man glanced back the way they'd just come from.

He looked back at Elsa, and she recognized fear in his gaze now. He must have realized that he had lost control not only of Elsa, but of everything. He took a step towards her, but flinched, and looked back again. There was a roaring sound that Elsa recognized as a straining engine. Another rumble shook the corridor.

'Ha!' said Elsa. 'It sounds as if your favourite girl just got away. If you know what's good for you, you'll stand aside and let me go too.'

He was caught by indecision – grab Elsa and finish her, or rush back and check on Jasmine?

Elsa took a surreptitious step backwards.

The engine roared again, and moments later there was a metallic shriek, the rending of metal. The man started towards the source of the racket, and Elsa tensed to run. He spun around and aimed a finger at her. 'No! You're coming with me.'

Ordinarily she would have spun on her heel and run for it as she'd hoped to seconds before. But if she was correct and help had arrived, she should run towards it not away. She feigned acceptance, and held up the length of chain to him. After a brief pause, he reached for the proffered chain. She let it drop. Air snapped from him in annoyance and he grabbed for the trailing chain. It was the moment she'd been waiting for: she dodged past him, and ran shrieking down the corridor towards the cavernous room they'd come from. With a bellow, the man hurtled after her, again trying to stamp on the trailing chain, but missing.

Elsa slapped through the plastic curtain and was again on the raised platform. Daylight flooded through the hole in the roller shutter. She thought she spotted movement, and hoped it was Jasmine running for her life. But in the next second the old truck hurtled back inside, and almost somersaulted into one of the deep pits. Scummy water gouted over it, but it didn't fully submerge, stopped by a sunken vehicle beneath.

The yawning hole in the shutter beckoned her, and Elsa started for it. To her left the man burst through the plastic curtain, and he stopped momentarily, stunned by what he saw. His gaze slipped from the hole, to his wrecked truck, to where a gap had been punched into the room where he'd confined Jasmine.

Elsa couldn't go for the stairs down. He would easily cut her off, so she vaulted off the platform and landed on the broken trestle she'd earlier demolished. Her legs were so weak they gave under her, and she spilled over the pieces, earning another graze when a broken end jabbed her ribs. Her pursuer charged down the steps, but she was unsure if he was coming for her or Jasmine. She scrambled up, and hobbled away. She was jerked to a halt: the trailing length of chain was wedged in the broken trestle. No! Not now! She yanked her wrists, but the hold on the chain was resolute. The man turned towards her. He glanced at the bolthole in the shutter, then at her and his mouth turned up in a facsimile of a smile when he spotted her bad luck. He began edging round, to block her escape route, watching as she strained to loosen herself. He stooped and picked up a leg from the broken table, wielding it like an ogre in one of those dark fantasies she used to picture. This time he was determined to smash in her skull.

A figure vaulted over Elsa from the platform, landing between them.

She was as stunned as her abuser at the sudden appearance of the tall, broad-shouldered man, especially when he held up a knife.

The newcomer obviously wasn't a cop.

He was clad in soiled denims, and his dark hair was plastered to his brow. He glimpsed once at her, and she caught a flash of turquoise, and his mouth turned up at one end.

Had she called it all wrong? Did her abductor have a confederate, who'd come to assist him now that things had gone haywire? Otherwise, why would a knife-wielding man be here?

'Is this ugly creep bothering you, ma'am?' he asked.

Elsa, who had defied every effort made by her abuser to knock her cold, fainted, but this time through sheer relief.

# FORTY

Sirens caterwauled in the distance. Through the rain and wind it was hard to tell how far away the police were, but they couldn't be more than minutes. Thank God Detective Ratcliffe had put away any doubt and brought plenty of officers, sirens competing.

Jasmine was slightly ahead of Tess, pushing through the foliage that obscured the path, but they were nearing the point where she'd entered the structure with Pinky, and that meant they weren't far from the Mustang.

They were soaked through, but Jasmine looked as if she could care less – she was only relieved to be out in the open air. Tess thought it remarkable that after weeks of confinement, suffering constant abuse, the young woman could put a foot in front of the other, let alone run.

They passed the animal trail Tess and Pinky had used earlier, and Tess urged Jasmine on. 'It's not far now, and then we'll be safe.'

'Wh-what about the others?' Jasmine asked and almost came to a halt. Tess ushered her on, one palm on her shoulder.

'We found Lucy and Maria; one of my friends got them out.' She *hoped* Pinky had got them out. 'That's when I came back to find you.'

'But what about Elsa?'

Tess thought of the screams she'd heard earlier, and how they'd abruptly ceased. The ensuing silence didn't bode well for Elsa Moore's chances of getting out alive, because they had been the screams of someone at death's door.

'Don't worry, I've another friend helping Elsa.' She wanted to add, 'If anyone can get her out safely it's him,' but she couldn't be certain Po had gotten to her in time. Best remain hopeful, she thought, and kept quiet.

'Elsa managed to ring you in time?' Jasmine asked, and again almost halted. 'Thank God!'

'Yes,' Tess said. She pressed Jasmine on. 'Thankfully she got out a call.'

She didn't understand the circumstances behind it, but now knew who was responsible for switching on Jasmine's cell. Elsa hadn't gotten out a call, but the fact that the phone had connected to a network had been enough to pinpoint its location. Without that one lead, she doubted she'd have found any of the girls in time. How ironic would it be if the girls' saviour were the one to pay for her heroism with her life?

Please, Po, she prayed silently. Save Elsa.

They rushed along the cinder trail, and came out on the low ground adjacent to the old foyer. There was a set of steps up to a dais that bridged an ancient gulley. But Tess didn't send Jasmine up them. When she'd first come down from the parking area, she'd come off the old wooden steps on to a foot trail. She looked for the way back up. It was muddy and rocky, not an easy route for Jasmine with her bare feet. 'That way,' she said, and turned Jasmine for the concrete steps. Jasmine's strength finally failed her. She paused at the bottom step, hands on her thighs as she bent and wheezed. 'Not far now,' Tess reassured her. 'We only have to go a little further, I promise.' She wrapped an arm around the girl's shoulders and supported her upwards. She could feel Jasmine's bones through the thin, sopping T-shirt and understood how emaciated she was; no wonder she lacked the strength to haul herself up those last few steps.

As they gained the platform, Tess spotted the wooden steps up to the car. If she had to carry Jasmine up them on her back she would. She looked for Pinky, but the angle didn't afford a view to where they'd left the Mustang.

'I'll help you up,' Tess said and offered her hand. Jasmine took it gratefully. But before she got going, Jasmine tilted her head up to the rain, and let it patter on her face. She licked the moisture gratefully.

'Come on, there're drinks in the car,' Tess told her.

Jasmine's dark green eyes sparkled at the prospect of quenching her thirst, and took the first step. Tess supported her, surprised by the strength in her injured wrist. There was a time not too long ago when she feared her hand would never recover from almost being chopped off.

'Hold it right there!'

A jolt of cold electricity shot through Tess. She recognized the voice, and couldn't comprehend how Calvin Hopewell had found his way to the remote site. She turned, bringing up the Ruger.

'Drop your weapon,' Hopewell snapped, even before she'd got a bead on him.

He had emerged unnoticed from the foyer building as she'd supported Jasmine on to the first step, and his stance was firm, his gun held steady. He was toting a semi-automatic Glock 17. The man had trained as a Marine, he would know how to shoot. Tess allowed the revolver to slip from out of her grip, and swing over, so that she suspended it by her forefinger through the trigger guard. She held it out by her side as she completed her turn to face him.

'Let's not have any Annie Oakley shit,' Hopewell said. 'Drop the gun and kick it over here to me.'

Beside Tess, Jasmine was struck dumb. She sank on her butt, and a moan of defeat wheezed out of her. Tess reached back to her, keeping hold of her hand, and gave a reassuring squeeze. The woman sobbed.

'There was a time when I considered taking you,' Hopewell directed at Tess, 'came very close to it too, until you stuck that gun in my neck. You aren't going to be as lucky a second time. Drop the gun, or I'll put a bullet in your gut.'

She dropped the revolver, and toed it away.

'That's better,' Hopewell said and edged forward. He peered past Tess at the person he was really interested in. 'Hi, Jazz. Long time no see.'

Jasmine buried her face in her shoulder.

'So you're going to try pulling that coy crap again? I didn't buy it then, sure as hell don't buy it now.' Hopewell took another step, but his aim didn't shift from Tess. His gaze swept over both women. 'Help her up, Tess,' he said.

'Can't you hear those sirens?' Tess asked. 'You must know you've no hope of getting out of here. Give it up, Hopewell.'

'I hear them. That's why I want you to get Jazz up. There's a car up there and we're leaving before the cops arrive.'

'No,' Tess answered firmly. 'She isn't going anywhere with you.'

Hopewell tilted his head, squinting at her. 'No? You aren't in a position to refuse. Get her up, or I swear to God I'll put you down then drag her the fuck to my car by her hair.'

'You won't touch her again, you son of a bitch!'

'Get her up. Last chance, Tess.' He pointed the gun at her face.

Tess peered directly down the barrel of the gun. It looked depthless.

'You'll have to kill me first,' Tess assured him.

'You don't think I will? You don't think I'll blow your fucking brains out?'

'Cal,' she said reasonably. 'You haven't killed anyone yet. You hurt some people, Maxwell Carter kind of bad, but you're not a murderer. Not yet. Let us go, forget Jasmine and leave. That's your only chance.'

Hopewell laughed. 'That's what you know. How'd you think I got here, bitch? Remember a guy by the name of Trojak?'

Tess couldn't help the frown that etched her brow.

'I made him follow you here,' Hopewell confirmed. Then he mimed shooting. 'Then . . . Pow! Put one in the back of his head. So you see, it's too late for him, and it's too late for me. NOW GET JAZZ UP!'

The savagery of his yell set Tess back on her heels.

The sirens were now so close that Tess expected cops to swarm down the steps any second. She had to keep Hopewell talking, buy them some time.

He stormed forward, and rammed the Glock into her throat.

'How does *that* feel? Enough to motivate you?'

Jazz pulled on her outstretched arm.

'Stay there, Jasmine,' Tess said.

'He's going to kill you,' Jasmine croaked. She attempted to stand, hanging on to Tess for support, but Tess shrugged her loose and she slumped down on her backside again. If she got up and Hopewell forced them to a car, there'd be no stopping him from taking them both. She was seriously encouraging a bullet to her throat, but she stood her ground.

'You're a brave one, I'll give you that,' sneered Hopewell. 'But bravery doesn't cut it. Get moving.' He pushed Tess around, just as she caught a flash of movement. Her face must have betrayed her surprise, because Hopewell suddenly snapped around.

Pinky, with his iron pipe raised overhead like a club, charged from the foyer.

Hopewell cursed, swinging the gun away from Tess. She screeched a warning, but it was too late, and Pinky's only hope was to land a solid blow to Hopewell's head. Tess threw herself on Hopewell, just as the gun fired.

Pinky stumbled and fell, the pipe sliding from his fingers.

No! Blackness swept Tess's mind as she watched her friend collapse only feet away. She fought the shock, pulling at Hopewell, who took a step towards Pinky and aimed at his head. She dug her fingertips into his face, and he jerked his head aside. She rammed her shoulder into him but he outweighed her by half again. He set his feet, and swung the elbow of his gun arm into her face.

Stunned, Tess dropped on to her backside, just as Jasmine launched at Hopewell. He caught her under the chin with his free hand, held her at arm's length as she squealed and clawed. He ignored her, sneered down at Tess, and said, 'You're proving more trouble than you're worth.'

He jammed the gun to Tess's forehead.

She was terrified, but at least Pinky was safe from an immediate *coup de grâce*.

# FORTY-ONE

The clusters of poorly etched tattoos on Jesse Randall's hide reminded Po of some inmates' body art he'd come across during his time at Angola, Louisiana's notorious maximum-security prison better known as the Farm. Mostly black inmates populated Angola, but there was a minority of white prisoners who formed allegiances and marked themselves to show it: mess with one, and you messed with all. But Jesse's tats didn't resemble any of those displayed by any gangs Po was familiar with, and he suspected they had been inked into his skin for effect. The horrific mutilation of Randall's face he did believe was a product of his time inside: that wound looked like a punishment delivered by another prisoner who took umbrage against the sex offender, to mark him out as a beast. To your run-of-the-mill, law-abiding citizen, his appearance would be intimidating, but the scary image meant as little to Po as the man's steroid-induced muscles. He looked like a fearsome monster, but it didn't make him one.

Po held his knife close to his right hip, but the shiny metal kept drawing Randall's gaze. He repeatedly made fake lunges at Po, the table leg swinging but falling short. He would launch a genuine attack soon, once Po was off guard, but he wasn't ready yet to test his weapon against a blade.

'Give it up,' Po told him. 'The cops are outside, and you're going to prison, f'sure. Come at me, though, and you're going down permanently.'

He couldn't begin to understand the mind of the psycho, but Po guessed Randall wasn't thinking clearly. His best bet was to run for it, to try to evade the police, but he wasn't showing any sign of trying to make a break for it. Randall kept up the ineffective lunges and stabs with his club, as if trying to find a way through to Elsa Moore, who Po recognized from the photographs shown him by Tess.

'It's over, Randall,' Po went on. 'I'm taking Elsa out of here and I'm not going to let you stop me.'

Randall's face pinched when he heard his name.

'Yup, we know who you are, and what you've been up to. You're finished; it's up to you how you want to go out.'

'I'll kill you!' Even at a shout Randall's voice slurred, as if forming words was troublesome for him.

'I'm not going to stand around and let you,' Po warned.

Randall took another clubbing blow, but this time followed the action with a stamp of his foot. Po didn't flinch. Randall backed away again.

'There's the door.' Po indicated the gaping hole in the roller shutter. 'You could try to run.'

The big man glanced once at the prospect of freedom, but he returned his glare to Po's knife, and shook his head. One option declined, he was weighing the others. Perhaps he thought Po was afraid of a fight, the reason why he'd offered a way out. Po wasn't scared to engage; it was simply that Elsa's safety remained his priority. The girl had fainted, but he could hear her coming around. Once she was able to move, then so could he.

The rain still thrummed on the roof, and the wind made a dull roar as it blustered over Quabbin Reservoir, yet a new sound could be heard. Police sirens. In his state of mind, there was no telling what Randall made of them, but Po guessed the police's impending arrival would force the muscle-freak's hand.

Elsa muttered something.

'You OK, ma'am?' Po asked, without taking his eyes off Randall.

'Trapped,' Elsa croaked.

'Move back along the table, try to free the chain,' Po suggested.

'I'm trying.'

Randall let out a shout and sprang forward, this time with commitment.

Po didn't dodge, because that would give the man a clear line at Elsa. He drove into Randall, getting up his left forearm, jabbing in with his right.

Randall's arm impacted Po's and the club whistled down over Po's head. The tip struck him low on the back, but most of the force had been redirected. His knife went in and out, but Randall gave no indication he'd been stabbed. He simply didn't know it yet. Po braced his legs, throwing his weight into the giant and forced him back. Randall disengaged, struck again with his club while he was moving backwards. This time Po had to take the impact on his arm, but thankfully he'd angled his elbow out, and the club glanced from him rather than breaking bones. He retracted his cramping arm. But darted out his blade to keep Randall on the back foot. Behind them, Elsa rattled free and fell on her side.

'Get up on the platform,' Po told her.

He had to trust she obeyed because Randall came at him again, this time more determined now that he'd hurt Po.

Po sank his weight, and the club missed his head by a whisker. He jabbed in, and sheathed his knife in Randall's side. The man's momentum pulled him off the steel with a sucking sound. This time he knew he'd been cut, and he slapped a palm over the wound. 'Naaaaaahhhh!' he hollered in denial.

'Too freaking right,' said Po.

Swinging his club, Randall charged, and this time Po was forced to dance aside. He spun on his heel, a matador avoiding the goring horns of a bull, and back-swiped his blade at Randall's body. The man's sleeveless shirt partially saved him, but he was still scored across the ribs. The punctures to his lower abdomen were more troubling; he simply didn't know he was bleeding to death. Unhindered by his wounds he battered at Po again, and then lunged after Elsa. She drove away from him, leaping and getting her elbows over the edge of the platform. She scrambled to haul herself up, but was too weak. Randall clutched a flailing ankle and dragged her down.

He raised his club, targeting her head, but Po crashed into him. They went sideways, Randall's grip wrenched loose. Po had an arm round the bigger man's body, rolling with him off the wreckage of the trestle. As they hit concrete, they spilled apart. Randall had lost his club, but so too had Po lost his knife. It was buried to the hilt in Randall's side.

Po found his feet first as Randall crawled clear.

He didn't resume his attack but went to the girl. She was stunned, barely able to get up, so Po lifted her towards the platform. She snaked an ankle over the edge, then slid on her backside, aided by Po.

'Go,' he said, 'leave this scumball to me.'

He turned as Randall came to his feet, emitting a howl of rage. Randall felt for the knife hilt, got his fingers round it, and yanked it out. Blood pulsed from him in three separate streams. He swayed as he studied the knife, then tried to staunch his ebbing life with the flat of his other hand.

Unarmed, Po beckoned him forward.

As reckless as his taunt appeared, there was purpose to it.

Drops of blood pattered the floor between Randall's splayed feet.

'Come on, you spineless freak,' Po taunted again, curling his fingers to draw in an attack. 'What's up, you can only hurt helpless girls? Can't handle it when someone gives you a real fight?'

Randall attacked.

He barrelled in, his arm swiping up to skewer Po's guts on the knife. Snapping back his hips, Po's crossed forearms met the upswing, and immediately he transferred his grip so both hands were around Randall's wrist. The force of the man's attack lifted Po off his feet, and as he braced his arms, he was carried a few feet as Randall continued to drive into him. As Po's heels contacted the floor, he was still pushed unerringly backwards. He allowed the man to strain to sheath the knife in him, and more blood gouted out of Randall's wounds. Po twisted under Randall's arm, from the outside in, without releasing his grip. As he pivoted, it folded Randall's arm back on his own elbow. Po yanked down, and Randall had two options: sit down or have his elbow snapped. Students of Aikido or Japanese ju-jitsu familiar with the *shiho-nage*, or four directions throw, were conditioned to going with it, and tumbling safely out of the lock, but Randall had no such skill. He attempted to meet force with force and there was only one outcome – the tendons supporting his elbow joint were ripped apart. Pain took him down on his back, even as Po stripped the knife out of his failing grip.

Po stood over the man, knife again near his hip as he prepared to open Randall up.

'Stay down. Trust me, after what you've done, I'll happily slit your damn throat.'

Randall writhed in agony, his crippled elbow cupped with his opposite arm. He moaned and thrashed seemingly oblivious to Po's threat.

Po eased back.

It would be easy to kill the man, and the temptation was great. He'd killed before, but never in cold blood. He sheathed his knife in his boot.

He glanced at Elsa.

She hadn't fled. She crouched a few feet back from the edge of the platform, watching Randall squirm. She appeared unaffected by the trauma he'd suffered, didn't even display any joy at seeing her abuser punished, and Po knew she was in shock. She was shivering, and not only through being naked in the chilly air. If she wasn't treated quickly she could go into a seizure. He pulled off his denim jacket. It was damp, spattered with Randall's blood, but it might help.

He reached up to her, offering the jacket, but she shook her head wildly. She wasn't looking at him.

Po turned quickly, just as Randall rushed at him in silence.

His disabled arm hung loose at his side, but his left hand slammed Po, and he was knocked away from the platform. Elsa scuttled backwards but Randall had lost interest in her. His rage was on the one who'd shattered his arm, and cut him to pieces. He stormed after Po, backhanding him, then aiming a kick at his legs. Off balance, Po couldn't avoid the furious attack. He grimaced at the cold fire burning through his thigh, his leg deadened, and was swept up by Randall, who took them to the floor in a graceless dive. The wind exploded from Po's lungs as he bore the brunt of the impact. Randall's fingers dug into his face as he climbed Po's body. He braced his knees either side of Po, and tried to grind his skull into the concrete. Despite a dislocated elbow, Randall went to punch with his right arm: it slapped ineffectively against Po's shoulder.

Po's advantage was that his hands were still free, and the man on top was losing strength fast. He got his arms up, knocking aside the hand on his head, and Randall braced it on the ground to stop from falling. Po bucked at the hips, and

Randall was dismounted, though not fully. Po squirmed out from under him, and then kicked with both feet at Randall's body. Before Po made it up, Randall had got his knees under him, plus one hand. His scarred face turned to Po as he pushed up from the floor, and madness shone in his one good eye. He was dying, but there was still fight in him. Po scrambled to meet his next attack.

But then Elsa was behind the kneeling giant.

Incredibly, she wrapped a length of her chain around Randall's throat, and yanked backwards. She was half Randall's weight, and severely emaciated, but she found strength from somewhere as she dragged him backwards. Surprise now filled Randall's features, then panic as the chains bit deep into his throat and cut off his breath. He pawed at the chain, even as he toppled on to his butt and was dragged across the floor.

'Elsa!' Po hollered in alarm.

But his warning came too late, or maybe she ignored it. Still hauling with all her might, Elsa pitched backwards into one of the deep trenches, and filthy water gouted around her. Inexorably, the chain tightened around Randall's neck, and his eyes bulged, his tongue protruded, and his fingers fell away from the chain. Trailing a wide smear of blood, he was dragged over the lip and into the trench.

Po scurried to the edge of the trough. The scummy water foamed with bubbles, but there was no sign of either Elsa or the man she'd just strangled to death.

'Shit!' Po snapped, and without pause dropped over the ledge and plunged beneath the surface. Floundering around, he reached and grasped, but found nothing, so tucked at the waist and dove deeper. He touched cloth, ignored it, and felt further up until he found Randall's neck, and the chain that encircled it. The chain was yanked taut, and he groped down its length until he found Elsa's bare wrists. She grasped at his arms in reflex, and he was glad. He kicked for the surface, trawling her below him. Towing two people behind him took every ounce of effort and yet he was barely making any progress, but unexpectedly he found something slick under his feet, and he kicked and pushed, until he was standing on a car roof. He broke the surface, gasping for air, then hauled with his last strength and was thankful when Elsa popped up alongside him. She screamed in panic, ejecting a plume of dirty fluid from her mouth. Po pulled her into his embrace and planted his feet. Randall didn't emerge from the depths, and Po could care less.

'It's done,' he soothed Elsa, stroking lank hair from her face. '*You* did it, Elsa. You're safe, I'm safe, everyone is safe now.'

# FORTY-TWO

Tess thought about Po, not the bullet intended for her brain.

It saddened her that she hadn't gotten to say goodbye. She briefly wondered where he was, and if he'd saved Elsa. She knew he'd do everything in his power to help her if the girl could be saved. The way he would fight to save her if he realized she was in peril. When first they met and she engaged his services as her guide to Louisiana she told him he wasn't her bodyguard, and wasn't expected to take a bullet for her. He'd proven he'd do just that for her – once placing himself between her and a madman's last desperate attempt at her life – and he would now. She hadn't known him long, but her feelings for him were the strongest she'd felt for anyone alive, and she'd also take a bullet for him. Yet here she was, and she wasn't throwing down her life on Po's behalf, but for his friend, Pinky, and for Jasmine Reed, and the other girls. How would Po take the news of her death? She pitied Hopewell for the weight of vengeance he was pulling down on him . . . but not much.

At the last moment, she'd slid shut her eyes; she'd no intention of having Hopewell's sneer imprinted in her mind as the last fleeting image she'd ever see.

As her thoughts had coalesced on Po's face, and his lazy smile and twinkling turquoise eyes, she'd sensed the pressure of Hopewell's finger on the trigger through the subtle movement of the barrel digging into her forehead. So what was he waiting for?

The gun barrel retracted.

She glimpsed up.

Cal Hopewell still loomed over her, but his gun was down by his side, and his head was tilted back at an odd angle, as if he was mimicking the way Jasmine had earlier thrown back her head to gulp down the rain.

What the hell?

Hopewell's silhouette appeared bulkier than before, and he seemed to have sprouted extra limbs. Tess shook her head to make sense of what she was looking at.

There was more than one man. Behind Hopewell a second figure craned back, his left arm looped around Hopewell's throat. Hopewell's head was pulled back, because the second figure was levering on a handle that jutted from his face. The Glock slipped from lifeless fingers as Hopewell was dragged a few steps backwards. Both men sat down heavily on the concrete dais, but the second man continued to grind whatever he'd rammed through Hopewell's eye into his brain. Hopewell's mouth hung open, there was no life left in him.

Tess could feel blood streaming from her nose from when she'd been elbowed. She wiped at her nostrils with the back of her hand, then reached for the dropped Glock with her bloodied fingers. She dragged it into her grasp, then glanced back in confusion when she felt hands on her. Jasmine hugged her around her shoulders, her head pressed to Tess's cheek. The young woman sobbed in relief, and Tess was certain she sobbed too, though she'd no time for it. She slowly extricated from Jasmine, assuring the girl it was all over, but with the gun now aiming at John Trojak as he sat numbly with Cal Hopewell slumped in his lap.

Police sirens now made a cacophony of sound, and from above them, Tess heard the voices of the first officers to arrive.

'Trojak?' Tess whispered. 'John?'

Trojak's head lolled, and she saw that one side of it was matted with gore. His gaze was unfocused, and it took him a few seconds to settle it on Tess as she pushed up off her backside. 'I . . . I only ever . . . wanted to help,' he whispered.

He let go of the piece of rusty iron he'd shoved into Hopewell's eyeball. Looked at the palm of his hand as if he didn't recognize it.

Jasmine spoke his name.

Trojak blinked and resettled his gaze on her.

'He warned me that Cal was coming home,' Jasmine said for Tess's sake. 'It's why I ran. If I'd known what was going to happen I'd have stayed put. Could anything have ended as bad as this?'

Trojak was critically wounded, and he had saved their lives, and he deserved Tess's gratitude. But she turned to Jasmine and said, 'Help him if you can.' She went to Pinky.

Lucy and Maria had come out of hiding, and they too crouched alongside Pinky. He had rolled on his back, and he stared up at the trio of concerned faces peering down at him as rain pattered on his face.

'Did I die and go to heaven, me?' he asked. 'I'm surrounded by angels!'

'Pinky, are you hurt bad?' Tess asked, her voice strained with emotion.

'There are benefits to having well-padded love handles, eh?' He was clasping his side where Hopewell's bullet had punched in and then out of him. 'Don't think I'm hit bad, me, just had some impromptu liposuction.'

He was making light of being severely wounded, but he was right; with the correct medical assistance he would make a full recovery, with only minor scarring to boast about later.

'Thank God, thank God,' Tess said, and placed her palm on his cheek, stroking gently.

'As lovely as that feels, you promised you were going to give me the number for that hunky male nurse,' Pinky said. His smile was a grimace of pain. 'Never a dull moment round you two,' he said, 'but for now I wouldn't mind things slowing down, me.'

'You're going to be OK, we'll look after you.'

'Nicolas might not be happy that I failed to save you,' Pinky said.

'You did save me, Pinky. All of us.'

She checked out Lucy and Maria. Both young women looked as shocked as everyone else, but also equally relieved that their nightmare was over: they at least owed Pinky for getting them out alive. If he hadn't gone at Hopewell with the iron pipe, then who knew where things might have ended for Tess or Jasmine.

Pinky craned round, trying to see behind him. 'Where is Nicolas?'

'I . . . I don't know,' Tess admitted. 'But you know him, he'll be fine.' She wished she felt as confident as she sounded.

Police officers swarmed down the stairs towards them. Tess

checked for Jasmine, and saw that she was supporting John Trojak's head in her lap. The man, for all Tess had thought him a troublesome burr in her hide, had become her saviour, and probably of them all. She hoped dearly that he'd pull through. Hopewell was dead and good riddance.

Police officers moved among them, first checking for weapons, then when seeing that the survivors were all in need of assistance in one form or another, melting into caring roles. Tess stayed beside Pinky until a uniformed cop took over, then she stood, scanning faces. A plain-clothed woman came down the steps, followed by a tall guy, and Tess identified them as detectives. The woman was perfunctory with her commands as she viewed the scene and directed her officers. Pinky, Trojak, and the three young women were all being administered to. Tess stood and faced Detective Ratcliffe.

'I'm Tess Grey,' she said. She hadn't yet put away Hopewell's Glock, and Ratcliffe eyed it cautiously. 'Thanks for coming, Detective Ratcliffe. Everything is fine here, but we're not finished yet.'

Ratcliffe had straight dark hair, clipped back behind one ear, and wore spectacles and a smudge of pink lipstick. Her features were fine boned. She could pass as a meek school ma'am if you ignored the intense intelligence burning in her gaze behind her rain-dotted lenses. She was counting survivors, and then her attention alighted on Hopewell. 'That isn't the Jesse Randall you warned me about?'

'He's Calvin Hopewell, another dirtball rapist.' Tess used the Glock to point at the derelict plant. 'Randall's still in there. There's another girl, Elsa Jayne Moore, and my friend, Nicolas Villere, still inside with him.'

Ratcliffe waved over the other detective. He approached, weighing up the presence of the gun in Tess's hand, then dropping any concern when Ratcliffe told him to organize a search.

'I'm going with them,' Tess announced.

'No,' Ratcliffe said, 'you're not. And I think it best you hand over that gun, Tess, before you go doing something stupid with it.'

Tess looked down at the Glock, and it surprised her that she still held it. She handed it butt first to Ratcliffe, with a nod at

Hopewell. 'It's his. He shot both those men you see over there, and was about to kill me with it.'

'You were lucky to survive,' Ratcliffe said. She handed Tess a handkerchief, which she dabbed at her nose with. 'There's time for details later, but how you stopped an armed man with only a lump of iron . . . well, lucky's the word.'

'I had help,' Tess said, but didn't offer any more. She turned from the detective. 'The details can wait,' she agreed, 'we need to get going. Po needs me.'

'Po?' The name meant nothing to Ratcliffe.

'My partner, Nicolas. I have to go help him.'

'I've officers looking for him.'

'They could take for ever,' Tess said, recalling the labyrinthine tunnels she'd tracked through, and stooped to pick up her grandfather's Ruger. 'This one is mine. I've a concealed carry permit for it, but if you want to inspect it, you'll have to wait until I can fetch it from Maine. I know of a quick way to where Randall was holding those girls. You coming?'

Detective Ratcliffe tucked back her jacket and displayed a gun on her hip. She placed her hand on the butt, and Tess thought for the briefest second that Ratcliffe was about to draw on her. 'Lead the way.'

Gratefully, Tess nodded at the woman, then turned and danced down the stone steps to the cinder path. Ratcliffe waved two uniformed officers to follow. At a jog, Tess retraced her steps back to where she'd rammed a gaping hole through the roller shutter. Behind them the lake danced with white caps as the storm pummelled it, but none of them paid the dramatic view any mind. As soon as they entered, the uniformed cops securing the cavernous room, Tess spotted Po, though only his head and shoulders were visible above the turgid water that surrounded him. He was holding a naked young woman in his arms, but Tess had never been happier to see either of them in such an intimate clinch.

'Hi, Tess,' he said and winked. 'I'd wave hello, but I have both hands full.'

# FORTY-THREE

The first real snow of winter had fallen overnight and through the next day. For years Tess had dreaded the first fall because of the ugly memories it always stirred. That was then, and this was now. She could now look on snow with a different slant, because although her old life had ended that fateful night, it had been the beginning of the new one she enjoyed now, and for that she was grateful.

She was enjoying a rare dinner date with Po, though they weren't alone. Emma Clancy and her brother Alex had been invited to help them celebrate. It was a low-key affair, in a small but favourite waterfront restaurant on Custom House Wharf that specialized in seafood, and was rustic and cozy. The snow twinkled in the lights as it fell gently over the Fore River. It was a Christmas-card-perfect scene, and the food and drink was good. She'd even got Po out of denims and boots into an open-necked shirt and suit jacket over chinos and shoes. Freshly shaved, with a neat new haircut, he resembled a dashing young Clint Eastwood. Normally reticent in company, he was more relaxed, and enjoying the laughter: he and Alex were more at ease with each other, which couldn't be a bad thing.

Emma Clancy ordered champagne, and once their flutes were topped up, she proposed a toast. 'To us,' she said, keeping things simple.

They clinked glasses, repeating her words, and drank.

'And to absent friends,' Po added.

Pinky had returned home to Baton Rouge, with a firm promise to return for Thanksgiving. The bullet wound he sustained had shortened his planned stay in Portland, most of which ended up in a hospital in Springfield, Massachusetts instead, and he was determined to come back to enjoy their company when the bullets weren't flying. He was healing well, and in good spirits.

'Absent friends,' Tess said, 'and unexpected ones.'

She was referring to John Trojak. Despite the impressions

gained from their first encounters with the man, he'd shown his true colours when he'd come to Jasmine and, by virtue, Tess's rescue. He was a good man, one who'd been used and abused in a way dissimilar to what Hopewell and Randall's victims had, but still a victim all the same. He'd done some bad things on Daryl Bruin's behalf; there was no denying it, but who was Tess to judge? It was all a matter of perspective, and in her opinion he'd paid penance for his old ways, both in the injuries he sustained and in saving the day. She'd even forgiven him for burglarizing her home, because had he not done so, events would have ended in a totally different manner. OK, so Hopewell had only made it to Randall's lair through Trojak's misdeed, but if not he'd have gone for Jasmine at another time and place, perhaps when none of them could have stopped him. In some versions of the story, John Trojak was a hero, and to be honest Tess was fine with that. He'd certainly earned the accolades: his stay in hospital had outlasted Pinky's, because the bullet Hopewell had fired at him had creased his already injured skull, and nobody could understand how a man with such a traumatic injury found the fortitude to creep up on the gunman and end his reign of terror with a piece of rusty iron he'd found beneath the dais where he'd fallen.

'Very unexpected,' Po added, but drank. He had buried the hatchet with Trojak, visiting the man's sick bed to shake his hand and thank him for saving Tess's life. As he left Trojak's room he'd bumped into the man's estranged wife, Veronica. He wasn't proud of himself for leaving her in tears when he told her John deserved better, but neither was he regretful: she needed to hear some home truths.

'What's going to happen to John?' Tess asked Emma.

'Nothing major. He's agreed to stand as a witness in the case against Daryl Bruin. In return he has been granted immunity from prosecution. If Bruin doesn't go down for corruption and blackmail, he will for his part in the attempted rape of Jasmine Reed. Maxwell Carter too.' Max had survived surgery, though he'd remained in a critical condition for a few days. His throat-cutting didn't excuse him his part in the attempted rape years before, even though his role had been minor, and he'd largely been pushed into helping Cal Hopewell and Bruin to get their evil way with the underage girl. 'It's only a pity Hopewell isn't around to stand trial; I can't help feel he escaped justice.'

'He got what was coming to him,' Po said, 'I'm only sorry I wasn't the one to catch up with him.'

'If you had we might not be sitting here like this enjoying great food and drink,' Alex reminded him. 'We'd be sending you food parcels in Maine State Prison. All's well that ends well, as they say.'

Po's eyebrows rose and fell, but he didn't reply. Alex was right, Po would have killed Hopewell, and it wouldn't have been seen as an act of self-defence, or to save the lives of others in peril, the way Trojak's actions had. He'd already gotten away with the death of Jesse Randall, though he'd tried to take the blame. The fact that Elsa's chain was still wrapped around his throat when all three of them were hauled from the water told a different story. Elsa wasn't being prosecuted: there wasn't a jury in the nation who would convict her after all that she and Randall's other victims had endured. In fact, Elsa had been hailed a heroine by the media, and in both Tess's and Po's opinion it was an accolade well deserved. The girl had not only fought back, she had got to a phone and led her rescuers to Randall's hiding place, and to Jasmine, Lucy and Maria. Her actions had put an end to the reign of terror of a sexual predator and murderer. She had appeared on TV talk shows, and was being pursued by the large publishing houses in New York for her story, on which she had already made a start – her dream job had always been to write. Hollywood producers were also allegedly sniffing around, and Tess and Po had joked about who would be their onscreen counterparts if Elsa's tale ever made it to the screen: Hugh Jackman and Scarlett Johansson had both been mentioned to playful shoves and chuckles of denial.

'I'm guessing there'll be some sort of posthumous inquest into Jesse Randall's crimes?' Tess asked. Emma had been in touch with Detective Ratcliffe, who was helming the investigation to discover the true length and breadth of the sexual predator's activities. Though four girls had survived their ordeal, there was yet to be resolution in the murder of Carrie Mae Borger.

'Definitely an inquest,' Emma replied, 'but I'm still unsure to what length. The girls have all been interviewed now, as have all of us. I imagine when it comes to it we'll all be called to give evidence.'

Emma had gained official commendation for having high-lighted the presence of a serial offender working their patch when she'd sent over Tess's report to Detective Ratcliffe. The praise did more for Emma's professional reputation than it did for Tess, and she was happy that her employer – and friend – had benefited. After all Emma had assisted her when Tess was actually working a private case, where she needn't have.

'I've a feeling Jasmine might be seeing the inside of a lot of court houses over the next couple of years,' Emma went on. 'She's a witness in the cases against Daryl Bruin, Maxwell Carter, Calvin Hopewell and Jesse Randall. My only hope is she doesn't do another unexpected flit.' She turned up her mouth in a lopsided smile.

'She has no reason to run any more. She's reconciled with her grandmother, Margaret Norris, and looking forward to starting a new job.' She raised an eyebrow at Po to pick up the explanation.

'Bar-Lesque is no more,' he said to looks of confusion from both Emma and Alex. 'With Bruin and Max Carter out of the picture, the business was left vacant, and with it the danger some decent people might lose their jobs. I've bought out the lease and Jasmine and Chris Mitchell will joint manage it. Not as a burlesque revue but as a retro bar and diner. I always did enjoy old-school rock and roll music and they're a perfect fit for the front of house jobs.'

Alex shook his head. 'Po, you mind me asking something, now you're practically my brother-in-law?'

'Go for it, bro,' Po said with a lop-sided smile of his own.

'You're a grease monkey, right? Where do you get all this money from?'

'You're afraid I'm still up to my old criminal ways?' Po teased.

Alex shrugged expansively. 'It has crossed my mind.'

Po took no offence. 'I was never *that* kind of criminal. After my father was murdered, I was the sole beneficiary of his life insurance. I was wise enough to invest it at the time, and as you might recall I didn't get to spend any of it when I killed his murderer and ended up spending a long term in the Farm. By the time I got out, the pot had grown quite a ways. I'd gotten used to being thrifty, so reinvested, and well, I even beat the economic crash a few years back. I'm not rich, but I'm comfortable enough that I can throw a little cash where it's needed most.'

'A true philanthropist, unlike Daryl Bruin,' Tess put in.

'You're rich and you still hang around that grimy old garage?' Alex wondered.

'What can I say? I enjoy tinkering with engines when I'm not pretending to be a private eye.' He raised his champagne flute at Emma. 'That isn't to say I'm too rich to be paid for my time doing just that.'

'Po, you earn every cent I pay you,' Emma replied, and she tipped her glass to him. 'But,' she said, 'you're still picking up the check for dinner.'

'F'sure,' he said. 'This one's all on me.'

'Wow! You're so generous, Po!' Tess grinned. 'We can't pass up an opportunity like that, guys.' She picked up the empty champagne bottle, and eagerly shook it at a nearby waiter.

# ACKNOWLEDGEMENTS

I would like to say thank you to my wife (and chief whip-cracker when my productivity becomes tardy), Denise Hilton, my literary agent Luigi Bonomi and the team at Luigi Bonomi Associates, my friend and fellow author Graham Smith, my fellow artist Karen Ratcliffe (not to be confused with a fictional homicide detective of the same name), and my editor Nicholas Blake and the team at Severn House Publishers, and also to all my loyal readers, who all played a part in the writing and publication of this book. I couldn't have done it without you.

Matt Hilton